EXPLORER 2000

Book One
Lost in Taldish Sector

by JB Stephens

A HAZELWOOD SELECT book
Published by Cheese Press Publishing

Book Cover by Jordan Hermitt & Holly Rutland

ISBN 979-8-89136-001-3

Cheese Press, LLC
100 Mill Street
Suite A
Lawrenceville, GA 30046

www.CheesePressPublishing.com

First Hardcover Edition, June 2024

For my wife and kids. Thanks for being the crew!

-JB

Chapter 1

Hidden in the growing shadows of towering skyscrapers, three cloaked figures ducked and twisted through deep alleyways in the city of Al-Enjar, the political and governmental hub of the Galactic Community, and home to the Community Council. The nearby skyways hummed with the activity of hovercraft busily buzzing along like huge bulbous insects, commuters heading home as the solar cycle came to a close on the grand city. As the sky of Octagon V slowly darkened, the automatic lighting system began to glow with a dim yellow hue.

The tallest of the three mysterious individuals halted the other two, which were significantly smaller. It held up its hand and motioned for them to stop, saying in a soft, silky voice, "Not yet your majesties. Hold a moment..."

Above them, on a small catwalk connecting two towers together, a pair of Star Guard officers patrolled. They were clearly identifiable by the tall figure, as they were wearing very distinctive blue camouflage with light body armor, complete with helmet and infrared goggles. Fearing the slightest sound or movement could give away their position, the stealthy trio in cloaks waited for the guards to pass.

Normally, the Star Guard would be helpful in a tight situation, but their involvement here could prove detrimental to the goal of the cloaked individuals. "Just a few more blocks," the tall one muttered, "then we'll be at the ferry station, and hopefully we can charter passage for you."

The coast was clear, so they quietly and quickly made their way forward. Only the soft pitter-patter of their feet could be heard in the near silent evening air. Ahead of them lay a warehouse district with a space station on the other side. With as much traffic as Al-Enjar saw, surely they could find a captain desperate enough to earn a few bits to help them make good on their escape...

A loud resounding *bang!* echoed from the belly of the little star-ship's engine room, followed by an angry "Ouch!"

A quick response was shouted from the upper deck. "All good down there, Commander?" a deep throated voice boomed.

"Yes, that's why I yelled 'ouch'," quipped back a woman's voice. Her hands covered in black soot and oil, Commander Kel slowly rose from the engine room of the vessel. She was a shorter Human with pale skin and autumn colored hair, built like a warrior. Kel did her best to wipe her hands with a rag, but the rag was already twice as filthy as she was. It did little more than smear the concoction of engine dirt further up her arms.

"Doggone this blasted hunk of junk!" fumed Kel, dismissing the engine room with a swift gesture. "That's the third time this week we haven't been able to clear out the exhaust pipes."

The other voice replied, "We'll get her up and running again, you'll see!"

"I wish I shared your optimism, Captain..."

At that moment, the owner of the booming voice swooped down the stairwell from the upper deck into the cargo bay of the ship, landing with a loud thud. His long, navy blue duster swished behind him dramatically. The captain of the spacecraft stood tall and almost stately in the flickering lights of the hold, his near seven-foot frame seeming to take up all the available room therein. He hailed from the planet Zen I, sporting gray skin, four muscular arms, snowy white hair, and eyes like the expanse of space itself. Fully clad in his navy blue and dark gray uniform, covered with ammo belts and bandoliers, the captain looked every bit the part of a heroic explorer, jutting his powerful square-shaped chin outward resolutely.

"Optimism is one of the best weapons in our arsenal, Commander," the Zennian retorted in a good-natured fashion. "We have to keep our eyes on the stars if we want to get there someday."

"Until then," Kel snapped back, "we have to figure out how to afford your optimism. The coffers are low, while repairs are high." She planted a wrench in the captain's hand. "So how about helping me clean out the exhaust pipes? We have a ferry charter in the morning, assuming this old rust heap will be ready."

The captain's demeanor sank a bit. "Another commuter bound for one of the Octagon moons?"

Kel noted the disappointment on her captain's face and tried to offer a brighter perspective. "Yes. And paying us handsomely to do it. Who knows, after this one we might be able to finally purchase a reservoir of G-Star fuel, instead of the Powerizer crud that keeps clogging the pipes."

It cheered her up a bit to see his countenance lift. "Indeed," he replied with renewed vigor. "After all, only hard work and determination will see us through. It's not as though a shipload of money is suddenly going to walk through the bay door, right?"

At that very moment, a soft voice called out, "Excuse me? Is this vessel available for charter?"

Both Kel and the captain whirled toward the cargo bay door, which stood open to the night air. Standing before them was a tall figure, shrouded by a black cloak and hood. The person pulled back the hood to reveal a Gonian man, whose thin, gaunt features cast strange shadows over his orange spotted skin under the glow of the bay lights. Like most Gonians, his eyes bulged from a narrow skull, but unlike many, this man had swept his head sprigs backward as if styling them in a hairdo, and under the cloak he was quite fashionably dressed.

"I'm sorry, but we've already chartered a ferry for today, due to show up in a few hours," answered the captain.

Kel, however, noted the Gonian's accouterments and interjected. "Uh, Captain, while I hate to oppose your authority on board the ship, might I request that we at least find out what the very well-dressed man is offering to pay?"

The captain seemed to grasp her meaning. "Right, Commander," he drawled, then turned back to the Gonian. "I am

Captain Burnay Nado, of the Explorer 2000. We have the last Explorer model still in operation, and it is at your service. How can we assist?"

The man seemed quite nervous as he began to reply, "The ferry service won't be for me. I need to secure your services for these two." He motioned to the two smaller figures that accompanied him. Kel found herself a bit shocked. She hadn't even noticed them until now! They were also covered from head to toe in black hooded cloaks. The Gonian continued, "I need you to take these children on board."

"Where do they need to go?" queried Nado.

"I need you to leave the system. They need to be taken to Taldish Sector."

Kel found herself even more shocked. "We're not exactly equipped for long range travel. I mean, we don't have a reactor for the main drive, our fuel situation is less than adequate, we have several repairs that need to be made, and – "

The mysterious man cut her off. "I am willing to cover all your expenses and pay a stipend on top of that. Your repairs and fueling can be done at the nearest orbital station. This must be done with utmost speed and secrecy."

Kel and Nado couldn't help sharing an excited glance. She quickly regained her composure. "How much is the extra stipend?"

"I have twenty thousand bits allocated to this venture. That does not include your expenses."

"Deal!" Captain Nado shouted enthusiastically.

"Captain, if I may," Kel halted him. She proceeded to speak in hushed tones. "This sounds too good to be true. We don't know anything about this guy, or these kids. What if he's a kidnapper, pawning the kids off on us because the Star Guard's getting too close?" She realized that may be far-fetched and added, "Okay, that might be a bit unrealistic, but it could be something like that."

As if able to hear their quiet huddle, the Gonian spoke again, saying, "I understand you may have reservations, so I brought this." He reached into a pocket on his vest and retrieved a small glimmering item.

Nado immediately recognized it. "That's a Galactic Community Council badge. Only the highest ranking members of the Council have one of those."

"I assure you I am operating under the most reputable intentions."

There didn't seem to be much left to argue, but still something felt off to Kel. "The children, though, who are they?"

"This is Princess Mara and Prince Jym," answered the Gonian.

"Prince and Princess of what kingdom?" Kel asked.

"I am not at liberty to discuss the identity of their majesties any further at this time. Besides, the less you know, the better."

Aha! thought Kel. *I knew there was a catch.* Then she spoke aloud, "We'll need more information if we're to carry out your instructions."

"Very well," the man sighed. "I will pay you an additional five thousand bits for no questions asked."

"Deal!" Captain Nado shouted even more enthusiastically this time. Feeling the need to protest further, Kel started to speak, but Nado covered her mouth and reiterated, "Deal."

Shoving Nado's large hands aside, Kel cautiously offered, "Shouldn't we convene with the doctor first? He is an officer on the Explorer."

"He'll go along with it," the captain dismissed her. But after a thought he added, "Albeit reluctantly..."

"I have one final question," said Commander Kel. "Is this payment physical currency, or were you planning to use Community credit?"

With an unsure expression, the strange man revealed a large envelope and showed the contents. Kel thought the notes and coins within seemed to glow and sparkle in the flickering work lights. She finally nodded, and at last, an agreement was reached. The Gonian addressed the small beings. "Your majesties, I need you to accompany these fine folks. They will see you safely to your destination."

Within a few minutes the trio had brought aboard the few possessions that the young monarchs had with them. Kel and Nado made sure they were as comfortable as possible in the compact bunking compartments of the upper deck. While the kids bade farewell to their mysterious benefactor, the two spacers began preparing for launch.

As they were closing ports, unplugging power anchors, and performing a final check of the auxiliary engines, Commander Kel sought out the captain. She found him in the engine room, attempting to blow the last of the soot from the exhaust pipes with compressed air. After getting his attention and shutting off the compressor, Kel whispered, "Captain, when was our commuter supposed to get here?"

Checking his timepiece, Nado replied, "It would have been about two hours from now. Why?"

"Just thinking out loud," the commander mused, "but what if we didn't set out immediately? What if we waited two more hours?"

With a rather dim expression on his face, Captain Nado stated, "Then we won't get the prince and princess off planet as quickly as possible, as requested."

"All I'm saying is that every little bit helps, right?"

"Helps what?"

Her frustration was beginning to mount against the obtuseness of her friend, so Kel felt she was going to have to spell it out for him. "My suggestion is that we 'prep' the ship for launch until our other ferry charge arrives. Then we can collect the money from the commuter, in addition to carrying out the duties of protecting our wards…"

Suddenly Nado's face lit up. "Oh, I got you! Two paydays in one. Good plan Commander, I like it."

"Then we're agreed?"

"Indeed!"

Breathing a sigh of relief, Kel continued her chores. *Sometimes talking to Nado is like expecting a girth-worm to perform quadratic equations*, she thought. But at least he was on the same page as far as collecting extra money for their excursion. *Better get the bridge squared away and make sure the controls aren't sticking like last time.* With that last pondering, Kel ambled to the upper deck and spent ninety minutes longer than usual on her pre-launch checklist for the bridge.

Busily working with the compressor, Captain Nado never even heard the hurried footfalls of their actual chartered passenger. It wasn't until he looked at his timepiece again and saw how much time had elapsed before he shut down the noisy compressor and commenced packing up all the components and hoses. It was only then that his ears sensed the brash voice coming from the cargo bay.

"Hello? I'm here for my ferry to Octo III! Is this the right place?"

Quickly, the brawny Zennian secured his equipment and sprinted from the engine room out to the bay. Before him stood a lithe figure, little more than five feet tall. She was chiefly humanoid in appearance, but with a messy mop of pastel purple hair atop her head. Dressed in a multicolor outfit with an oversized sweater and carrying only a small duffel, the young woman looked more like a wayward vagabond than their usual dignitaries and businessmen.

"Captain Burnay Nado, of the Explorer 2000, at your service," the captain introduced himself.

"My name's Schiff," responded the woman. "Shape-shifting entertainer extraordinaire!" She giggled awkwardly then offered an addendum. "Though 'extraordinaire' might be a bit much...not many people have need of a shape-shifter these days. It's kind of hard to market that as a unique skill when there's a whole race of us out there. Though I suppose we are somewhat rare, I haven't met another 'shifter in the entire Octo system. I s'pose I should be grateful for the gig, some big company kickoff meeting for a new software startup. I'm mostly in it for the food, they have great snacks at these things! Have you ever tried grilled minio? It's good stuff let me tell you!" Schiff suddenly stopped herself mid-rant. "I'm blathering, aren't I? Blast it! It's a thing I do whenever I'm in a new and/or unknown situation. Which is most of the time, considering I'm a traveling entertainer..." She slapped her head, seeming clearly embarrassed as far as Captain Nado could tell. Schiff mumbled, "There I go again. Maybe you can just show me to my quarters?"

Unsure how else to handle things, Nado just said, "Of course," and proceeded to direct Schiff to the upper deck bunking area. But as they were headed up the stairs, the princess met them halfway. Nado was caught off guard. "Uh, Princess, what are you doing out of your compartment? Is something wrong?"

Princess Mara's yellowish skin seemed even paler now, somehow. "Yes. Very wrong. You should not have wasted time."

"What do you mean?" Nado nervously asked. "We were prepping the ship."

"No. You were waiting. And now the danger is upon us. I have sensed it."

"Sensed what?"

"That."

The tiny princess pointed out the bay door. Nado and

Schiff both followed her gaze until they saw the dark entity that approached the ship. It moved with precision, each piece of its frame in perfect harmony with the rest, whirring and clicking with every step, a veritable symphony of factory-fresh machinery. The being paused when it came within a few steps, and then it issued forth a vocalization. The voice that exuded from the thing was clinical and cold, yet strangely almost suave.

"Greetings crew and passengers of the Explorer 2000," it announced. "This unit's designation is H-8-RED, an assassin robot of unrivaled sophistication. You will hand over the prince and princess or face dire consequences." After issuing its eager sounding threat, the robot's ocular sensors began to glow red, and it readied a hefty plasma carbine.

Thinking fast, Nado reached for his communicator, bellowing orders. "Commander Kel, get us in the air! Now!"

The device crackled a response. "We have to close the bay doors first, captain."

"No time! This is an emergency! GO NOW!!!"

Outside, Captain Nado could see the robot calmly resume its measured pace towards the ship's entrance. "I see you have chosen dire consequences," stated the thing. "So be it."

Plasma bolts began singing through the bay! The captain pushed his charges up the staircase and out of harm's way, drew a small derringer from his belt and returned fire. A couple of shots connected but did little against the robot's armor plating. That was okay though, he only needed to keep it occupied and focused on him. The assassin kept its pace, closer and closer to the rear of the vessel. It was almost in range. Nado felt the Explorer shake and jerk as her liftoff thrusters ignited underneath, pushing her skyward. That was all they needed.

"Commander!" he yelled into the communicator. "Ignite the port and starboard engines!"

"We haven't achieved full takeoff elevation yet!"

"Kel! Ignite the engines!!"

Her voice buzzed through again, "Alright, alright! But they seem sluggish...wait, did you really spend two hours cleaning the exhaust pipes and not finish cleaning them?!"

Nado, still in a firefight with the robot, quipped, "I hardly think this is the time!"

"Captain, if there's still grime in the pipes, we'll backfire on ignition!"

His eyes narrowed, and the captain smiled slyly. "I'm counting on it. Punch it!"

The old starship grumbled and groaned, then with a massive jolt, the rear thrusters belched forth a stream of soot, grime, and fire. The blast pushed the assassin robot backward, but it dug its feet into the asphalt. Chunks of the pavement were ground out until the robot finally lost its footing and was blown through the air, a nearby warehouse halting its flight with a sudden **smash!**

The Explorer sailed through the midnight sky, barely clearing rooftops and struggling with balance. Unsecured supplies careened from the ship, falling through the open bay door. Nado's eyes fell on the airlock switch, located near the open door. Utilizing all four of his muscular arms, Nado maneuvered spider-like across the bay, as high winds threatened to rip him right out of the ship. Upon reaching the switch at last, he heaved with all his might, hanging on for dear life until the heavy airlock doors finally sealed. With the pressure beginning to equalize, Nado could feel Kel regaining control of the Explorer. With a heavy sigh, the captain collapsed to the floor as the Explorer 2000 took to the stars.

Two clerks stood with a report in hand, just received remotely on their data-pads. They exchanged a concerned look. One of them eventually spoke. "His lordship must be informed. As senior clerk, I will take on the duty...of designating you, junior clerk, to deliver the report." The other started to argue, but the senior clerk stopped him. "No debate. I hold seniority, it is my decision. Go, and remember not to look his lordship directly in the eye. Good luck."

The junior clerk followed the long beryllium corridor to a large door, which slowly opened on approach, revealing a dark chamber within. A luxurious runner ran the length of the room, with orange lights on pedestals glowing like torches placed periodically along the way. The richly embroidered runner flowed from the doorway until it reached a set of stairs, leading up to a throne obscured in darkness. The person who sat thereupon was veiled from sight amidst the near ethereal blackness. All that could be seen were the booted feet of the occupant, and a table full of bottles and glasses of various beverages.

"Lord Hex?" the clerk began. "We just received a report from the assassin unit. It appears it was unsuccessful in apprehending the children. They boarded a small vessel."

A cold, low voice rumbled from the throne. "What vessel?"

The clerk gulped. "It was an Explorer model, milord."

"Explorer? To whom is it registered?"

"Uh…records state it is captained by Burnay Nado, milord."

For a moment there was utter silence. Then a roar erupted from the shadowy heights! "BLAST!!!" A strong hand struck several drinks from the table, shattering them on the floor far below. The clerk cringed, but Lord Hex apparently regained a calm demeanor. "That is the last person I wanted to become embroiled in all of this… did they leave a heading with the port master?"

"Yes, milord, but it was very vague. Taldish Sector was all they said."

A low growl reverberated throughout the room. "Thank you for the report. Now, leave."

Needing no additional prompting, the clerk bolted out of the massive entrance, leaving Lord Hex alone. Or so it seemed. Another figure strode from the shadows behind the throne, tall and regal in stature, seeming almost to float around the huge structure.

"Your little pet failed," said the being.

"Not as spectacularly as your aide," Lord Hex shot back. "The prince and princess would never have escaped without his help. And you let him swipe your council badge from right under your nose."

"Watch your tone," hissed the other man. "Remember, you were elected by the council as Marquis of the Hexagon only due to my commendation. Now fulfill your end of the bargain and capture those abominations before they cause any real damage to my galaxy!"

Lord Hex could not contain a cruel chuckle. "*Your* galaxy? Ha! They really make you squirm, don't they?" The other man only glared hard. "Very well," Hex continued, "I'll take care of it. At least my assassin captured some valuable intel. I have many allies in Taldish Sector. And if all else fails, hopefully my dreadnought will be completed on schedule."

"Just get those kids, and either dispose of them, or deliver them into my hands!"

The Marquis du Hex, lord of the Hexagon system, narrowed his eyes and grinned slyly. "Worry not, my friend. As soon as I have those children in my grasp, you will be the first to know..."

Chapter 2

Thankfully, the orbital station above Octagon V was unusually quiet and serene. Despite the bars, taverns, gambling dens, small-time casinos, and hostels, it seemed that the typical debauching types had either already gone home or been arrested by Star Guard personnel. The shops and bazaars were just beginning to commence business for the new standard cycle, while all the less reputable establishments were closing, tossing any remaining patrons to the streets.

But all of this felt odd to Kel, like the calm before a storm. Walking the avenues of the station, she sensed herself fighting the urge to check every dark alley with her pistol. Every set of flashing lights appeared to the commander as robotic assassin eyes, leering at them with hate and bloodlust. She shook the feeling long enough to navigate to the nearest parts store, a place they knew well and had done plenty of business.

Commander Kel made her way towards *Wheeler's Used and Abused*, the proprietor of which was an old friend. Alongside her strode Dr. Rox Garrison, a Human man, and the third officer of the

Explorer 2000, who had spent many a long, sleepless night patching up Kel and Nado after various run-ins with the more nefarious individuals who frequented their usual haunts. Smugglers, thugs, muggers, bandits, even simple drunks had all tried to thrash the Explorer crew at some time or another, but somehow Nado always managed to come out on top. Luck was the only thing that made sense to Kel. The captain had an uncanny knack for being the luckiest brawler in any fight.

For now, they walked at a brisk pace, Kel keeping her mind focused on the task at hand. Get to *Wheeler's*, get the needed parts, and get back to the Explorer before anything else had a chance to go wrong. They may have outsmarted the mechanical menace at the docks, but Kel figured it was only a matter of time before even Captain Nado's luck ran out.

"I always forget how long the walk is from the docking bay to the shop," Rox muttered.

His utterance jolted Kel from her thoughts. "I know, usually the captain and I handle this," she replied. "But someone had to stay on the ship and keep an eye on the kids."

The doctor ran his hand through the thick brown hair on his head, allowing it to drift down into his well-manicured beard, pausing to rub along his jawline. Kel noted the indeterminate expression on his face, as the station streetlamps highlighted the salt in his beard and the silver in his hair. Without losing a beat, Rox responded, "You mean someone who knows how to deftly wield a firearm had to stay on the ship and keep an eye on the kids."

Though his words seemed pointed, he offered the phrase with a soft lilt in his voice, allowing it to flow without seeming like a retort.

His calm bearing was rarely abandoned, but in times of duress the doctor was known to fret and fuss like an overbearing parent. Still, in this moment, Kel was aware that there was something else lurking beneath the surface of the doctor's words.

"You disapprove of the captain's decision?" she voiced.

"Disapprove?" answered Rox. "I don't know about disapproval so much as disappointment that my opinion in the matter was not acknowledged, or even sought out. As is common with the Explorer's commanding officers, the guns and wallets did the primary thinking."

"You would have done differently?"

"I didn't say that. I only think it would be beneficial if we had a chance to review all the facts as a full crew before diving into yet another wild venture filled with various unknowns."

Kel frowned. "I asked every question I could conceive! Everything seemed to be in order, and I might add, Nado made the final call and was the one who decided to exclude you."

"I'm not trying to point fingers or lay blame," Rox assured her. "This was a good business decision in regards to the capital involved. But there was again unforeseen danger that almost led us to disaster."

"It's a big universe filled with a lot of danger!" the commander protested. "How are we supposed to foresee it all?"

"That's not what I meant," Rox attempted to sooth her. "I'm sorry I said anything. It wasn't my intention to start a fight."

"I'm not fighting," mumbled Kel. "If I was, trust me, you'd know it."

Throwing up his hands, the doctor sighed, "Just forget I mentioned it."

"Why are you so difficult to talk to?"

"Me? I wanted to have a civil discourse!"

The pink glow of flashing neon lights above them halted their discussion. Kel simply stated, "We're here. Let's be about our business and move on."

As the lights of the small shop flickered, the two silently walked under an archway with a barred gate that had been retracted. Inside, the store was lit by a dull blue hue from the expiring fluorescents that hung from the ceiling, ghosts of a better time when the station was new and fresh. Now everything was run-down, rusting, and falling apart. *Much like our ship*, Kel thought. Greasy, oily, soot blackened spacecraft components littered every shelf, bin, barrel, and crate, jam-packed into the minuscule market bearing the signage "Wheeler's Used and Abused." Now to find Wheeler himself.

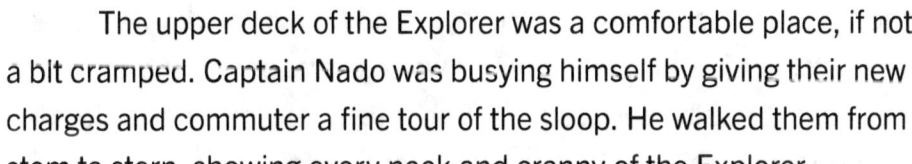

The upper deck of the Explorer was a comfortable place, if not a bit cramped. Captain Nado was busying himself by giving their new charges and commuter a fine tour of the sloop. He walked them from stem to stern, showing every nook and cranny of the Explorer.

The bridge sat at the prow of the craft, elevated a few steps above the crew quarters, while behind it was nestled a dining cabin, which also served as the "war room" when necessary. A very tiny galley kitchen surrounded the table, with meal preparation paraphernalia adorning the walls down both sides. Periodically spaced between the kitchen utensils and appliances were hefty magnetically sealed doors, the port side leading to individual bunking compartments, each furnished with a set of bunk-beds, a small dresser, and a few shelves built into the walls. The doors on the starboard side instead opened into a small medical bay, the operating room and sleeping quarters of Dr. Rox, and also the only shower on board. Much care had to be taken to ensure water rations were not depleted when bathing while in transit. At the rear of the galley/dining cabin was a final door, the only portal to the captain's cabin, wherein Captain Nado stored his most prized belongings, namely trinkets from the precious few adventures they'd had. Among them he kept a primordial sawtooth Fangorian skull (won in a card game), a weird pink crystal that was a gift from an old man calling himself a wizard (Nado and Kel had saved him from getting beat up by hooligans), and a still glowing lock of hair from a Lorian, an extremely rare sight to see off their home-world (they had assisted her in navigating Al-Enjar to reunite with her people and get home).

At the fore of the galley was a hatch that led down a short metal ladder into the most spacious area aboard the Explorer, the cargo bay. Inside this metal honeycombed miniature warehouse dwelt a plethora of storage crates, each containing various supplies they would undoubtedly need, dehydrated food, sealed water cases, cannisters of fuel, a small armory's worth of weaponry, and the like. The cargo bay also housed a small shuttle, barely big enough for three grown creatures, that was used for rapid transit to and from space stations and planets that had no landing space for larger craft.

The aft of the cargo bay acted as the airlock, with two hefty hermetically sealed bulkhead doors maintaining a barrier between the occupants and the dangerous void of space beyond. Only a very small area lay between the two bulkheads, allowing for pressurization and depressurization if needed for short spacewalks. Turning to the fore of the cargo bay would reveal the final room of the Explorer 2000, the engine room. Sporting twin port and starboard forward thrusters and an intricate series of less powerful underbelly thrusters for takeoff, as well as a Casimir warp drive for long-range travel, the Explorer was clearly designed for reaching uncharted space. Carefully positioned away from the engine casings was the massive water reservoir, used for the shower, galley faucets, medical sinks, as well as both the water and oxygen recycling units.

The hull of the ship consisted of a plasti-steel alloy, designed to be lighter than most metals, but just as durable and sturdy, allowing for easier liftoff and landing, requiring far less fuel than larger vessels. Small, clear, acrylic plastic windows dotted the ship in various places, bunking compartments, captain's cabin, and the bridge, granting passengers and crew an opportunity to view the expanse of space while traveling. The ones on the bridge were somewhat larger, giving the command crew a better field of view for maneuvering in spaceflight. One large viewing portal spanned a fair length of the ceiling of the galley but was usually covered by a protective plasti-steel barrier, only opened when the craft was gliding or halted. It certainly could never be exposed when engaging the warp drive.

Completing the tour, Nado escorted the group outside the ship to grant them a fine view of the custom color job he and Kel had painstakingly applied. The Explorer had been donned in a thick coat of metallic blue shuttle paint, with a slight yellow tint applied to the exterior of the windows. The port and starboard forward thrusters exhibited flame decals running the length of each, and Nado was quite proud to point out the name of the ship, grafted in glimmering silver on the hull. The solar panels used to recharge the massive batteries that powered most of the ship's basic functions were currently within their protective housings, thus he sadly could not display them. But he could talk about them! Nado proceeded to inform the newcomers of the power of the luxonite crystal panels that had replaced the traditional silicon panels due to the enhanced capability of the crystals to absorb and transmit sunlight. They were, however, much weaker as a result, requiring the housings for warp travel and potential combat.

After the excursion around the Explorer, Princess Mara and Prince Jym appeared rather exhausted, so Schiff suggested that they get some rest. Meanwhile, she and Nado retreated to the galley, plopping themselves down in the cushioned swivel chairs at the table each with a hot beverage in hand. Nado sighed heavily as he mused, "I tell you, my one great love in life is the Explorer 2000. She's everything I ever hoped for in a ship. And now I finally have the chance to get her out there, into the far reaches of the universe." He paused, noticing Schiff. "After we drop you off at your destination of course," he hastily added.

She didn't seem off-put by his statement, supplementing the conversation with, "My destination has changed." Her expression grew into excitement as she spoke. "I'm coming with you guys!"

Nado, however, was a bit off-put. "Um, that isn't exactly covered by your fee..."

"Fee, schmee! If that tussle at the docks was any clue at all, I'd say you guys are in real trouble! And if I'm doing my math right, you're transporting Vampyrials while being chased by assassins." Schiff paused. Nado felt the tension in the room thicken.

"Vampyrials?" he questioned.

"Sure!" replied the ever-chipper Schiff. "You didn't recognize them? I had my doubts at first, I mean, no one's really seen any for a hundred years! I don't know all the history, but you can't mistake that pale yellow skin, not to mention the orange-y eyes and those all-natural black tattoos. I only know 'cuz, it's a weird request, but I've been asked to shift into Vampyrial form from time to time. Did you know they're born with those tattoos?"

The captain was lost in thought. "Vampyrials..." he pondered. "I do know the history. It's been one hundred and twenty-three standard GC years since the last Great War and the defeat of Prime Executor Mantis. His attack on the fledgling Galactic Community was barely repelled, but the formation of the Star Guard by the first Grand Marshal saved the day."

"What happened after that?" Schiff interjected.

"They hunted Mantis' followers to the ends of the universe," answered Nado. "The Grand Marshal believed the threat ended after Mantis' death, but that original Community Council feared that they'd only made him a martyr, and worried about a vengeful insurrection by the other Vampyrials. So, they ordered a genocide."

"That's horrible!"

"Maybe, but they felt it was the only thing to do. The Vampyrials under the Prime Executor had what many believed to be magical powers. It wasn't magic of course, but the Vampyrials had learned how to transform their natural proclivities for sensing dark energy fields into manipulation of those energy fields, using it to terrible effect!"

"Wow!" exclaimed Schiff. "If those two are really that rare, you're right. You'll definitely need my help!"

"I didn't say – " Nado started.

"In exchange for my shape-shifting services, my short-range teleportation blink, unnatural ability to bluff, and the morale boost I'm sure to bring along, all I ask is room and board."

"Well, I – "

"Won't take no for an answer? That's what I thought you'd say!" Schiff rose from her seat. "Thanks for the drink, I've got to get my quarters set up to be a bit more homey. Cheers Cap!"

And with that, the strange young woman bouncily pranced back to her room, leaving Nado confused and bewildered. "Did I just hire another crew member? On accident?" He decided to shrug it off and just roll with the punches, however weird they might be.

Octagon V's orbital station was still largely asleep, so no one noticed an odd scene taking place in a shadowed corner. The legs and boots of a Star Guard patrolman slowly disappeared from view, being dragged into an unused maintenance tunnel. A metallic hand meticulously wrapped around the entrance hatch, gently closing it. The owner of the hand methodically remained out of sight.

Light clanging could be heard from the rear of Wheeler's Used and Abused informing Kel that the shopkeeper was present. She called out, "Wheeler? What are you messing around with now?"

But there was no response. Instead, the noise suddenly quieted, and only muffled whispers crept from the back room. Kel worriedly shot a glance at the doctor, who raised his eyebrows in fear, his eyes growing wide. The tough commander whipped her duster aside, reaching for the trusty pistol on her hip. She motioned for Rox to hide, and cautiously inched closer to the caged cashier's counter, behind which lay the source of the mystery.

The doctor, never one to countermand, quickly slipped around a towering shelf of miscellaneous piping, silent as the grave. After making sure he was in a safe location, Kel hunkered down, staying low so as not to be seen over the counter-top. Reaching the cashier cage, she swiftly turned, putting her back to it, craning her right ear upward to try and hear more of what was happening as the whispering continued.

"Maybe they are gone?" a gravelly, scratchy voice offered.

"Don't be ssstupid!" came the hissed retort. The second voice was also scratchy but sounded more feminine to Kel. "They did not sssay they were leaving, did they? Go sssee where they are, and I will continue our…interrogation."

Here they come, thought Kel, waiting to see who the ruffians were. She stayed poised with her back to the cage, hiding underneath the lip of the counter-top. Her head turned towards the usually locked door that led to the back area, keeping her pistol at the ready. The door handle turned, hinges creaking lightly as the door swung wide.

Out stepped a huge brute, a hulking Kriton, whose black scales glistened under the fluorescent lights. A long snout filled with fangs grimaced sourly, as the thug's beady eyes scanned the room, his thick tail swishing back and forth. Heavy body armor made Kel think twice about trying an opening volley with her pistol, and the massive rifle in his hands gave her even more reason for alarm.

"Who'ssss here?" the big Kriton called out. Long strides allowed him to cover nearly half the store in just three steps. "Wheeler ish closhed for bushinesh at the moment. Come back later!"

Thinking fast, Kel ducked inside the cage through the open door. She had no doubt that Rox could stay hidden, the more pressing matter was getting to Wheeler. Thankfully, no more doors separated her from the back room, only a lightweight curtain. Kel silently locked the cashier's entrance. *That ought to keep the big guy out of the way temporarily*, she supposed. The commander then peeked through the curtain.

It was difficult to make much out from her vantage, but Kel was pretty sure that the second voice belonged to another Kriton, who stood near the middle of the room. Dead center sat a chair containing a skinny little Pyrian, Wheeler himself. He was tied up and begging for mercy, an act that only earned him a slap from the second Kriton.

"Quiet you!" she harshly whispered. "Or I will sssmack you around more until Schlaar getsss back. The only thing I want to hear from you ish what you have done with the protection money."

"I told you," the skinny little Pyrian whimpered, "I already paid this month!"

That bought him another slap. "Liar! Give ush the bitsss you owe!"

Kel couldn't take any more. Breathing deep, she rolled into the room, landing in a kneel and aimed her pistol. The Kriton was quicker than she'd anticipated though, snatching Wheeler's whole chair and using the Pyrian as a shield. It was a standoff!

"Who are you?" the Kriton woman bellowed. She shook Wheeler. "Who ish thish?" Then back to Kel. "You'd besht lay down your weapon, or your little friend will be ssslashed to ribbonsss!"

Commander Kel surveyed the room. Several things shot through her head simultaneously, the sharp fangs and claws on her adversary, the danger of losing Wheeler or herself, the great lummox outside who had certainly heard the commotion, and the long light fixture dangling from twin chains.

"Okay," Kel said softly, pulling her hands back and aiming her gun at the ceiling. "I'm backing off, lady. Whatever you say."

"That'sss right," grunted the Kriton. "You do as Shtrepp sssaysss."

It seemed that Shtrepp was satisfied with Kel's actions, so the clever commander took the chance to make her move. She fired a quick shot toward the ceiling, and her blast connected with the light fixture! The super-heated plasma bolt quickly snapped the flimsy chain, and the fixture swung down onto Shtrepp's head! The Kriton shrieked in pain as the glass splintered across her face and the hefty metal fitting smacked her across the room. Wheeler was dropped to the floor, and Kel wasted no time in subduing her opponent. Using the assailant's own leftover rope, she tied Shtrepp to some piping on the wall. One goon was dealt with but that still left…

"Shtrepp!" hollered Schlaar from the other room, pounding on the locked door. "I'm coming!"

Kel rushed from the back room into the cashier cage to see Schlaar about to bash in the entire doorframe with his massive foot. But as soon as he caught sight of her, he instead leveled his heavily modified electro-rifle in her direction. Worse than a taser, electro-rifles fired a powerful projectile that not only ripped through flesh but shocked the victim with over five thousand volts in the process!

Less than ten feet away, Kel was bound to be hit. But just as Schlaar readied his shot, the mountain of piping and parts behind him began to shake and sway. An avalanche of engine components rained down on top of the Kriton, toppling him to the floor. Atop the crashed pile stood a triumphant looking Rox.

"You're not the only one who's good in a fight around here," he stated. Kel just smiled weakly.

The two of them checked in on Wheeler who, despite his frail frame, had only suffered minor bruising from the dastardly duo. "I'll be alright," he wheezed, rubbing a scruffy beard with spindly fingers that resembled suction cups. "I've suffered worse than these two. Couple of second-rate fists-for-hire that couldn't string two cohesive sentences together between the pair of them. Bah!" He spit in Shtrepp's direction. "It'll take more than that to shakedown ol' Wheeler!"

Within a few minutes they had also tied up Schlaar and Wheeler had notified a Star Guard dispatcher of the incident. Troopers were on route to arrest the crooks. Wheeler turned his goggled eyes towards Rox and Kel.

"But now, on to business," the slim Pyrian declared. "What do you need this time, Kel? A few more cannisters of Powerizer for the next ferry? I've got a great deal on – "

"I'm going to stop you there, Wheeler," Kel said. She showed the envelope full of money. "We need an overhaul. I need to outfit the Explorer with all new parts, I want a whole case of G-Star fuel, and I need a reactor core for the Casimir drive."

Inspecting the bits, Wheeler laughed, "Hoo-boy! You ain't kidding! How'd you get this kind of coin, you rob somebody?"

"Call it investment funds," replied Rox.

"Whatever you please!" the unkempt merchant quipped. "I've got one reactor core left. Could've sold it a while ago, but I kept it in stock hoping this day would come. It's all yours!"

A short while later, Kel and Rox were on their way back to the ship with a motorized dolly carrying their new purchases in tow. They bid a fond farewell to Wheeler, who still laughed in delighted surprise that the Explorer was finally leaving the system. "I sure will miss my best customers," he cajoled. "But I'm glad that the captain is going to be able to live his dream."

It was quite some time later when Wheeler's shop bell dinged again. He shouted from the back, "It's about time you got here! What, is the Star Guard in a competition to see which patrol is slowest?"

The short Pyrian approached his cashier counter and abruptly halted. Before him stood a tall copper-colored robot with glowing red ocular sensors. It was covered in heavy plating, dressed in a sleeveless brown leather duster, and carried a plasma carbine on its back. Wheeler felt very unnerved at the sight of this thing, his green skin growing a bit pale. He rubbed at his nasal cavities nervously.

"Greetings," the robot vocalized.

"You're here for these grunts?" Wheeler pointed at Schlaar and Shtrepp.

The robot merely glanced at the two Kritons, then back at Wheeler, and offered a brusque, "Certainly. In addition, this unit is investigating an unrelated crime. Two persons of interest were smuggled off of Octagon V. You will relay all known information regarding the Explorer 2000, as well as all crew and/or occupants."

Wheeler was aghast. "Smuggling? That doesn't sound like them…wait, is this some kind of scam? Who are you anyway?"

The robot flashed a badge in Wheeler's face. "This unit's designation is Star Guard officer 48721, as denoted by this badge. Now, divulge the information."

Chapter 3

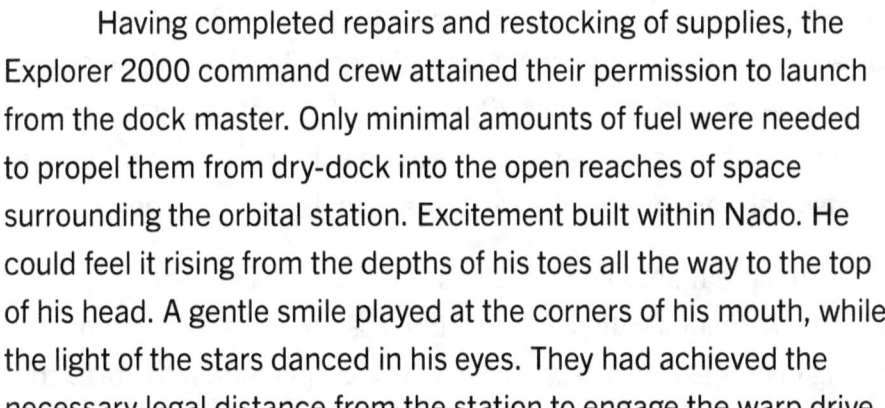

Having completed repairs and restocking of supplies, the Explorer 2000 command crew attained their permission to launch from the dock master. Only minimal amounts of fuel were needed to propel them from dry-dock into the open reaches of space surrounding the orbital station. Excitement built within Nado. He could feel it rising from the depths of his toes all the way to the top of his head. A gentle smile played at the corners of his mouth, while the light of the stars danced in his eyes. They had achieved the necessary legal distance from the station to engage the warp drive.

The drive had been used before of course, its power being needed to generate the necessary force to simulate gravity on the vessel. But they had only ever had enough basic power cells for this function. A fusion core was required to actually activate the main purpose of the drive, deep space travel.

"It is time," he murmured to himself. Then aloud, "Commander Kel, set our heading for Taldish Sector."

"Aye captain," Kel responded, tapping keys on the navigational computers. "We have our course."

The captain spoke into the onboard intercom system. "All passengers and crew of the Explorer 2000, prepare for warp travel in one minute." He proceeded to count down from sixty aloud, anticipation growing with every second. For the first time in his life, Captain Burnay Nado was taking his Explorer model ship into the expanse of space. It was a dream come true, a lifelong goal from childhood realized! Upon reaching the end of the countdown, Nado gave the command, "Engaging the warp drive!"

Captain Nado flipped a series of switches, sending the signal to the warp drive that made it rumble and hum. Everyone aboard could see through their view ports as a shadowy bubble began to envelope the ship. Outside, it seemed that reality itself warbled and blurred, bending and stretching around them. Anyone watching would have seen the Explorer 2000 suddenly seem to zoom out of existence, but the crew barely noticed the shift, protected within the dimensional warp bubble that had been created around them.

In mere moments, the Explorer had arrived at their destination. Instantly, the warp bubble dissipated, leaving them floating in open space. Kel and Nado worked in tandem to utilize the air jets and bring the Explorer to a complete halt. The ride was over, but Nado's joy hadn't diminished. "That was incredible!" he shouted. "I mean, I've been on vessels that used warp travel before, but I've never commanded it myself! What a thrill! Let's do it again, let's go somewhere else!"

Calming him down a bit, Kel interjected, "Captain. We've entered Taldish Sector. That was where we were asked to go."

"Quite right, Commander." Nado settled himself. "I suppose we should take a few cycles to assess the next steps." He paused, wondering what the next steps should be. One warp and they'd already completed the mission at hand. Now what? The Gonian hadn't given them any further instructions.

As if sensing his confusion, Kel offered, "Maybe we can confer with the prince and princess to see if they know what to do."

"Excellent suggestion, Commander! Let's secure the ship and convene in the war room."

After taking time to double check the cargo bay and the engine room, Nado and Kel gathered the rest of their travelers in the galley, each taking a seat around the long table. Nado scanned the room, trying to present the appearance of a hardened spacer with years of experience. The captain started by going around the table and making sure they were all acquainted with each other's names, titles, and respective roles.

"If I haven't said so before," he began in his most intimidating sounding voice, "I am Captain Burnay Nado, the executive officer of the Explorer 2000. All decisions aboard this vessel go through me." His voice softened and wavered a bit as he continued, "Well, most decisions go through me. Some go through the other officers, and many are discussed in a triage… but I also handle much of the piloting, gunning, and minor repairs." Nado cleared his throat briefly. "Kel, why don't you go ahead next?"

Smiling and shaking her head, the commander said, "I'm Commander Kel, navigator and mechanic."

Without prompting, Rox continued the round. "Dr. Rox Garrison, medical officer and resident chemist."

"I'm Schiff!" The nimble shapeshifter didn't miss a beat, speaking overly dramatically. "The captain hired me for any stealth missions, spy work, or gambling that needs doing. I also deal with the morale of the crew, and onboard entertainment."

Kel took that moment to exchange a look with Nado, a look that he clearly recognized as perturbation. He shrugged back at her trying to indicate that it wasn't his fault, but she just rolled her eyes as a response. Nado waved it off, as silence fell across the chamber. Gradually, all eyes turned to the children, Mara and Jym, awaiting their input. But the kids only sank in their chairs, both looking as though they wished to be invisible.

"It's okay," Kel softly addressed them. "You're safe with us. Whatever you were running away from before can't hurt you here. Our job is to protect you."

"I'm Prince Jym," the boy stated, but his sister motioned for him to be quiet.

"Jym!" she reprimanded. "You know our rule. We never talk about it with anyone. For our safety and theirs."

"No Mara, I'm done being quiet all the time," argued Jym. "We have to trust somebody if we're ever going to find mom and dad!"

Scowling deeply and pursing her lips, Mara mechanically rose from her chair and regressed back to her room. Everyone expected the door to be slammed violently based on her expression, but the girl simply closed it in a controlled and purposeful manner. Eyeing her brother until completely out of sight, it was obvious that Mara wanted Jym to know how upset she was with him.

As soon as she was gone, Jym's head dropped. He closed his eyes and sighed, but still spoke. "Sorry. Mara's just very protective...

and scared. We've been in danger for a long time, and that danger is still out there."

"Who are you trying to escape?" Schiff wanted to know.

"We aren't sure. But we know that someone, for some reason, wants us dead."

"What about that Gonian fellow who paid us to escort you?" the captain asked.

Jym shrugged. "You mean Uncle? He never told us his name. Just said to call him our uncle. He picked us up from the Human flotilla after we were awakened from our stasis pods." Though the crew was filled with questions, they all decided to let the young prince relay his tale in his own time. He kept going. "We don't know much, but apparently we were found in stasis pods on a derelict ship by salvagers. The logs recorded by our parents stated that their pods were activated automatically when there was an issue with the life support systems. They fixed it temporarily by diverting all other power to it. So they had to use the only escape pod to try and get help. But they never made it back." Jym stopped.

"Is that all you know?" the doctor prompted him.

"There's a little more. Uncle told us that because of what we are a lot of people were scared of us and wanted to let us die. But the council voted, and the decision was that we would be kept in stasis on the Human flotilla. I don't know exactly what happened, we were pretty groggy from the cryo-sleep, and Uncle didn't talk much about it, but we were awakened from our pods and rushed to the Octagon. We lived in seclusion with Uncle for a time, but he said it was getting too dangerous, so he brought us to you. That's pretty much it."

"That's not it." Everyone jumped a little. Mara stood by her doorway, having returned unobserved. "Whoever is after us has nearly unlimited resources, so they aren't going to quit just because we left the Octagon. They're going to keep coming. They see us as a threat, a danger to the universe, powerful and vicious monsters."

Schiff gave a gentle smile. "Sweetheart, you can't let others dictate your identity, and you can trust me on that. You're not any of those things."

With a grim look on her face, Mara replied, "Don't be so sure."

Several standard cycles had passed following the awkward meeting with the kids, and no clear plan had yet been implemented. Kel was taking stock of their supplies in the cargo bay. The Explorer models were equipped for quick travel to uncharted sectors then back to base, but they weren't exactly meant for long periods of space gliding.

"We need to find a nearby planet or station to resupply," she mentioned as Nado stepped into the bay. "Aimless footling about in an endless void might not be good for our life support systems. We're going to start getting low on water soon."

"Which means low oxygen as well," the captain finished her thought. "Let's check the nav charts and see what's close by."

They took a quick jaunt up to the bridge to look over the maps and charts. Binders full of navigational information were piled inside a cabinet embedded under the command console. The pair rifled through the pages searching for the entries on Taldish.

"Here," called Nado. He showed Kel the pages of his binder. "We're roughly in this vicinity, not far from that solar system."

"Is that the Rellis system?" Kel queried.

"Yes. One habitable planet, Khardan."

Kel looked up. "That's the Kriton home-world."

"I'm well aware of that. Is that a problem?"

"No, no problem at all," Kel quickly dismissed. Her recent run-in back at Wheeler's was still fresh in her mind. But it was a big universe after all, and word couldn't travel that fast with Schlaar and Shtrepp incarcerated, especially with the couriers of the Rover Express on strike.

"Very good," she heard Nado saying. "I'll inform the rest of the crew."

"Kritons," she mouthed, her words barely above a whisper. "Eh, what are the odds?"

"Thanksss for the ride," Schlaar growled to their newfound friend as they disembarked from the small shuttle. "It'sss good to be back on the home-world."

"We'll be shure to let you know if we sssee your quarry," added Shtrepp. "But how can we contact you?"

The pilot handed them a tracking fob. Schlaar and Shtrepp looked at each other knowingly. It was a bit unreliable, but the fobs acted as radio beacons, pinging satellites and bouncing the signal along until it could be received by the partnered fob.

"And we ssstill get a bonusss payment if we sssubdue them?" Schlaar double-checked.

Red ocular sensors glowed from the darkness of the shuttle's cockpit. "Indeed. This unit will pay handsomely for any assistance in the capture of the Explorer 2000 crew."

"After resupply on Khardan, where to next?" Rox asked the captain.

"I'm not entirely sure," Nado answered. "But we'll just take it one step at a time. It's all we can do for now."

Giving a nod, the doctor retreated back to the med-bay. As Nado began securing the galley utensils for landing, Princess Mara slowly approached. For a moment, she just stood and stared at the floor, as if waiting for something to happen. But Nado deemed that allowing her some leeway was the better course of action.

Minutes of uncomfortable silence agonizingly passed before the princess at last spoke. "You said we were in Taldish Sector?"

"Yes, Princess," the captain replied.

"How much do you know about it?"

At this question, Nado lit up. Knowledge of space exploration, history, and astrography were his favorite subjects. "Quite a bit actually. Taldish Sector got its name from the Aronite explorer who discovered it. It isn't his name though, his name was Grandos. Initially it was named Grandos Sector, but when he found out that the races who inhabited this sector were rather hostile and difficult to liaise with, he submitted a name change to the council." Nado paused to see if his story was being well received. Mara had taken a seat, leaning forward with wide eyes. Jym entered the room and joined her.

Nado resumed his tale by saying, "You see, Grandos had a bitter rival. He himself was an explorer, retrieving information from the field. All his findings were submitted to an Aronite astrographer, an interstellar map-maker, named Taldish. Taldish was fiercely jealous of Grandos and would repeatedly question his findings and force him to make asinine adjustments to his reports. So, in retaliation, Grandos submitted the name change, attaching his rival's name to one of the most dangerous and hated regions of the universe.

"Taldish was furious when he discovered the treachery! This led him to his own retaliation, albeit far more lethal. Taldish invited Grandos to his home under the pretense of reconciliation. But upon reaching the fourth course of the meal, Grandos began to feel ill. His vision blurred, his body broke out in sweats, and his temperature skyrocketed! He knew he'd been poisoned so he fled from Taldish's home to the nearest hospital. Unfortunately, the poison was made from the deadly yix root, for which there was no antidote. Grandos died on the operating table, but not before relaying his story.

"There wasn't enough evidence to convict Taldish of the crime according to Aronite law. But Aronite law still caught up to him, not for the poisoning, but the name change that Grandos had submitted. You see, after Grandos' death, Taldish attempted to change the sector's name back to that of his rival. But Aronite law stated that only the original explorer could submit name changes, and upon the explorer's death the name that had been chosen could never be changed again! Unable to undo his terrible mistake, Taldish was forced to live with that shame and ridicule for the remainder of his life."

"Wow," exclaimed Jym. "You sure know a lot about interstellar history."

"It was a primary field of study when I was in the collegiate academy," Nado said proudly.

Mara spoke up again. "Who are the dangerous races that live here? Are they still hostile?"

"Excellent question," the big Zennian responded. "Our current heading is for the planet Khardan, home to the massive, scaly Kritons. They've been a major source of difficulty to the Galactic Community, but never fought any wars against them. Then there are the furry, predatorial Ranjemans of the planet Ranjeman. Don't ask them for help with naming conventions, you can probably tell why. They are very territorial hunters, but again, not warmongers per se."

"Among the worst are the Gnarfs. They call their home-world Urkasak, and it is ruled over by a monstrous warlord named King Bë-Konn, whose crimes include raiding, looting, piracy, illegal scavenging, and hostile invasions of colonies. Taldish is also home to the Hexagon, once known as the Heptagon. It was intended to be the sister government to the Octagon, acting as the Community Council's extension in Taldish. But their leader, Prime Executor Mantis, built an interplanetary weapon of mass destruction, which he tested on one of his own moons! He killed millions of his own innocent people, and then went on to wage war against the Galactic Community, nearly bringing the GC to the brink of extinction!"

"What race was Mantis?" Mara wondered.

At that moment Kel entered the room, interrupting before Nado had a chance to answer. "Captain, I hardly think this is the right story at this time."

"But I was just getting to the best part," protested the captain.

"I think the kids need their rest before we set down on Khardan," Kel insisted. "Come on your majesties, let's get you settled." After escorting them from the room, the commander dragged Nado to the bridge, lecturing him. "Have you forgotten what race Mantis was? And what race they are? They're already struggling with a universe that they think hates them for being Vampyrials. You really think telling them the history of the worst Vampyrial of all time, the one that led to their near genocide, is the right thing to do at this juncture?"

Nado felt the heat of frustration rising inside him. "Well excuse me, Miss Queen-of-all-things-relating-to-the-Vampyrial-children-we-are-currently-escorting…never mind, that started better in my head."

"All I'm saying is that perhaps we should keep the whole evil Mantis thing to ourselves for now."

"Fair enough."

"Come on. It's almost time to plot our landing vector. I'll be hailing their control tower as soon as we're in range."

The Explorer 2000 set down amid a cloud of swirling dust and debris upon the surface of Khardan. As spaceports went, it wasn't the worst, but it also certainly wasn't anywhere near the best. Primarily coated in dirt, the small port consisted of little more than a smattering of buildings, a control tower, and a few maintenance hangars.

Captain Nado led the crew in debarking from the ship, except for Dr. Rox who opted to stay on board and keep an eye on the ship itself. All around them they could see desert and brown, rocky mountain ranges as far as the eye could see. Heat from the local sun beat down on the dusty ground, causing distortion on the horizons. It made for a good climate for the cold-blooded Kritons though. Their own attempts at space travel had been highly hampered by this fact, a problem that they'd had to solve with heavy, specialized space suits.

Beyond the port, Nado could make out a town. The buildings resembled giant round shells made of hardened sand and rock. Above ground there wouldn't be much to see, but Kriton architecture wasn't made for the surface. They resided in underground facilities, lined with natural insulation for retaining the correct temperature. Among the few innovations of the Kriton people was their magnificent insulation and vast improvements to HVAC systems.

On initial approach the town felt empty and almost eerie. But they soon heard the sounds of raucous behavior emanating from the bowels of the strange structures. One dome in particular was significantly louder than the rest.

"I wonder what this place is," mused Nado, unable to read the sign.

"It says 'saloon'," noted Schiff.

This surprised Kel. "You can read the Kriton language?"

"Oh, yes," the shapeshifter replied. "In my line of work, sometimes folks want you to emulate the languages of whatever you shift into as well."

"Huh," Kel grunted. "I guess you're pulling your weight."

"You might find me quite valuable to have around," quipped Schiff in a good-natured manner. "I contain a multitude of unseen talents!"

"Saloons and barkeeps are a good place to get information," the captain proclaimed. "Kel, let's you and I head inside and see if they know where we can restock and resupply."

"Good plan Cap," said Schiff. "The kids and I will mosey around town and see the sights!"

"I'm not sure that's a good idea," Kel started to say. But Schiff had already whisked the children down the street to the next set of structures.

"They'll be okay for a few minutes," Nado assured. "We'll only be here for a bit, then we'll catch up." And he led the commander through the arched entryway and down a long flight of stairs into the boisterous basement below.

Sitting on barrels in a dimly lit corner of the noisy bar at a ramshackle table, Schlaar complained to Shtrepp in their native tongue. "I don't trust that Star Guard robot. When did the Guard start using robot patrols? And when did they ever let crooks like us go?"

"Shut up!" his partner fussed. "What is the Human saying? 'Don't look at horse mouths' or something like that."

"I don't know what that is supposed to mean. You don't know what that means either! What even is a horse?! What a stupid saying!" Schlaar slammed his drink on the table.

Shtrepp reproached him. "Cut it out! We don't want to draw too much attention, there are bounties out on us as well. Two thousand, eight hundred, and thirty-four bits is a lot to owe to someone like Trell."

"Trell is murg larva dung! I hate his stinking guts! We shouldn't owe him anything."

"Well we do owe him, and if we ever want to pay off that loan, we'll have to come up with something. And that robot gave us the answer. We find that Explorer crew and bust them up! Then we get paid."

Schlaar grumbled, "I'm not so sure about that. What are the odds that the Explorer crew will show up on Khardan? And even if they did, what are the odds they'd land on this side of the planet? And if they somehow did that, how can we expect them to waltz right into this saloon and announce their arrival like idiots?"

At that moment, all attention was directed to the entrance stairs as a big, booming voice proudly announced, "Hail friends! I am Captain Burnay Nado of the Explorer 2000! We are in need of assistance and require directions to the nearest market to procure water and food for our spacecraft. Can anyone help us?"

Shtrepp gave a smug look across the table. "You were saying?"

"I stand corrected," Schlaar growled. "I suppose they are complete idiots."

"And we are incredibly lucky. Activate the fob and let's see how fast we can form a posse. Gnash and his boys are around here somewhere."

With a nod to the barkeep, the two thugs slunk from the room, disappearing into another chamber. Emergency escape tunnels led to the surface, giving the perilous pair the perfect secret exit. They quickly shimmied and clawed their way out, splitting up to cover more ground and grab as many willing hands as they could. If they were able to get to the local thieves' guild fast enough, the gang boss Gnash would undoubtedly want a piece of this action...

The tiny shuttle was chilly and dark, but that didn't bother the H-8 assassin unit. It needed no warmth, no light, no sustenance. A blinking orange bulb attracted the robot's attention, the tracking fob. Against all odds, the Explorer 2000 had managed to cross paths with its Kriton lackeys. Computing the spaceflight rapidly in its processors, the deadly automaton deftly maneuvered its craft towards Khardan, programming and protocols demanding that it seek and capture its prey.

Chapter 4

The saloon had fallen deathly silent following Captain Nado's pronouncement. Kel could see every dark, beady eyeball returning her stare. If a shootout was imminent, she couldn't tell. These patrons had apparently perfected the art of their gambling faces. After a few moments that felt like an eternity, eventually the clientele went back to their carousing.

Slapping her forehead, Kel mumbled, "Captain, do you really think running around announcing ourselves like that is the wisest thing to do?"

"What do you mean?" Nado asked. "We need resources. They might know where to find them."

How dense can you be? Kel wondered, but out loud she said, "This place is filled with a brood of Kritons. You know, creatures that are typically found in the employ of less than reputable individuals?"

"Kel, I'm shocked at you!" jibed the captain. "I know you're a Human, but I thought racial profiling was only done by the Humans on the Community Council." He then added in a more serious tone, "And the Aronites of course...all Aronites."

"Hey newcomersh!" the barkeep called. "You need sssupliesss?"

"There, you see?" Nado joked at Kel. "Helpful barkeep, never fails!" To the barkeep he replied, "Yes, my good man. We need fresh supplies for space travel."

"Try the ssstore three doorsh down on the wessst ssside of the ssstreet," the barkeep informed them. "They should have what you need."

"Fantastic! Thank you!" Nado turned to leave.

"Wait, wait! When you go to pay for the provisionsss, sssay 'khanakhat.' If you do, they will give you a dissscount."

"You, sir, have been more than helpful. You have my deepest appreciation." Once more, the captain and commander attempted to exit.

"Wait, wait! Make shure you vishit the weather ssstation before your departure. Make shure conditionsss are right for takeoff. There could be sssandsssstormsss in the area."

"We will. Your concern for your fellow sentient is admirable." Shaking the barkeep's hand vigorously, Nado turned to go.

"Wait, wait!" the barkeep yelled again.

"Oh, what now?!" Nado was starting to get agitated.

"How about a couple of roundsss? On the houssse!"

Captain Nado held up his hand. "No, thank you. Kriton grog isn't exactly my drink of choice, though I do truly appreciate the gesture."

"Could I interessst you in a few gamesh at the tablessss?" offered the barkeep. "I'll even ssspot you a few bitsss."

Kel watched as the barkeep surreptitiously checked a timepiece. "Captain, we need to go. Right now."

"As my first officer has mentioned, we are on a strict timetable," Nado said to the barkeep. "While I am in awe of your immutable hospitality, we do need to leave. Thank you."

"Wait, wait!"

"No!" Nado firmly bellowed. "Thank you, goodbye." As they ascended the stairs to the surface, he whispered to Kel, "Talk about being helped to death."

"I don't think he was being helpful, Captain," Kel returned. "He was checking the time. I think he was trying to delay us."

"There you go with the profiling again," jested Nado.

"I wasn't – never mind. How about you take care of the supplies while I track down Schiff and the kids?"

"Sounds like a plan to me."

The two split up, Nado heading to the west side of the street towards the store, with Kel hurriedly jogging in the opposite direction. She was anxious to get the rest of their group gathered safely back on the Explorer. Her eyes quickly scanned every side street and alley, searching for any sign of the others. Something was wrong, very wrong. She just couldn't shake the feeling that they'd blundered into a trap.

An expansive underground warehouse awaited Captain Nado as he descended another flight of stairs inside the general store that the barkeep had indicated. Huge steel shelving lined the walls, extending all the way to the ceiling. They jutted towards the center of the complex, creating aisles between each set.

The center of the storehouse was littered with bins and crates overflowing with all manner of commodities, arranged in a simple block pattern that allowed space for walkways around them. One section was designated solely for the Kriton-sized specialty spacesuits which hung from a series of sturdy racks. A band of Pyrian workers bustled past Nado on their way to the freezers in the rear of the storehouse.

Ah yes, a Pyrian Union Force, Nado thought to himself. *Being cold-blooded, they'd have to have someone else work the freezers.*

There was so much to see and shop for, so the captain made sure to take his time, enjoying the sights, sounds, smells, and free samples of exotic meat dipped in rare spices and sauce. They even had discounted game tablets! Nado couldn't resist the urge to check every single aisle, shelf, bin, and freezer to see what wonders may await.

It was nearly an hour later before he had finished his circuit of the massive market, bringing along the list of items he had selected for purchase. When he reached the checkout counter, there wasn't even a line. This place was the best! Nado made a mental note to come back to this warehouse whenever they needed a resupply in the region.

"Ish thish everything you need?" the cashier asked. She was smaller and more slender than most Kritons.

"Yes, and can you add the spaceport delivery fee, please?" the captain requested. "I certainly wouldn't want to have to lug all of that back to the port by myself!"

"Sssomeone will be happy to ashisht you," the cashier slurred.

"Oh, one more thing!" Nado had almost forgotten. "I have a discount code, 'khanakhat'."

At that, the cashier looked up from her work. She looked a little afraid of the word, even shuddering slightly. "I sssee," she murmured. "Are you by yourshelf?" The captain nodded. "Very well. I will factor that into your cosht." She then knelt down and retrieved a long string of stickers from under the counter. "Here, put theshe on. Thish denotesss that you are a preferred cussstomer. Have a good day sssir."

"I love this store!" exclaimed Nado. "You have a good day too!" He paid for the order and proceeded to exit via the gigantic staircase. The captain couldn't help but relish the experience as he ambled up the steps. It had been exhilarating to shop in an alien bazaar for the first time in his life! A rush of enthusiasm flowed over him as he breached the surface again, sunlight washing him in its radiance.

But sunlight wasn't the only thing that fell upon the unsuspecting Zennian. Hidden from view on the domed rooftop, three Kritons in black leathers crept along, waiting for the chance to pounce. As soon as the tall spacer was fully in the open, they swooped in like opportunistic pack hunters, tackling Nado to the ground!

A ghostly quiet had shrouded the small town, the only activity being dust devils swirling across the wide dirt roads. Instinctively, Kel's hand slid to her hip, wrapping around the hilt of her pistol. She was nearing the far end of town when a figure strode into the center of the street and squared itself off against her.

"You are part of the Explorer crew, yesh?" the person wheezed. The figure raised its head, black scales glaring in the sunlight, dark eyes staring hard. Then the eyes widened in recognition. "YOU!"

Kel knew her assailant instantly. "You!" she shouted, almost at the same time. It was Shtrepp, armed to the teeth with guns, knives, and an ugly-looking electric prod dangling from her belt! Kel wasted no time. She drew her pistol and fired several shots in Shtrepp's vicinity, running for cover behind a building entryway.

Super-heated plasma bolts whistled through the air past Kel's head as Shtrepp returned fire, hollering, "Schlaar! It'sh her! The one from Wheeler'sss! Shoot her!"

Before Kel had a chance to look for the lumbering Schlaar, he revealed his location with two powerful blasts from his electro-rifle! The bolts exploded against the wall just above Kel, causing tiny electrical shockwaves to burst across it. Her ears were ringing, making the commander quite disoriented. She tried to shoot back at Schlaar, but he had ducked out of sight atop a roof on the other side of the road.

"I'm in a terrible position," Kel grumbled to herself. "Got to get to better cover…"

The commander tried to get a look at her attackers, but more shots pounded the walls of her slim cover, sending debris into her eyes. Ears ringing, eyes stinging, and heart pounding out of her chest, Commander Kel flung herself into the open, firing wildly in all directions! Barely able to see through tear-blurred vision, she bobbed and weaved across the street to a thin entrance of a smaller structure. The walls were hard and unforgiving as she slammed into them, squeezing through the slender crevice.

"Don't let her get away!" screeched Shtrepp.

Inside a structure, Kel figured she had an advantage, until she checked her pistol to discover there was only one shot left in the cartridge. *I need a look around, see what I can use*, thought Kel. After brushing the dust from her eyes and allowing them to acclimate to the darkness, she could see pelts adorning the walls, alongside spears, composite bows, and huge curved knives. *It must be a hunting lodge*, she supposed. There was a fireplace at the rear wall, a skin of hardened plate hanging above the mantle. Tools for lighting the fireplace were scattered across the hearth. *That gives me an idea...*

Outside, Schlaar and Shtrepp cautiously crept toward the entrance to the lodge. Schlaar slid from his rooftop hiding place, meeting Shtrepp at the door. They took up positions opposite each other and proceeded to converse quietly in their native tongue.

"I saw her go inside there," whispered Shtrepp. "If we rush, we can surprise her."

"The entry is too thin for my power pack," muttered Schlaar, motioning to the apparatus on his back that powered the electro-rifle.

"Dump it," his partner hissed. "It's close quarters anyway. Use your claws and teeth!"

"And when I get shot, then what?"

"Then I blow Gnash's signal horn, and we get his whole gang to join the chase!"

Schlaar finally agreed, doffing the power pack and abandoning his favored weapon. On a quick count of three, the duo turned to bust into the lodge. But the moment they turned to go, something else burst out. It was draped in a shroud of hardened plate, with blazing torches in each hand. The Kritons shrieked and roared as the heat stung their eyes, rubbing at the pain vehemently. Kel shed the plated skin and in a split second had to decide which target she would take the shot at, heavily armed Shtrepp, huge and toughened Schlaar, or...there was a power pack on the ground next to him. She didn't hesitate. Kel fired her last shot.

Schlaar recovered with just enough time to see the commander level her shot. Panicked, he roared, "Hit the dirt!" throwing himself on top of Shtrepp. The two were launched down the street as the power pack exploded from the impact of Kel's plasma blast! They tumbled to the ground in a tangled heap. Feeling rather proud, Kel afforded herself a brief smile, but then noticed an oddly shaped device at Shtrepp's mouth. The Kriton woman blew into it, and an awful noise erupted from the horn.

"Uh, oh," moaned Kel, as a light tremor shook under her feet, and a thundering could be heard in the next street. It was the sound of no less than a dozen more Kritons, all decked in black leathers, careening towards her! "Where are Schiff and those kids?" she fumed. "We have got to get out of here."

The wily commander slipped from the road, getting out of the open and hiding behind another building before the horde had a chance to see her. Despite her labored breath, she could hear a scratchy, gravelly voice not too far away shouting, "I've got the kidsss! Go get the captain and firsht mate!"

Kel peered out just enough to see the group of Kritons sprawling out across the road, pulling Schlaar and Shtrepp from the ground. She then saw the owner of the voice she'd heard, another Kriton in black, escorting the prince and princess through the throng. *No! They've got the kids!* she worried. *That's my primary target.*

Carefully snaking between the buildings, Kel eventually caught up to the kidnapper. She was out of ammunition, but the thug didn't know that. Maybe it would make for a decent bluff at least. She heard muffled murmurings just around the domed wall next to her. The commander whirled around the edifice and aimed her pistol!

Standing before her was an unexpected sight. There was Schiff with Mara and Jym, alone. Not a Kriton in sight. "Wait, what?" was all that would come out of Kel's mouth.

"Did I fool you too?" Schiff excitedly queried, her eyes laughing. "I heard the brutes in the street, heard your firefight, and then heard the commotion of even more on the way. So, I shifted into a Kriton form and slipped the kids right past the guards!"

"It was awesome!" Jym exclaimed.

"It was pretty cool," agreed Mara.

Kel just breathed a sigh of relief. "Schiff, the more time we spend on this particular mission, the more I like you. Come on, let's get back to the ship."

The girth and weight of Kritons notwithstanding, the three grunts that currently held Nado against the ground were no match for his Zennian strength. The captain shoved upward with all his might, knocking the goons back. Armed with only one of his plasma pistols, Nado was certain that this battle would be better fought with fisticuffs.

"I'll have you all know," the captain uttered, "I have three rules when it comes to brawling. Number one, never fight if you don't have to. Number two, remember there is no such thing as a fair fight. Number three, if you must fight, always draw first blood!"

Emphasizing that last word, Nado elbowed Thug One in the face, blocking a body shot from Thug Two with his lower arms. Thug Three tried to bite at Nado but was caught by the throat and received a powerful uppercut to the jaw. Thug Two twirled and came back with a clawed slash at the captain's face, but he dodged and kicked Two in the gut. One and Three attempted a tandem attack, both leaping at Nado's shoulders. Reaching out, he grasped their collars, thumped Two in the face with his lower fists, and slammed One and Three together, their scales crunching from the impact.

Thinking his foes defeated, Nado dusted his hands. But Kritons are made of tougher stuff than he realized. Thug Two charged headlong at Nado's gut, while One and Three recovered. It took all four of Nado's arms to stop Two's charge and keep him from gnawing a hole in the captain's belly. Meanwhile One and Three circled in front of the Zennian, and One launched Three through the air with his tail! Three landed on Nado's head and shoulders, while One dashed around, slashing the captain across the back with sharp claws.

Acting fast, the captain felt he had little choice but to let go of Two, allowing the monster to bite his flank, just under the ribcage.

But with all four arms, he grabbed hold of One's tail as the brute jetted past. Nado used One's own momentum to swing him into the air, smashing him down on Three, who still sat on the captain's shoulders, his teeth sunk into the left side. Three collapsed to the ground, utterly stunned. One had bounced off of Three, so Nado used that as leverage to continue wielding One as a flail, crashing him into Two. The trio of troublemakers thudded into the dust, unconscious. Nado winced from his multiple wounds but had little time to relax before two more Kritons wandered by. They were arguing with each other but stopped when they saw him.

They looked like they'd been through a battle themselves, covered in scorch marks and singed armor. Both were still armed heavily however, the female wearing bandoliers of knives and carrying several small firearms, the male toting a nasty electric prod in one hand and a large pistol in the other. They aimed their weapons at him instantly, and Nado knew there was only one tactic he could employ in this situation.

"I surrender!" he shouted, throwing his hands in the air. "Please don't shoot!" They held their fire, so he talked more. "I really don't understand, why are you all attacking? Did I do something to offend your culture?"

"I am Shtrepp, and thish ish Schlaar," the female growled. "We are being paid to hunt and capture the crew of the Explorer 2000."

"If I may ask, how much are you getting paid to do this?" Nado queried.

Schlaar answered this time. "Two thousssand bitsss. We need the money."

"What for?"

"We owe much to another."

Shtrepp grew antsy though, shouting, "Enough of thish! Why are we talking when we could be shooting?!"

"Because I might be able to help you!" countered the captain, hastily. "How much do you owe?"

"Two thousssand, eight hundred, and thirty-four bitsss," Schlaar replied.

Nado thought for a moment. It would cost him certainly, but it would be worth it if it got these goons off their backs. "Back on my ship, I have a primordial sawtooth Fangorian skull. It has a market value of around three thousand bits to the right collector. I'll give it to you."

"Why should we trussst you?" Shtrepp was obviously not convinced.

"Because you've got guns aimed at me," Nado stated. "It'd be pretty stupid of me to try and bluff right now."

The two Kritons shrugged at each other. "Makesss sssenssse to me," Schlaar muttered. "And I've had more than I wanted of sssstruggling for thish money already. I sssay we go with him to hish ship."

"Fine," snarled Shtrepp. "But no funny bushinesh."

Nado had no intentions of anything of the kind in his condition. "That would also be a foolhardy decision considering my injuries and, once again, the guns aimed at me." As they started to head for the spaceport, he asked one final question. "Out of curiosity, who was paying you to capture us?"

The remaining crew arrived at the Explorer 2000, ready to embark and hunker down for safety. But as they approached, Kel spied a small craft that had been landed right next to their bulkhead doors blocking the entrance! "Oh, you have got to be kidding me!" she blurted. "What moron situates their craft right next to another like that! You'd have to be an utter imbecile to do something like that!" The hiss of air escaping from the airlock interrupted her tirade, indicating that the occupant of the small shuttle was emerging. "Good. I can give them a piece...of...my...mind..."

Kel's words slowed as the pilot marched forth. It moved with perfect precision, a red glow emanating from its head. A cold vocalization issued from the fog and dust that swirled around the tall frame. "Greetings crew of the Explorer 2000." The air cleared and the assassin robot stepped forward. "You will hand over the prince and princess or face dire consequences."

"Oh, come on," Kel groaned.

"Hey, isn't that the robot from Octo V?" Schiff pointed out.

"Get down!" yelled Kel, yanking Schiff and the kids behind a low row of rocks.

"You continue to choose dire consequences," declared the robot. "How illogical."

The robot commenced firing at the row of rocks, chipping away at the tiny boulders little by little. Kel looked at Schiff and quipped, "Well, it's been fun. Short, but fun."

Suddenly, the two noticed Mara start to rise from the rocks. "The energy fields are strong here," was all she said, and stood erect.

"What are you doing?" cried Schiff.

"Do you want to get killed?!" Kel warned.

But it was as if the sounds of shouting and gunshots faded into obscurity for Mara. She stood steadfast, unwavering and unfaltering. Stubbornly staring down the computerized killer, the little princess lifted her right hand. The H-8 unit took aim. Mara closed her eyes and waited.

Time seemed to slow as the report of the carbine resounded in the spaceport. A plasma bolt sailed unerringly toward the princess. At the last nanosecond, Mara's eyes snapped open, her hand flexed, and the burning projectile halted mid-flight. As fleetingly as she had stopped the blast, Mara whipped her wrist, sending the shot straight back to its origin, ripping through the assassin's metallic plating!

Mara's hand twisted around, and the robot was then lifted off its feet, limp as a ragdoll. With blood trailing from her nose, Mara thrust her arm forward, sending the H-8 flying backward into its shuttle. The thing crashed inside, the red glow of its ocular sensors finally dying. Jym rushed to Mara's side.

"Mara!" he cried out. She glanced at him weakly and collapsed, exhausted from the expulsion of power. Schiff also ran to assist, but Kel only stood shocked. That certainly explained why someone very powerful within the Galactic Community wanted these kids either under control or dead. It was just like the stories that Nado had told.

There was no time for such musings now though, so Kel turned her attention to the downed assassin. The robot lay crumpled within its shuttle, tossed against the wall like a bag of trash in a landfill. She could still hear a hum coming from its interior though. The power core was still active. This thing could be reactivated! She snatched its plasma carbine for good measure.

They all took a few minutes to reconvene and try to figure out how to get the shuttle moved so they could board the Explorer when Kel caught sight of the captain approaching. Something was wrong however, he was being escorted by Shtrepp and Schlaar! "Everyone find cover," Kel ordered. Then she called to the hoodlums, "You let our captain go, or I'll give your wretched bodies some new orifices!"

"Hold your fire!" hollered the captain. "Everything's okay!"

"What?"

"We talked it over. Turns out, they can be bought by us as easily as by that robot!"

Kel looked over her shoulder at the subject of that sentence. "Huh. Well, good thing you made friends. Something tells me they weren't going to get paid after all."

Confused by that statement, Nado concluded the trek to the Explorer. The groups quickly swapped tales, and the Kriton pair agreed to help the crew muscle the shuttle aside so they could get on board their ship, and Nado could retrieve their prized skull. As they were setting about the work, Schlaar grunted, "Now we can pay off what we owe to Trell!"

Nado perked up. "Trell? You don't mean Gren Trell, the gentleman crime lord, do you?"

"None other," responded Shtrepp.

"Then I'm really glad we worked something out! Trell is one of the worst out there, you should never do business with him!"

Schlaar rolled his eyes. "Now he tellsss ush!"

"There'sss only one problem left," mentioned Shtrepp. "We asssked for help from the local thievesss' guild to catch you all."

"They're led by a nasssty guy called Gnash," Schlaar informed. "He'sss not looking for a quick payout like we were though. He wanted your ship, your sssupliesss, and your headsss on pikesss. That'sss the only way we were able to get hish help ssso fasht."

"That explains why there was a small army chasing us around town," noted Schiff. It was at that moment they all heard the telltale cacophony of propellors whirring in the distance, sounding as though they had actually kicked a nest of giant, angry, stinging insectoids. Schiff looked around. "Hey, what's that noise?"

Schlaar and Shtrepp exchanged a look. "Gnash!"

Chapter 5

The heat of the Khardan sun brutalized the Explorer 2000 crew, who were desperately heaving with all their might to shove the H-8's shuttle aside. Drenched in sweat, they continued to shove and shunt. Even Nado, together with Shtrepp and Schlaar, was having a tough time getting the vessel to slide across the dusty ground. Though it was a tiny spacecraft, the shuttle was still incredibly stout and weighty.

"I don't understand," grunted Schiff, "why we couldn't just fly the shuttle out of the way."

"Because," Kel replied between hefts, "the robot's precision landing...can't be replicated...by us." She paused for a breath. "If we try to launch...we might damage the Explorer...ugh!"

"Could Mara move it with her powers?"

Jym joined the conversation. "She drained herself dealing with the robot. She's in no condition to do anything like that."

"Besides," mumbled Mara, "it doesn't work that way. It isn't telekinesis, I can't just move whatever."

"Let's go team!" encouraged Captain Nado. "We're running out of time!"

Indeed, time was growing short. The drone of Gnash's propellor-powered hovercraft amplified as the flying machines drew ever nearer. Nado shook his head as he contemplated their circumstances. Time wasn't growing short, it was already gone.

"Never mind," he stated. "We have no other recourse. We must stand and fight. Everyone, battle positions!"

The misfit band scuttled about, each preparing for combat in their own way. Shtrepp tossed two spare pistols to Captain Nado and scurried behind the shuttle for cover. Schlaar checked the power levels of the electric prod and the ammunition of his own pistol, stomping to the opposite end of the small craft for protection. The captain himself reached inside the robot's tiny ship, picking up a large piece of plating that had dislodged. He hefted it as a shield with his upper arms, his lower set dual wielding Shtrepp's pistols. Schiff helped Jym carry Mara to the interior of the shuttle, well out of sight, then she positioned herself to help reload weaponry. Kel also ducked inside the shuttle with the robot's carbine, but a wild idea crossed her mind. She gradually turned around until she was facing the disabled assassin unit.

Peering through the modular binoculars that hung from his neck, Nado tried to get a good view of the incoming threat. Three hovercrafts soared in their direction, stirring up a minor sandstorm in their wake. The crafts bore a unique design, each with two seating pods only fit for a single operator. The pods were round and had an open top, their underside housing the engines and maneuvering props. In one pod sat the pilot, a gunner in the other.

Two were identical in design, but the third that flew in the middle of the formation instead sported three pods, one pilot and two gunners. Situated in the pilot chair, perched as if on a throne, was an individual who could only be Gnash himself. It an odd sight to be sure, but Gnash's features were that of an albino Kriton, bearing snow-white scales and gray eyes, one of which was marled with a foul scar.

"Incoming!" yelled Captain Nado.

With a roar of sputtering engines, the storm descended on the crew! Belt-fed automatic gatlings spit a slew of projectiles all around. The captain's makeshift shield absorbed several shots, allowing him to return the favor. Shtrepp and Schlaar laid down covering fire, while Kel was noticeably absent from the fray.

"Commander!" Nado thundered. "We could sure use some help out here!"

But the commander was busily piddling with the H-8 unit. She had pried open the hatch that gave access to much of the thing's central processing cores. A mess of circuitry, wires, motherboards, and more awaited within.

"What are you doing?" asked Schiff. "Mara just toasted that thing, we don't want to wake it back up, do we?"

Determination written all over her face, Kel declared, "We do if I can reset its IFF programming."

"IFF? What's that?"

"It stands for 'Identification, Friend or Foe'," Kel excitedly answered. "I'm no robotics engineer, but I do recall how to do that. Just need a few more seconds..."

"I'll see if I can buy you those seconds," Jym proclaimed, ripping a long piece of shrapnel from the shuttle wall. Before Schiff or Mara could stop him, the young prince dashed out into the hailstorm of gunfire.

Nado, Shtrepp, and Schlaar were barely able to hold off the assailants, as the hovercrafts circled like carrion birds. Suddenly Jym appeared, running to the middle of the battlefield. He gathered all his strength, and with a burst of energy exploding beneath him, leapt high into the air, sailing toward one of the hovercrafts.

Mara, watching from inside the shuttle, feebly reached toward her brother. "He didn't use enough of the energy field. He won't make it." The princess balled her fist and thrust her arm in Jym's direction. His failing flight was at once renewed, and he zoomed forward at an alarming speed! Holding his shrapnel sword aloft, the prince infused the sharpened metal with dark energy, slicing his hovercraft target in half. As the pods whirled out of control, Jym managed to alight in a perfect three-point landing, and the crashing craft burst into flames behind him.

That was one down, but two remained, still raining a steady barrage. The young monarch fled from the fight, his own nose bleeding from the use of his abilities. Mara had fallen unconscious, and Kel had yet to join the fight.

Sweat poured down her face, as Kel dexterously poked her fingers into the cranial cavity of the robot. There was the circuit board that governed the IFF programming. One quick electrical short, and it would be reset. But one false move could result in anything. For all Kel knew, the unit could have a self-destruct feature built in.

"Schiff," she murmured, barely above a whisper, "I need you to locate the power core on this thing. Should be just under the chest plating. When I reset this circuitry, I need you to power it up. Hopefully performing the reset in tandem with a reboot of the whole system will keep it from malfunctioning, or worse, self-destructing."

"Self-destruct?" a nervous Schiff questioned. "As in 'blow up'? It might blow up?!"

"Not if you do exactly as I've instructed. Ready?"

"I guess so..."

"One, two, three!"

The hum of the power core intensified, and the robot's ocular sensors lit up again. They were not red however, but a soft yellow. It turned to Kel. "Greetings."

"It worked!" cheered Kel. "Robot, can you – "

"This unit's designation is H-8-RED, an assassin robot of unrivaled sophistication."

"Yes, yes!" Kel hurried the thing. "We know all that!"

"Detecting a reset to IFF parameters. This unit recognizes you as Commander Kel of the Explorer 2000 but does not register you as a foe."

"That's great, now deal with the threat outside!"

For a moment, it appeared as though the robot was thinking. Then it jerked its head at Kel, snapped it towards the shuttle door, then back at Kel again. "Aye, commander. This unit was armed with a plasma carbine. Do you know the whereabouts of said equipment?"

"Here!" Kel thrust the weapon into the robot's chest. It took the carbine, rapidly checking it for any damage, then to make sure it was loaded. Powering up the weapon with ease, the H-8 evenly waltzed into the raging skirmish outside.

The captain and their new Kriton allies were outmatched and outgunned, and all three were down to their last remaining, all too precious, rounds of ammunition. As the gunship hovercrafts continued to pummel the crew, the robot strode coolly into the midst of the action. It swiveled its carbine into position, fired two perfectly placed shots, and then turned back toward the crew as the last two hovercrafts spiraled to the dust!

Coughing and wheezing, Gnash emerged from the wreckage and sputtered, "You're all dead! I'll have that ship, everything on board, and your headsss on pikesss, you batch of – "

His words were cut short by a final plasma blast from the robot's firearm, as the murderous machine whipped its arm over its shoulder, pulling the trigger without looking back. Gnash stood stunned, sunlight spilling through a cauterized hole located center mass. Not wanting to give the guild-master a chance, Nado, Shtrepp, and Schlaar riddled him with the last of their ammo. As the albino Kriton fell flat, everyone began to relax. The fight was over.

Hours later, the Kriton pair had their skull reward, and the Explorer 2000 had once more taken flight to the expanse. The young monarchs lay in their berths, resting after their display of power. Schiff and Kel filled Dr. Rox in on their misadventures while he patched up Captain Nado.

"Good grief," the doctor said lightly. "It feels like we jumped out of the frying pan and into the fire, doesn't it?"

"It was incredible!" exclaimed Schiff. "I've never done anything like that before!"

"Neither have we," Kel chuckled. "Whatever is going on with those kids is unlike anything any of us have ever dealt with. They're in a serious load of danger."

The atmosphere of the med-bay shifted, suddenly darkening and intensifying. The trio looked at each other, even Schiff's perky attitude getting crushed by the weight of their thoughts. They had gotten extremely lucky. Kel glanced at the captain, lying unconscious in one of the sleeping pods on the bay wall. His wounds were fairly severe, two bites, one to the abdomen and another to the upper left shoulder, and several large lacerations across the back from the claw attack.

Rox noticed her gaze. "I've done my best to treat him. I had to give him a double dose of anesthesia to knock him out. Acetaminophen for the pain, a large amount of disinfectant, more stitches than he's ever had before, and about half our supply of clean bandages to fully wrap him up."

"He really took a beating this time," Kel muttered. "We can't just keep wandering aimlessly. We need a plan of action. If we don't take initiative, whoever is after the kids is going to catch us eventually."

Walking to the gurney that sat in the center of the bay, Rox motioned to the H-8 unit that lay deactivated upon it. "First things first, we need to talk about this being on board. I probably don't need to say it, but I don't like the thought of being trapped in space with an assassin unit."

"Maybe the robot can tell us who sent it?" Schiff offered.

"Not a bad idea…," mused Kel.

"Wait a minute!" Rox halted them. "That thing has caused enough mayhem, don't you think? It's apparently been hunting us since the Octagon."

"Yeah, but Kel reprogrammed it," Schiff elatedly informed.

"You did?" questioned Rox.

The commander couldn't look the doctor in the eye. "Not quite. I didn't fully reprogram it, but we did reset the IFF parameters. It saved our lives in that fracas. I don't think it's a hazard anymore."

"That's got to be the most insane thing…"

"Rox, what if we could actually reprogram it though?" Kel pondered. "I know a little of robotics, and with your help – "

"Kel, I'm a physician, not an engineer."

"I know that, don't patronize me! I just figured you have a mind for meticulous work, perhaps we could – "

"As I've had to reiterate to the captain many times, the title 'doctor' doesn't make me an expert in all fields of science," said an exasperated Rox.

"Forget it!" Kel heatedly spat. "I'll do it myself."

Sighing, the doctor relented. "You don't have to do that, I'll see what I can do – "

"No, no! You don't get to change your mind now!" argued Kel. "Schiff will help me."

"I will?" uttered a surprised Schiff, who had been watching the exchange like a ping-pong match.

"You ask for my help, I say no, you get furious," complained Rox, "then I say I'll help, you get even more upset, and say you don't want it. You are impossible."

"At least I'm not an old grump!" Kel quipped.

At that, the doctor tried to de-escalate the impassioned debate. "Perhaps we should all get some rest first? I'm sure we'll feel better after a good sleep."

No one was contrary to that suggestion, so they headed into the main hold, leaving Nado asleep in the med-bay. On their way out, however, they nearly bumped into Mara and Jym, who were attempting to piece together a snack. The siblings nervously shifted, their expressions betraying the look of toddlers whose hands had been caught in the proverbial cookie jar.

"You don't have to be afraid," Kel calmed them. "It's okay for you to help yourselves if you're hungry."

"I thought you needed to keep a close watch on rations," stated Jym.

"We do," affirmed Kel. "But you guys are part of the crew. As long as we keep a record of what's been eaten, and don't gorge ourselves, it's fine. Get some food."

Hearing this, the kids wasted no time in securing a small meal. While they ate, the rest of the crew just quietly observed. Mara and Jym both gulped their respective nourishment as if it were the only meal they'd had in several cycles. It became evident that the use of their abilities had far-reaching consequences.

"Now that the two of you are rested," the doctor began, "maybe you'll let me give you a checkup? Those nosebleeds are cause for quite a bit of consternation, and clearly your…gifts…have a potent effect on your appetites."

"We'll be fine," Mara asserted.

Between munching, Jym added, "It's happened before, it'll happen again. Happens every time."

"That doesn't mean it should," persisted Rox. "Please, just a quick checkup. I want to be sure you're both healthy and unharmed."

"Why?" Mara wanted to know.

The doctor smiled. "Because I'm a doctor. And because I care about you."

That seemed to catch the children off guard. They stared at one another, a fleeting look of confusion shared between them. There was no doubt that it had been a while since anyone had treated the siblings with even a modicum of tenderness. With a sorrowful countenance, the doctor traded a glance with Kel. She understood his sentiment and felt similarly. Her heart ached for these kids. A life on the run with a ragtag band of spacers was no life for children, they needed their family. But no one spoke, leaving the thick cloud of stillness hanging heavy in the air.

Rather uncharacteristically, Mara broke the silence. "We'll take the checkup. We haven't been to a doctor since right after we fled from the flotilla."

"Good." Rox presented another gentle smile.

Jym then timidly addressed Kel. "Last cycle, the captain was telling us about Taldish Sector. You stopped him when he started talking about Prime Executor Mantis. Mara asked what race Mantis was, but we never found out. I want to know."

Her gaze drooping toward the floor, the commander responded quietly, "He was a Vampyrial."

"He had powers like ours, didn't he?"

"According to the histories, yeah, he did."

"That's the real reason people are scared of us and want us dead, isn't it?"

Kel nodded. "We think so."

"That's what we figured." Now it was Jym's turn to let his face fall. "Are you guys going to try and get rid of us too?"

"Never!" rang a voice from the med-bay door.

"Captain Nado, you should be asleep!" scolded Rox. "Goodness knows I gave you enough sedatives to knock out a Hydromedan whale..."

But Nado waved him off. "Prince Jym, Princess Mara, you two are a part of this crew as much as anyone else aboard. You are not mere passengers, a payday or payout, nor are you simply components of a mission. You are individuals, people, a fact that many within the Galactic Community overlook. We are not defined by our outward race, but by the tenacity of our spirits, and the content of our hearts. And from what I've seen in our endeavors so far, the two of you have more heart than the explorers of old." The captain wobbled a bit. "And now I'm feeling woozy. I believe I shall take a seat."

Nearly faceplanting straight into the galley deck, Captain Nado managed to flop himself clumsily in one of the chairs. He eased back, breathing hard and wincing while holding his left side. With flaccid eyelids, the captain gripped the edge of the table as though it were a lifeline, holding fast as dizziness overwhelmed him.

"Cap, you look awful," Schiff bluntly told him. "You really should go back to sleep."

"As soon as we adjourn this meeting," he returned groggily.

Kel took command of the situation. "In that case, we'd better wrap this up quickly. Captain, we were actually all headed to bed, then discuss what the next phase of our mission should be."

"I see." Nado shook the torpor from his head. "In that case, I call this war room conference to a close. Let's all get to bed."

The garrulous Zennian rose to his feet and promptly lost his balance, slamming to the floor with a loud thump. Everyone rushed to his aid, assisting in lugging his burly bulk back to the medical bay pods. Weary and worn, the crew sought solace in serene sleep.

After a peaceful rest, the crew reconvened around the galley table with a simple breakfast of rehydrated eggs and fruit slices. Reinvigorated by sustenance and sleep, the crew gathered in their usual formation with Captain Nado at the head of the table, flanked by Kel and Schiff. The doctor sat near the med-bay door, while the kids sat on the far end of the table next to their bunking compartment doors.

"Alright," Nado commenced the discussion, "I'd like to hear everyone's suggestions for where they think we should head next."

"I still liked Schiff's idea," noted Kel.

"I had an idea?" Schiff queried.

Kel rolled her eyes. "About reactivating the robot to find out where it came from, who sent it."

"Oh yeah, that one!" beamed Schiff.

"That's a decent plan of action," Nado agreed.

"Debatable...," was the doctor's input.

The captain scanned the room. "Any other ideas?"

Jym raised his hand. "Mara and I were talking about it before our sleep cycle. If we're Vampyrials from the Hexagon, maybe we should go there to see if we can find some answers about where our parents might be. Maybe they're on the Hexagon itself, waiting for us to come home."

"Is that where you grew up?" Schiff asked.

"We don't know," Mara answered, a melancholy warble in her voice. "Our mom and dad never told us the name of the planet we grew up on. I remember being really little and they taught us basic academics and trained us how to control our abilities. Then one day they said it was too dangerous and whisked us off to those stasis pods on that ship. The next thing we knew, we were fleeing the flotilla."

"I guess it's possible that your parents are on the Hex system," comforted Schiff. "We'll look for them there, right Cap?"

"I would," started Nado, "but if we're going there, we'd have to get permission from the warden of the Hexagon."

"Warden?" questioned Jym.

"About every decade, the council elects a new person to act as the overseer of the Hexagon," explained Rox. "They don't want anyone stumbling across anything they deem too dangerous, so they have it guarded zealously by a warden."

"We don't know who the current warden is," Nado finished his thought. "But if we find out, perhaps we can file a request with them. I can do some research."

"Meanwhile, I still say we see about that robot," Kel grimly stated. "If it can tell us who sent it, maybe we can get ahead of this person, or even lay a trap to catch them."

"I'm not sure about that," argued Rox. "Even if it doesn't malfunction and tells us where it came from, who's to say that we can do anything about this mysterious enemy? We talk a good game when it comes to 'laying a trap' or 'getting ahead of them', but this individual seems to have plenty of resources on hand. Certainly more than us anyway..." He trailed off, obviously feeling as though he were outnumbered.

Kel noticed his waning bravado and swallowed her pride. "Your concerns are valid, Rox. There are a ton of unknowns surrounding this. But I feel like that's all the more reason for us to see what that H-8 unit can tell us, if anything at all. You're right, it's a long shot. Might be the only shot we have though. Maybe there's a compromise we can reach?"

"Thank you." Dr. Rox looked at her with unmistakable gratitude. "I appreciate that. Can we reactivate it without giving it full autonomy?"

"I think so," replied Kel. "But it'll take an extra set of hands."

"I'll be happy to help."

Captain Nado rose from his seat slowly, still a bit unstable from his injuries. "Then we have reached a decision. Good conference crew. Let's go interrogate an assassin."

It took Commander Kel no small amount of time to locate the plethora of wiring and circuits that she assumed controlled the robot's motor functions. With Rox and Schiff assisting, they cautiously clipped the wires and deftly deactivated the circuitry. Occasionally, Nado would interject with a phonation, "Ah!" "Oh!" "Careful!" "Oof!"

Kel finally had enough. "Captain, maybe you'd be more at ease waiting outside?" she requested, barely keeping her fiery temper under control.

"No, no, this is fine," Nado responded. "Ooh, look out!"

"WILL YOU GET OUT OF HERE!!" Schiff screamed. Everyone stared in shock. "What? He's making me crazy."

Backing away, Nado meekly mentioned, "There is still the matter of researching the identity of the Hexagon's current warden, perhaps I'll just do that." He slipped from the bay.

Painstaking minutes passed before the task was at last complete. They were ready to activate the H-8-RED assassin robot again. The kids found Nado and brought him back for the interrogation.

"You're sure this will work?" the doctor asked of Kel.

"No," was her honest reply. "But we did the best we could."

"I suppose that's all I can ask for," conceded Dr. Rox.

Hearts beating in their throats, they all waited with baited anticipation for the reactivation of the robot. Kel hit the switch. The power core thrummed as the yellow ocular sensors started to radiate once more. Everyone jumped back as H-8 sat upright!

"I thought it couldn't move!" shouted the doctor.

"So did I!" Kel retorted.

"Greetings crew of the Explorer 2000," the robot recited. "This unit's designation is H-8-RED, an assassin unit of unrivaled sophistication. Sensors indicate that multiple motor functions are unavailable."

They all breathed a sigh of relief. At least part of Kel's plan had worked. "Look Red, we've all heard the intro before, you can stop saying it," she groaned.

"Very well," the robot clinically returned, "this unit will no longer identify itself."

In another part of the room Schiff leaned over to Nado. "Sorry about before. Any luck with your research?"

"All is forgiven," whispered Nado. "Unfortunately, we currently have no access to any records that might indicate who the warden of the Hex is. Hopefully it's someone who'll be willing to assist us."

Meanwhile, the commander continued her interrogation. "H-8-RED, can you inform us of the identity and whereabouts of your former master? Who sent you to kill us?"

"As you are recognized as a friendly by this unit, that information can be freely granted," answered the H-8. "This unit was formerly commanded by Lord Hex, also known as the Marquis du Hex, the current warden of the Hexagon system."

A shocked silence fell across the room. Then Nado quipped, "Someone willing to assist us. Well, so much for that notion."

Chapter 6

Across much of the surface of the planet known as Urkasak was an expansive sprawling of humongous trees, wrapping almost entirely around the equator. This was the preferred biome of the Gnarf people, who lived in enormous pyramid-like structures, the spires of which peeked out above the green, verdant, jungled canopy. Massive mountain ranges bordered the jungles, separating them into naturally formed provinces.

A lone shuttle lighted in a clearing near the largest of the pyramids, and a lone figure strode forth. Well dressed in a sage green underlay with gold colored lightweight body armor, the person moved with a strong and even gait. His dark gray cape shimmered with a metallic sheen, flaring dramatically in the breeze, a heavy hood obscuring his face in deep shadows.

Trailing the figure was a floating hand truck, hovering just above the ground via a series of powerful magnetized machinery. Canvas tarps concealed the unknown goods that filled the hand truck. A crude stone thoroughfare led from the clearing in the direction of a gigantic palace, upon which was located an impossibly steep column of stairs leading to the uppermost levels. Swiftly activating the machine with a small remote, the individual began the long march towards the pyramid palace ahead, his goal at the topmost layer.

Therein lay the lair of the leader of all the Gnarf kingdoms. The palace throne room glistened, bedecked in a coat of precious metals, accented by gemstones and jewels. A row of guards bearing thick shields and polearms with vibrating sawtooth blades, and dressed in hide armor, stood at attention on either side of the chamber. Crystal pools lined the walls, as mossy, floral vines dangled above them.

Upon a mountainous throne sat the Gnarf leader, his piercing eyes leering from under layers of wrinkles that threatened to engulf his entire face. Rough horns protruded from his head, holding aloft the king's incredibly large crown. Like all Gnarfs, his skin was bronzy and hairy, and his immense nose turned upward above a pair of tusks that jutted from his wide maw. Long, pointed ears pierced with countless rings spread like wings from the sides of his ugly mug, while his triple chin rested on a corpulent, barrel shaped body.

The wanderer entered the hall and addressed the Gnarf king. "Oh, great Bë-Konn, High King of the Gnarfs, I bring tribute worthy of the god-killers." He finished with a bow.

Bë-Konn hefted his fat frame from the throne. "Hex-man. What gifts have you brought to the Gnarfs?"

"See for yourself, great king," Lord Hex answered, yanking the canvases from the hand truck with a flourish. "I give you new weapons from the star gods. Fire-breathers, thunder-makers, and sunburst shooters." Revealing what lay within, Lord Hex stepped aside to give the king a good view of the flamethrowers, sonic grenades, and missile launchers he'd packed. "There are also plenty of power cells to keep your new weapons functional for quite some time," he added.

"Hmph," snorted King Bë-Konn. "As always, Hex-man, you come with good tribute and flowery words, but your presents also always come with a price. What favor do you seek now, dark and wicked trickster?"

"You are so untrusting, dear king," soothed Lord Hex. "The task I ask of you is a simple one, but one that requires a great deal of cunning and effort. I'm sure you can handle the effort, it's the cunning that concerns me."

The king growled, snarling, "Do not insult us Hex-man! Remember who you are speaking to!"

"You'd best do the same," Hex coolly returned. "You should not forget that I am a god."

"You should not forget that we are the god-killers! The only thing that keeps us from devouring your essence is that none of us wish your evil abiding in us!"

"No, the thing that keeps you at bay are my displays of power," the marquis corrected. "Shall I remind you?" He raised his left hand, fingers ready to snap.

"That will not be necessary," Bë-Konn acquiesced, allowing his facial muscles to relax. His jowls flopped against his practically non-existent neckline again, seeming at once to merge with the rest of his flabby physique. "What is the task you have for the Gnarfs?"

Satisfied with this response, Lord Hex laid out his plan. "I want you to take your sky-beasts and scour the stars looking for another specific sky-beast. It is named 'Explorer 2000'. It is wandering this sector of the heavens. Your patrols may discover it in the open heavens or docked at one of the star kingdoms. I have here an inscription of their names and likenesses."

"Why can you not do this yourself, Hex-man?"

"Because you have a vast and numerous people, capable of covering more distance than that of a single god," Lord Hex flattered the king. "But listen, when you come across the crew, they are to be remanded into your custody to await my arrival. You are to keep the captain and the children alive and unharmed, if possible."

"What of the rest of them?" inquired Bë-Konn.

"At least two on board are of the race of the star gods. They'd make a fine feast, I'm sure." Twirling theatrically with a swish of his cape, Lord Hex confidently paraded out.

The podgy potentate waited until he was sure that the trickster god had left, then summoned his militant second-in-command. "General Hämm!"

Fortunately, the general was not far off, standing in attendance in the next chamber. A stout Gnarf in heavy armor, General Hämm stood a full head taller than the king, sporting a gold ring that hung from his nostrils. His wide waist displayed a belt of shrunken Human heads, while his own dome was adorned with a helmet made from the skull of some enormous alien animal.

"What is your request, my king?" the general saluted his monarch.

"The Hex-man has another task for us," replied King Bë-Konn. "He wants us to hunt for a sky-beast named 'Explorer 2000' and capture the crew within."

Hämm shook his hefty head. "With respect, my king, I do not trust the Hex-man. He is evil and will punish us if we fail."

"I know. But he has offered us great tribute to accomplish his request." Bë-Konn's fat fingers indicated the hand truck loaded with weaponry. "To defy the Hex-man may be a fate far worse than failing him."

"I will do my king's bidding," General Hämm conceded. "What are your orders?"

King Bë-Konn's countenance intensified. "Take the entirety of our sky-beasts, sending our fleetest messengers ahead. Those messengers are to deliver word to our envoys and patrols stationed on the star kingdoms, informing them of the Hex-man's mission. Roam the heavens General Hämm, until the Explorer 2000 is captured. Then the Hex-man will have his prize, and perhaps we will finally be free of his cursed presence!"

Following the H-8's shocking revelation, the crew of the Explorer had busied themselves with their normal cyclical routines. An odd sensation of gloom enveloped the ship, everyone feeling the weight of uncertainty. As if by rote, Kel wandered the bridge, checking the flight and navigation consoles repeatedly. In the med-bay, Dr. Rox read through medical texts that he'd studied countless times before, while Schiff sat in her bunking compartment perusing through her petite parcel of belongings.

Captain Nado occupied himself with the task of inventorying all their supplies, including the arsenal. His own two plasma pistols needed cleaning and maintenance, as old gun oil had gotten stuck in the barrel, and the heating elements for the ammunition cartridges needed a recharge. While he was at it, the captain also cleaned and repaired Kel's pistol and checked her old scoped .308 sniper rifle. Sometimes the classic ballistic firearms were truly best. Tried and true, and often more reliable than super-heated plasma bolts, the ballistics also offered a longer range than the more technologically advanced artillery.

They'd have to dock at a spaceport or station in order for him to inspect the Explorer's defenses though. Her hull was in fine shape, but they hadn't engaged the magnetic shielding, or the turret lasers. Thinking long and hard about it, Nado hoped that any dogfights in the Explorer could be avoided. Size and maneuverability were probably their only real defense against whatever forces Lord Hex may have in store for them.

Then something else in the bottom of the container caught his eye. It glinted from the shadows, refracting the glow of the cargo bay work lights. As if in a dream, the captain reached in to retrieve the object. Small and round, its metal surface was cold to the touch. He turned it over, allowing the item to rest in his palm. It was a badge.

Suddenly Nado was a child again, merely five standard years of age. A memory sprang forth to the forefront of his mind, a kindly person placing that badge in his hand. *"You're an explorer,"* the memory said in a young voice, *"a hero of the universe!"* Nothing to really write home about, the medal he held had been clearly crafted by an untrained hand. But it was all too precious to him. Everything he'd ever striven for, summed up by that tiny article.

"What am I doing?" the brazen Zennian suddenly mumbled aloud. "We should be executing a plan, not moping about." He spoke into the communicator pinned to his lapel. "Commander Kel? I'm calling another war room meeting. Right now."

Assembled around the table in minutes, the crew of the Explorer waited in bewilderment for what their intrepid captain had to say. His dire expression surveyed the room, bold and fearless resolve etched upon his face. "All the struggles we've all encountered to get to this point, all the hardships we've endured, and one piece of bad news is enough to send us all spiraling into this depressive state. No! We have a plan, and we should stick to it."

"Um, Captain," interrupted Kel. "There's still that teeny, little problem called...Lord Hex!"

"I know," Nado declared. "But thanks to your ingenuity with that robot, Commander, we now know who our adversary is and exactly where he's likely to be."

"Yeah, right where we want to go!"

"Precisely! What better tactic than to hide right under the nose of the very person who seeks you? It's got to be the last place they'd expect us to go!"

Dr. Rox rubbed his eyes. "How can we slip past his defenses though? It's not as though we have any kind of radar cloaking capabilities." Kel shot the doctor a corrective glare, so he clarified. "I'm not arguing against the idea. It does seem like our best bet to find answers for the kids. But I do think we should be armed with all the strategies we can invent so as to circumvent obstacles we will unquestionably come across."

"Agreed," said the captain. "I wonder if there are any cloaking devices available in this sector."

"Doubtful," Kel mentioned. "That's military grade tech. The Star Guard and the Flotilla Protection Fleet are probably not going to share with folks like us."

"But this is Taldish Sector," offered Schiff. "They don't have jurisdiction here. There might be something like that on the black market." The officers gave her a perplexed glance. "I'm just saying. The black market, that's common knowledge, right? I mean, it's not as though only pickpockets, thieves, and fences know about that sort of thing, right? I'm not saying that I've been any of those things, mind you, but maybe I have..." She trailed off.

Jym reached out to Schiff. "Don't worry, Mara and I are outlaws too. You're in good company." They shared a brief smile.

Nado continued. "There should be a space station not far from our current position. We can stop there for the last of our supplies, and perhaps to 'shop around' for a cloaking device."

"We'll need to stock up on whatever we can get," interjected Rox. "The med-bay has a few needs as well, and we won't be able to resupply at the Hexagon. Remember, those are war-ravaged worlds that have been basically dead for over a century. And what's our backup plan if we can't find a cloaking device?"

The princess voiced a question. "I sensed that your ship's warp drive uses dark energy manipulation for rapid transit and for artificial gravity. What if we tried to warp directly to the planet, then – "

"No way!" Kel cut her off. "That's literally impossible, I mean we'd impact the surface for sure, probably ripping a hole in the atmosphere in the process!"

"Let me finish!" snapped Mara. "I think I can control the energy field that the drive utilizes and stop the ship before that happens."

"That's an incredibly precise set of steps you've devised," Kel cautioned. "I'm also worried about what it could do to you. The Explorer is a lot more to manipulate than a plasma cartridge or a robot body."

"I told you, it doesn't work that way," Mara reminded her. "The weight and size don't matter, just the density of the energy field."

"Okay, that's a lot more energy being thrown around. Are you sure you could handle that?"

"I'm sure."

Kel sighed. "Alright, but I'm not sure I could pilot accurately enough to pull off a stunt like that. You'd have to be a robot – " She stopped herself mid-sentence. Everyone looked toward the med-bay.

Ending the silent stare, Jym asked, "Can the H-8 do that?"

"It piloted that shuttle pretty precisely," Schiff responded.

"The question in my mind is this, can we trust it to do what we want?" remarked Dr. Rox. "I have my doubts."

"Let me talk to it again," Kel requested. "I'll see what it can do."

"Then we have a new plan!" proclaimed the captain, beginning to bark orders. "I'll finish checking the cargo inventory and making a list of anything we'll need in excess. Doctor, can you do the same for medical needs? Commander, when you're done questioning the H-8 meet me in cargo to complete inventory, then we'll head to the bridge and navigate to the station."

"What can we do?" inquired Jym. Mara stood next to him, at the ready.

Nado beamed at them. "Go through the bunking compartments and make sure all loose articles are secured. Then do the same for med-bay and the galley."

"Aye, captain," they both saluted, and set about their newly assigned duties.

"And me?" Schiff chimed in.

"I could use an extra set of hands in cargo," the captain announced, and the two of them clambered down the hatch to the lower deck.

Amazed, Kel watched everyone scuttle about, completing their tasks. She had to give Nado credit, for all his nonsense, aloofness, silliness, and sometimes thick-headedness, he had a way of inspiring people. Maybe he wasn't the most skilled or experienced captain, but he was her captain. He was her dearest and fondest friend. But, on to business, time to deal with that robot again. Kel had it moved to her bunking compartment, which barely had enough space for the two of them. She reactivated the power core again.

After the telltale thrum of the core and the brightening of those yellow eyes, it started to repeat its usual recitation. "Greetings, Commander Kel. You will notice that this unit did not offer designation, as memory dictates that you requested identification be removed from the standard salutation."

Kel covered her face. "Oh, blast that's even worse. H-8-RED, from now on you can just say 'greetings' when you're activated. Nothing else is needed."

"Very well. Updating speech patterns."

"H-8-RED...that's a mouthful." Kel thought for a second. "Can I just call you 'Red'?"

"Very well. Updating response patterns. This unit will respond to the moniker 'Red'."

"Excellent. Red, aside from assassination protocols, what other capabilities do you possess?"

Red stood temporarily silent. Then it uttered, "In addition to highly sophisticated assassination protocols, this unit is equipped with computer engineering programming, infiltration programming, linguistics programming, and tactical piloting programming. This unit also features an artificial personality."

"Personality?" Kel wondered. "What are your notable personality traits?"

"Two personality matrices were uploaded to the memory core to produce a personality as close to sentience as possible," informed Red. "Most notably, this unit is programmed to be cynical, intimidating, jaded, opportunistic, strategic, and sarcastic."

"Sarcastic. Great," muttered Kel.

"Your tonal inflections indicate that you too are a utilizer of sarcasm," Red noted. "This unit will counter, you're welcome." Its last words dripped with sardonic flair so thick it was as if they'd been smothered in mocking molasses.

"Red, forget the sarcasm," Kel ordered. "I'm more interested in your piloting programs. Do they include navigational protocols?"

"Indeed."

"Good. I want you to plot a course for the nearest space station and fly us there."

"This unit will comply," Red responded. "And while unnecessary, this unit's speech patterns deem that an addendum is applicable in this circumstance."

"What 'addendum' is applicable?" Kel quipped.

"This unit is capable of spaceflight, but if that is your only requirement, you are vastly underusing the highly advanced assassination protocols for which this unit was constructed."

"Is that all?"

"That is all, Commander...for now."

Kel pointed her finger fervently at the bridge. "Just go fly the ship."

"This unit will comply," Red retorted in a mocking tonality, promptly marching toward the command center.

"I might have to kill that thing anyway," griped Kel, making her own way to the cargo bay. On arrival, she located Nado and Schiff busily rummaging through multiple boxes and cannisters. The commander picked up a spare clipboard and commenced her own count. "Did you guys already check over here?"

"Not yet," answered the captain.

Kel ripped open a container only to be surprised and

dismayed by what she discovered. "Captain, why do we have this?" She held up a ball of synthetic fibers unraveling it to reveal a specialty Kriton spacesuit.

"Oh," came Nado's sheepish reply. "I thought we could use it."

"How? None of us are Kritons!"

"What if we added one to the crew?" exclaimed Schiff.

"Don't encourage him!" Kel snipped.

Nado shrugged. "It was a good deal. They were on sale!"

"There you go, they were on sale," Schiff cheerfully chirped.

"I also grabbed a few game tablets, I thought they'd make excellent birthday presents!"

"We can't waste money on stuff like this!" the commander lectured. "Just because the Gonian paid us well doesn't mean we have an unlimited supply of money!"

Nodding, Nado affirmed, "You're right, of course, Commander. No more frivolous purchases. I got very excited. It was my first time in an off-world market."

"It's okay," Kel forgave him. "I suppose you didn't go too crazy, just the spacesuit and a few games."

"Um," the captain murmured, "well, there might be a couple of other oddities that made it on board."

"Do I want to know?"

"Probably not."

"How upset will I get when I discover said oddities?"

"Probably a lot."

"Would it be better if I go complete some other task?"

Nado snapped his fingers. "Come to think of it, no one was assigned to the preflight checklist of the engine room."

"I'll just do that then," Kel excused herself, leaving her clipboard in Schiff's hands.

The rumble of the warp drive sounded just fine as they all completed their duties and strapped in for the flight to their next destination. Vortex was the only name on record for the space station in question. Presumably, they'd be there momentarily, as the shadowy warp bubble once again consumed the vessel.

Red's voice echoed throughout the Explorer 2000. "All hands, prepare for warp travel. Initiating Casimir drive on the captain's mark."

"Let's go," Nado gave the command.

"Engaging warp drive," the robot mechanically mentioned.

Captain Nado leaned forward with anticipation. "Lord Hex, whoever you are, we're coming for you, and we will not be defeated or deterred." With that, the Explorer 2000 blinked into oblivion, carrying the crew to the subsequent phase of their grand plan.

War drums beat incessantly as General Hämm processed to his great sky-beast. The Gnarfs had collected a vast amount of the metal beasts over the decades, blending and fusing many of them together to craft one massive flagship. The general donned a power pack, withdrawing a nasty sword from its sheath. He attached a cord to the hilt of the weapon, activating the blade. It whirred and roared as the spiky chain rotated with deadly speed, threatening to dice anything in its path.

Hämm held his jury-rigged chainsaw sword aloft as thousands of Gnarfs boarded their own sky-beasts. He thundered his approval with a mighty war-cry, the soldiers bellowing their response. Observing the ritual from far above, King Bë-Konn stood upon the terrace of his palace apartment. "Go, my armies!" he rumbled. "Darken the heavens with your sky-beasts, blot out the celestial lights. It is only a matter of time before the Explorer 2000 is within our clutches."

"Are you sure this is wise, my king?" a low voice queried from behind.

"Flogg," acknowledged the rotund ruler. "Stop skulking in the shadows like slime and come out where I can see you."

Obeying the high king's command, a short Gnarf in purple attire with a feathered headdress emerged from the darkened corner. "Your grand vizier will submit."

King Bë-Konn then huffed, "Now what were you saying? Questioning my wisdom, I believe?"

"Of course not, my king," Flogg prattled. "I would never dream of it. I do not question the king's actions, only the loyalty of those in command of this venture."

"You, a measly advisor, think General Hämm, a war hero, unworthy?"

"I merely wish to bring to my king's attention the fact that Hämm did openly oppose you in front of subordinates. He sought to oppose the Hex-man's desires."

"So what? You believe that you should oversee this?" laughed Bë-Konn. "And to what end? Do you still seek the throne, vizier? Do you forget that our customs dictate that only a direct descendant, a lesser king, or the general of the armies can be in line for the high throne?"

The smaller Gnarf bowed his head low. "If it would please my king, I continue to assert that the oracles I have received give me cause to suppose that it would be a good future for our people if a mage were to succeed you rather than a warmonger."

This time Bë-Konn guffawed so loudly that it shook dust from the pillars. "Very well, seer, I give you leave. Take your priests and your own sky-beasts and go! If you find the Explorer before the general, I will add your name to the roster of potential successors."

Bowing even lower, Flogg grimly smiled a toothy grin. "Then let the race begin."

Chapter 7

Vortex bounced and thumped with strange alien tunes, played across a public announcement speaker system. It permeated every nook and cranny of the station, bass resounding and drumbeats pounding. Finding a place to carry on a quiet conversation was nigh impossible as the music pervaded the air.

Mixing with the audio in competing discordance, the unmelodious cacophony of street vendors hawking wares, garbled conversations desperately trying to be heard above the din, and the occasional hum of a cleaning apparatus threatened to drown out any other sound. The station was abuzz with clangorous noise, even escaping the main corridors by ducking into a shop or eatery did nothing to mitigate the clamor. It seemed the only place to go on Vortex to find silence would be to launch oneself out the airlock into the vacuous void beyond.

From the outside, Vortex appeared on approach to be a giant top, spinning in the middle of space on the border of an asteroid field. Vessels of all make and model were tethered to the various docking points littered around the belly of the station. It was accommodating to all sizes, from battleships to frigates, to sloops and schooners. Vortex could quarter any vessel, because Vortex wanted them all to feel welcome. Not out of any sense of hospitality though, but because the proprietors and vendors who worked the rough and tumble station wanted to swallow as many naïve and gullible saps as possible.

Having disembarked from the Explorer, Nado and his crew found themselves immediately bombarded by the sounds and smells of Vortex. It proved to be too much for Princess Mara, who opted to stay on board the ship with Rox. Carrying the doctor's shopping list, Kel set out with Jym and Red, leaving the captain and Schiff to gather the remaining goods. They had determined to stock up on extra water and thruster fuel, seeing that food rations and the armory were in decent order.

"Let's do our shopping and be out of here as fast as we can!" Kel practically had to shout to be heard.

"You worry about the medical supplies," Nado hollered back, "and we'll see about the cargo and…that other thing we discussed."

"The black market!" Schiff unnecessarily clarified. "We'll look for the black market!"

"Schiff, we probably don't want to go around announcing that," cautioned Kel.

"Oh, right. Sorry!"

"We'll meet you back here when we're done," instructed Nado. "If we're not here, just wait for us. Can't use the communicators here, the signal will get lost!"

Kel saluted the captain as a response, not wanting to damage her vocal cords any further by yelling above the station noise. She and Jym looked for the nearest station information kiosk to try and figure out where the closest medical supplier was located. Ever vigilant, Red dutifully tagged along behind them, plasma carbine at the ready.

Meanwhile, Nado and Schiff briskly sped in the opposite direction, their eyes peeled for general goods and the potential nefarious hustler who might have information regarding a cloaking device. Nado knew it was a tall order, but if they could actually find one that was compatible with the Explorer's systems, that could be their ticket onto the Hexagon worlds. At this point, anything to help the kids was better than flying blind. He was adamant that they would not quit until the prince and princess had answers.

There was one trivial section of Vortex wherein could be found a slice of stillness. Buried deep in the sub-basements of the structure dwelt a band of emissaries from Urkasak, led by their ambassador, a sagging sack of Gnarf flesh named Boxie. A former lover of the high king, she had been banished when he claimed she had stolen gems from his private hoard. Of course, no such thing had taken place, she was simply taking him up on an offer to lavish herself with his finery.

Lies! All of it had been lies, a ploy to lure her into betraying herself. Bë-Konn's treachery knew no bounds. There was another woman, and he had wanted to get rid of poor, misused Boxie. Of that she had no doubt.

But here, she was queen. Here, all would obey the voice of Boxie the Beautiful. She toyed with the piercings in her nose and ears, bangles dangling from her wrists and ankles. Her kingdom may not have been in the luxurious palaces of Urkasak anymore, but now she had a place of her own in the star kingdom of Vortex. And it was hers, all hers.

The rooms of her embassy had been decorated with silken trappings of scarlet and gold, draping from the ceiling and walls in ornate fashion. A throne of pillows squished under her obscene obesity, nearly as flat as the once-puffy mattress foundation. Human dancers writhed before her day and night, dressed in rags. Let Bë-Konn and the others eat the gods. She would rather see them suffer as slaves begging for her favor.

A disturbance arose on the far side of the room. Her guards, whom she referred to as "Boxie's Best," were blocking entry to another Gnarf. The guards pushed and shoved, but still the interloper refused to leave, insisting he had to see her. She could hear the commotion clear across the chamber, the unwanted guest causing quite the scene. This was getting out of hand, ruining her appetite. That was something Boxie the Beautiful could not abide! She rolled from her pillowed peak and onto the floor, plodding to the point of the problem.

"What is the meaning of this?!" shrieked the agitated ambassador. "I am trying to enjoy my supper and god-dance, and you burst in unannounced to spoil my evening! You'd better have a good explanation."

The uninvited Gnarf showed a data-pad. "Boxie, there is news from – "

"How dare you!" blurted Boxie. "Address me by my full title, you slop-eater!"

"Yes, milady," the Gnarf visitor sighed. "Ambassador Boxie the Beautiful, I bring news from the home-world. All Gnarfs in Taldish are to be on the lookout for a sky-beast bearing the name 'Explorer 2000'. The Hex-man requested that they be remanded to our custody, and we are hunting them by order of the high king. Their names and likenesses are on this data-pad."

Boxie pondered that for a moment. The high king, Bë-Konn himself. If she could achieve this glory, maybe that would be her chance to regain her status, end this banishment, finally have the opportunity to go home again. "Thank you, messenger," she drawled. "You may go." After his departure, she turned to her guards. "Boxies! Send patrols across the station, checking every docking bay. Should the port-masters refuse to share their manifests with you, rough them up! If the Explorer 2000 is here, we will be the first to find them!"

Having purchased the final reservoirs of water and fuel that they needed, Nado and Schiff began their hunt for the likely unattainable cloaking device. Nevertheless, they persevered, searching high and low, suffering the never-ending drone of the station's blaring PA system. Many simply turned them away in the search, until Schiff started shifting into the matching race of whatever person they spoke to. That finally yielded some results. They followed the trail to one of the lowest chambers in Vortex.

They were led to a small storefront, a sickly yellow fog wafting from within. Therein they found the proprietor, one Ickshen by name.

"I do not know why they sent you to me," wheezed the short, round fellow. Covered completely in a strange biohazard suit, the shop owner bustled about, frequently pausing his activity to suck some of the amber gases into his vented mask, following the action with a contented sigh.

"Ickshen? The device?" the captain reminded.

"Ah, yes," replied the shifty merchant. "Believe it or not, I actually had one recently. It was a prototype that a former employee designed. Needed work though. I fixed it up proper."

"Do you still have it?"

"Not anymore. You just missed it." Ickshen drew another long breath on the fog. "Ah, that's good. Your cloaking device though, it was purchased by a local gambler."

"Do you know the name of this gambler?" Schiff interposed.

"My memory isn't what it used to be," said the chubby cheapskate. "Bits usually refresh it from time to time though." The captain and Schiff rolled their eyes at each other, both placing a few coins in the shopkeeper's hand. He went on, "I remember now! You're looking for a fancily clad gent in the upper quarter. He's an odd sight on Vortex, a Lorian man. You'll know him by the luminescent blue skin and golden hair. Goes by the name Vin."

"Let's hurry!" Nado motioned to Schiff. "If we can find this Vin character, maybe we can barter for the cloaking device!"

As the captain and his cohort exited the fog-filled façade, Ickshen couldn't repress a chuckle. Waiting until they were out of earshot, he muttered, "Oh, and I almost forgot to mention his last name, Trell. Vin Trell, son of Gren Trell. Too bad you didn't have a few more bits, I might have remembered sooner." Ickshen allowed himself a long, wheezy laugh. "Good luck!" His laughter grew until it devolved into a coughing fit, making him double over and clutch his chest. Another inhale of yellow fog seemed to soothe his condition.

Racing from the shop and making a mad dash for the elevators, Nado and Schiff had a hurried conversation. "I couldn't tell under that suit," Schiff panted, "but what was that guy?"

"Indubitably, a Baldin man," replied Nado. "The squat size, the circumference of the body, the stubby arms and legs, definitely Baldin."

"They don't usually travel far from the Octagon," mentioned Schiff.

"True. But this fellow hardly seemed the typical sort of Baldin."

As the racket of Vortex built again in their ears, the pair decided against further dialogue until they were in a locale that better supported such endeavors. Impatiently, the captain tapped his foot vigorously while the elevators leisurely lifted them upward. Every time the elevator paused to allow more passengers on or off, he sighed, exasperated by the seemingly sentient silos, as if they were purposefully delaying their ascent. Nado looked upward, and though he knew better, the motion helped him feel as though he were influencing the lifts to move faster.

Pharmacies were abundant on the station, but few held all the provisions that Rox had asked them to retrieve. Kel and the prince feverishly strived to locate something that would work, eventually landing at a hole-in-the-wall clinic. On their way inside, they spotted what appeared to be a gaggle of guards, all wearing very distinctive, matching black and maroon body armor. They talked to the staff, and though the nurses were hesitant, they ultimately agreed to a bargain. All the remaining items on the list were sold to the commander at a marked-up price, but at least they had everything now and could get off this earache of a space station.

"Who are those guys outside?" Jym asked one of the nurses.

"Who, them?" she responded, pointing at the armor-clad individuals outside. "They're part of the Vardens, supposedly local law enforcement."

"I guess it's good you've got some protection, huh?" noted Kel.

"Protection? From the Vardens?" the nurse said in a mocking tone. "The only time we get any real law and order out of those guys is when their palms are greased. The only people they really care about serving are the guild of sleazy and corrupt businessmen that run this space station, the Yildi. And don't ask me any questions about them, no one knows much of anything about the Yildi."

"Interesting, thanks for the info," Kel cordially remarked. She then mouthed to Jym, "Let's get out of here." He only nodded in response. They started the trek back to the docking tether of the Explorer but hadn't even made it halfway when they were stopped in their tracks, spotting a strange scene taking place. Five gruff and gnarly Gnarfs were dragging a short Sorogan man, practically lugging him by the eyestalks. Black bruises on his silvery skin evidenced the fact that they'd beaten the poor fellow, the rips and tears in his blue jumpsuit reinforcing the notion.

Kel could barely hear the Sorogan's voice above the uproarious station speakers as he shouted, "I told you, I don't know where they went!"

Something about the whole situation sat wrong with Kel. She felt a twitter in her stomach that told her this was related to them and the kids. It was then that she recognized the Sorogan. He was their port-master. *Please don't look this way,* Kel's mind buzzed. *Please don't look this way.*

It was as if the Sorogan heard her thoughts, his eyestalks uncannily swiveling in their direction. "There!" he pointed them out. "That's them! I recognize that robot!"

Heartburn rose in Kel's chest as the Gnarfs dropped the Sorogan and headed straight for her and Jym. One of the bulky brutes addressed them. "Stay right where you are! By order of Boxie the Beautiful, we are restraining you!"

"Run!" shouted Kel. "Run, run, run!!"

Grabbing Jym by the hand, she took off in a dead sprint. Boxie's guards gave chase, but their cumbersome bodies did make it somewhat easier to outmaneuver them. Leading the ruffians from corridor to corridor, the commander's eyes shot all around, desperately trying to find a place to hide. "The robot," she fussed. "Of course he recognized the robot." She fired a glare at Red. "I knew bringing you along would end up being a bad idea!"

"Do not blame this unit," Red returned. "It accompanied at your insistence."

"Shut up!" Then spotting an obscured alleyway, she said, "This way!"

Unfortunately, though Commander Kel was adept at many things, she couldn't possibly have known the entire layout of a space station she'd never frequented prior. The alley was a dead end, a maintenance corner filled with rattling pipes. The passageway muffled the music of Vortex, but offered little else in the way of protection.

A snorting chortle echoed in the tiny access wing as all five of their pursuers filed in. The commander leaned towards Red. "You're the assassin here, how about you, I don't know, shoot them or something."

The robot swiftly scanned the area. "That would be unwise, Commander. These pipes contain flammable gases that would erupt and engulf us in fire should a wayward projectile strike them."

"Then what would you suggest?"

"Only one tactical solution remains," stated Red. "We must surrender."

"Leave them to me," Jym interjected. The boy took hold of one of the pipes, ripping it from the wall with a yank. Carrying it like a sword, Jym's hand crushed the end of the pipe, forming it into a hilt.

The Gnarfs displayed their spiked gauntlets with sickening smiles, large battery casings betraying their functionality as electrified weapons. At the same time Kel could see warping and blurring around the edges of Jym's pipe. He was infusing it the same way he'd done on Khardan. As the combatants squared off, even the thumping of the overbearing music began to fade.

The first of the Gnarfs roared and the battle erupted! He charged forward, his four comrades flanking him, two on each side in a V formation. A firestorm of fists rained upon Jym, the Gnarfs' arms flailing like windmills. But the young prince moved like lightning, as smooth as flowing water, and as deft as a bird in flight.

First, he zipped under the Gnarfs' legs, springing up at their aft. Now back to back with the first Gnarf, Jym swung the pipe straight over his head without looking, smacking the Gnarf on his crown! The second and third Gnarfs whirled to engage the prince, both swinging haymakers. Ducking beneath their strikes, Jym allowed the Gnarfs' fists to slam into each other. At the same time, he swiped the legs from under the second Gnarf, tripping him, then whipped upright using the momentum to bring the pipe sword around in an arc, pummeling the third Gnarf's face

Gnarfs four and five tried to assault the prince, but he blocked the incoming strike from four and dodged the punch from five. With a vicious grunt, Jym slammed the full force of his energy infused pipe into the gut of Gnarf five, then reversed course and brought the metal melee weapon upward to clash with the jutting chin of Gnarf number four. All five were down.

Blood trailing from his nostrils, Jym dropped the pipe and fell to his knees. Kel rushed to his side, quipping at Red, "How's that for a tactical solution?"

"That was not accounted for," the robot replied. "Updating combat assessment options."

"That was a rhetorical question…"

"You did not specify."

Kel eyed the machine. "Just help me get the prince back to the ship."

"Of course, Commander."

At long last, the elevator ride had concluded, allowing Schiff and Nado to disembark at the uppermost floor. The volume of the bellowing melodies was significantly decreased here, and the level was also significantly smaller than the main floors. An open shaft dominated the center of the floor, a thin railing being the only thing separating the occupants and a dangerous fall several stories long. Hanging from the lofted ceiling were several chandeliers on pulleys.

On the outer ring, multiple dens of vice were open for business, two of them casinos that brightly flashed with neon lighting. Both were busy, both were filled with patrons, and both looked equally dangerous. But of the two, only one had a long line waiting to be allowed entry, a huge Kriton bouncer blocking the way.

"That's the place for a guy like Vin," Schiff pointed out. "I'm sure of it."

"How do we get past that guy?" Nado wondered. "I'm sure we're not on the list."

"I have an idea," answered Schiff. "Follow me." She snuck into a deserted corner, leading Nado along, where she proceeded to transform. Shifting to the form of a Lorian woman, Schiff left no detail out. Perfectly adorned golden hair, pulsing blue skin, limpid white eyes, and sharp facial features. Even her clothing was affected, bending and ebbing until it reflected that of a slender evening gown, sparkling with silver sequins.

Looking at the captain with pursed lips, Schiff's words practically sang in an alto voice, "I'm Jeniffe, and I need a Lorian man to win big for me."

"That ought to work," mumbled a surprised Captain Nado. "But what about me?"

"You're my bodyguard, silly," Schiff mockingly said, strutting from their shadowed hiding place with utmost confidence.

They approached the bouncer, bypassing the queue. "Get in line like everyone elshe," he growled.

"I'm here at Vin's request," Schiff calmly declared.

"Ha! Ssso are they." The bouncer pointed out a plethora of women in the line, all clamoring to be let in.

"I guess Vinnie-winnie will be lonely tonight then," pouted Schiff. "I'm sure you can explain why his very expensive arm candy never showed at the tables." She turned to Nado. "Come Crusher, it's a long trip back to Noxus. I should have known better than to accept an import job."

That seemed to shock the bouncer. "He paid to have you imported from Noxusss?"

"He did."

"I need to sssee the bill of sssale," the bouncer asserted.

"Show him Crusher," Schiff ordered to Nado.

The captain panicked in his mind. What was he supposed to show? He reached into his coat pocket, wishing to goodness there was something in it. Paper crinkled, it was the receipt of his purchase at the Khardan bazaar! Nado flashed the bill then rapidly replaced it.

"Wash that written in the Kriton language?" asked the bouncer.

"Of course," answered Schiff. "Everything was arranged through Gnash's connections."

Again, the bouncer was aghast. Nado worried that Schiff may have taken the deception too far. Name-dropping a now deceased crime lord may not have been the greatest bluff. The bouncer, however, went from shocked to impressed.

"Gnash, huh?" he grunted. "Go on in."

Though leaping for joy on the inside, Nado repressed the urge to do so physically. Instead, he tried his best to look the part of a dour protector, staying close behind Schiff as she waltzed into the casino. They both looked around, seeing automated tables for all manner of games scattered across the main floor. On the far wall were a series of private chambers.

"That's where we need to go," Schiff informed. She led them in a wide circuit, allowing them to peek clandestinely behind the curtains of the exclusive areas. On the third attempt, the duo spotted their man. Vin was easily distinguished from his compatriots, a lone Lorian amidst a sea of Kritons, Gnarfs, Pyrians, and Humans.

Without skipping a beat, Schiff paraded through the curtain with gusto. "Hello, darlings, mind if I join?"

"We're all full up," Vin started, until he glanced up, "but we can make room for another, if they're someone as fantastically gorgeous as you." He kissed her hand in greeting. "I'm Vin, an emerging entrepreneur. You are?"

"I'm Jeniffe," said Schiff. "But you can call me whatever you like."

"Who's that?" asked another patron, indicating Nado.

"That's Crusher, my bodyguard. A girl can't be too safe these days."

Vin relaxed in his comfy, high-backed chair. "If you're playing, the ante is no less than one thousand per hand. Can you afford that?"

"Please," Schiff giggled. "That's a child's game. I'd rather play for something more tangible."

Vin was confused. "Like what?"

"I heard through…various sources that you recently procured a specialty device for hiding one's presence. I want to play for that."

"You're very well informed," smiled Vin. "But if I'm to put that up for bid, you'd better have something just as valuable to counter."

"If you win," Schiff retorted, "I'll grant you a private date with me, just the two of us." Vin only appeared mildly interested, so she literally upped the ante. "And my Crusher here will owe you a favor."

Now Vin's eyes lit up a bit more. "He's got an extra set of arms. I think he could handle two favors at once, don't you?"

"Done." Schiff offered her hand again, Vin kissing it even more lustfully than before. Not wanting to waste too much time, Schiff sang, "Let's play."

"It's a quick round of 'endurance'." Vin stared hard. "Are you sure you're up for that?"

Smirking, Schiff responded, "I'm up for anything."

"Alright."

The game was simple. Everyone went around the table placing their hands on an electrified pad. They would roll dice to see what voltage got pumped into their bodies, betting on how long they thought they could keep playing. Whoever could not endure their shock was unable to remain in the round and play for the pot, immediately losing their bet.

Everything grew quiet around the table. The bets were placed, hands were positioned, and dice were given to each player by the automated moderator. One by one the participants rolled their dice, receiving shocks in accordance with their respective rolls. Round and round the table they went, dropping one after another until the only ones left were Schiff and Vin.

Thankfully, Schiff had continuously rolled lower, Vin taking the greater amount of electrical abuse. It was her turn again. She picked up the twenty-sided die, casting it onto the table with a graceful flick. It turned up a twenty, the highest roll possible. Nado gulped as Vin grinned maliciously. The shock pad hummed with current, but Schiff held her ground, convulsing violently.

Vin's turn. He too rolled a twenty. "Oh, come on!" he moaned. Shouting in agony, he yanked his hand from the pad. Schiff had won! The cloaking device was theirs!

"Good game," the shapeshifter consoled her opponent. "It was well played."

"Here's your prize." Vin handed over the parcel, in good sportsmanship.

It was then that the Gnarf nobleman at the table received a ping on his data-pad. He glanced at it, then at Nado. He looked again. Nado noticed, and sensed something was amiss. Tapping Schiff on the shoulder, he craned his head toward the exit.

"Well, we should be on our way," she gushed, striving to maintain the lilt in her voice.

"At least give me a chance to win it back," urged Vin.

"Not today darling," Schiff resisted. "We have a busy schedule to attend to. Some other time perhaps."

"Hey!" the Gnarf interrupted. "I just got a picture of that guy on my pad. He's Captain Burnay Nado of the Explorer 2000. He's wanted by Ambassador Boxie the Beautiful." For a moment, no one budged. "There's a reward!" Every hand in the room began to scramble for a weapon.

The captain glanced at Schiff. "Now would be a really good time for you to use that short range teleport blink I believe."

"I can't," she replied.

"What? Why not?"

"I'm not really good at it," Schiff sheepishly answered. "We might end up outside the station for all I know!"

"Then we run!" shouted Nado, scooping her in his right arms. Using his left arms, he barreled through the other gamblers out of the private chamber. Winding through the maze of games, Nado raced for the exit!

Chapter 8

———— ◦◯◦◯◦◯◦ ————

Darting from one hiding spot to another, Kel led Red cautiously back toward their docking bay. Resting in the machine's unfailing mechanized arms, Jym slowly recovered from his exertion. The commander spied the area from their latest hideaway. More of Boxie the Beautiful's minions had joined the chase. Patrols littered the streets, threatening to uncover them at any moment. Timing was crucial to exacting their escape.

"Red, anything on your internal radar?" Kel queried.

"Gnarf patrols will pass by in approximately ten seconds," answered the robot.

"We'll wait for that opening, and make a break for the ship," instructed Kel.

"Protocols dictate that a firefight would be highly successful in this environment."

"No! Gunfire must be avoided, there are too many civilians in this area. I don't want anyone getting hurt."

The seconds passed more like minutes, but soon enough the patrols meandered past, creating an ample window for them to slip by. Only a few roads more, and they'd be at their docking bay. Hopefully the captain and Schiff would already be waiting for them, and they could launch out of this nightmare.

They were rounding the corner when a seedy street hustler jumped out and barred their process. "Hello there, fine folks!" he began. "I know what you're thinking, he can't have anything that'll interest us, but I couldn't help but notice that while you have a fine-looking pistol, you haven't got a fine-looking holster to match!" He opened a large rolling case full of ornately decorated pistol holsters. "Take your time and take your pick! Prices vary, but I can be flexible."

"Can you please flex aside?" Kel quipped. "We're in a bit of a hurry."

"Hurry?" said the pushy purveyor. "No worries, I can operate on a tight schedule. When can I squeeze you in for an appointment?"

"Never!"

"Oh, you are a tough customer, but look, I have the full line of articles right here, it'll only take you a quick second to choose."

"I don't want to – "

The hustler spoke quickly, but smoothly. "Listen, I didn't want to advertise this in front of a crowd, but for you I'll make an exception. This is a today-only offer, I'm knocking twenty-five percent off the full price of any item you want. That's a huge deal, considering these babies are top of the line goods, custom made too."

Kel had reached the end of her restraint. "Red, would you please remove this obstacle from our path?"

"Certainly." The robot's calculating computer brain settled on what it deemed an appropriate action, promptly booting the man and his wares across street with one speedy kick! The commotion drew the attention of a Gnarf patrol.

"Crud!" groaned Kel. "That's not what I meant, you dumb bucket of bolts!"

"You did not specify in what manner the obstacle should be removed," Red coldly informed. "Protocols dictated that was the most efficient method of removal."

"Stop talking, just run!"

"Again, this unit reiterates that a firefight is both imminent and effective."

"RUN!!"

"Complying." Still porting Jym in its arms, Red mercifully complied, and they both jetted from the scene with the patrol hot on their heels.

"You know," Kel panted, "for a robot, you don't seem to take orders too well!"

"This unit is programmed to be self-reliant and self-sufficient," Red stated. "These programming protocols allow for a certain level of non-conformity should the circumstances call for it. However, they do not permit outright defiance, which in many cases is unfortunate due to the recurrent lack of logic that seems to be prevalent in the fleshy blob brains of sentient beings."

"Are you finished?" retorted Kel.

"Not at all. However, you seem to be running short of breath, so this unit recommends finding a safe locale for a brief respite before continuing this discourse."

"Love to," Kel grumbled, "but first we have to lose those patrols you so helpfully managed to attract!"

"This unit will comply." Red shifted Jym into its right arm and reached out with the left, its robotic precision perfectly in rhythm. The left hand snagged a lighting pole, and the machine kept its pace, twirling around the post and using the centrifugal force to swing itself airborne, bowling over the Gnarf patrol with its long legs. Red continued churning its legs, landing into a full sprint that rapidly caught it up to Kel. It then hauled her onto its metallic frame and ducked into a side street that led to a small diner. Red hurried around the restaurant to the rear of the building where the commander was able to catch her breath. She leaned against the wall, hands on her knees, attempting to heave the pain in her chest away. A quick jaunt was one thing, she could be quite lethal across short distances, but a marathon runner Kel knew she was not.

"There has to be a better way to do this," she muttered.

"Again, this unit reiterates that a firefight is both imminent and effective," repeated Red, the sarcasm in its voice all too noticeable.

"I told you, too many civilians," Kel reminded. "We're already being hunted by Lord Hex, and now this Boxie character, who's probably working for Hex if I had to guess. The last thing we need is someone else putting a bounty out on us for injuring an innocent."

"Assassination protocols dictate – "

"I don't want to hear another word about protocols!" fumed the commander. "I just want to rest a minute, then try and make it this last leg to the ship."

"Very well, Commander. This unit will comply." Red moved to a more advantageous position to act as lookout while Kel recuperated.

There was little to do but make a break for it, as Nado leapt over tables and chairs, Schiff still in his arms in Lorian form. The cloaking device was secure in her grasp, so he sustained his fervent surge for the doorway. The bouncer was receiving instructions via his earpiece and moved to halt their getaway.

"Blast!" fretted Nado. "Now what?"

"Hold me out in front of you and close your eyes!" Schiff told him.

"What?"

"Just do it!"

Nado did as the little shapeshifter asked, plowing ahead blindly. He felt her shake in his outstretched arms then heard the most awful shrieking, roaring, blood-curdling noise he'd ever heard in his life. Afraid to look, the captain kept his orbs shut until he heard Schiff's normal voice again.

"You can open your eyes!" she shouted. "It's safe now!"

Allowing himself to see again, Captain Nado glanced around at the carnage that lay before him. The bouncer and casino patrons that had been chasing them now writhed on the floor, their own eyes a milky white. They moaned in horror at whatever Schiff had done, joined by several of the hopefuls that had been standing in the queue. Nado felt a bit bad for them, but at least his departure point was clear.

The elevators dinged ahead of them, vomiting a throng of commuters. Too many egressed, the ebb and flow making the crowd denser than Nado would have liked. A quick dive between the closing doors wouldn't be possible without harming someone in the process. The clever captain checked his surroundings, his eyes falling on the chandeliers precariously positioned in the open shaft.

Schiff followed his gaze. "Are you thinking what I think you're thinking?"

"If you're thinking I'm thinking about those chandeliers, you're thinking correctly," Nado unwaveringly answered. "Otherwise, think again."

"I thought that's what you were thinking about," Schiff happily related. "Let's do it!"

"Here!" Nado thrust a pistol into her hands. "Hold them off while I grab the fixture."

A once-excited Schiff now appeared rather unsure, holding the pistol as if it were a foreign object she'd never even seen before. Meanwhile, Captain Nado mounted the thin banister and with a heavy breath launched himself into the air! Not daring to peer downward, he fixed his gaze on the chandelier in front of him, all four hands clawing to reach it. Just as his leap began to succumb to the station's artificial gravity, Nado's fingertips managed to catch the edge of the fitting. He held on while the chandelier swung out of control, fighting to attain some level of balance.

Schiff watched, having converted back into her natural form. A voice rang out above the tumult, "Give me back that cloaking device you petty crooks! My dad sent me to get it!" Whirling around, Schiff saw Vin wandering out of the casino, rubbing the milkiness from his vision. The gambler locked eyes with Schiff. "You!" he shouted. "You're a 'shifter!"

As Vin tore at her, she shunted the pistol into the sash around her waist and entered a wide stance. Spreading her arms to match, Schiff turned her left side toward her aggressor, her palms outward with fingers pointed up. Vin charged at her with a wild jab which she easily parried with her left wrist, rotating her arms in a cycle. Her right hand swung around, fingertips flowing straight into Vin's chest in a jab. Schiff's hand recoiled, striking again at her target, this time aiming for his neck. She finished the attack by stabbing Vin in the abdomen with the palm of her right hand. The garish gambler stood paralyzed.

"That's the value of a nerve attack," Schiff said in a sing-song manner, proceeding to steal every bit from his coat and pant pockets. "And now I'll just relieve you of a few more items." She grabbed his wallet, expensive timepiece, and his gaudy belt buckle. "That should do it. Bye, Vin, have a nice life!"

Just at that moment, the other patrons burst from the casino entrance, pulling the bouncer to his feet. Casino guards had also joined the ruckus, all of them now thundering at Schiff. They were just about to reach her when a pair of strong arms grabbed her from behind, yanking her out over the abyssal shaft.

"Here we go!" yelled Nado, bouncing the chandelier's pulley. It gave way and they plummeted down toward the main floor of the station. Right before they smashed onto the avenues below, the other end of the pulley caught, halting their descent with a sudden jolt. The captain's grip was unable to hold on, causing the pair to fall further. A well-placed fruit stand with an awning broke their fall, springing them to the ground with a thud!

Disoriented, Captain Nado shook his head. "We're not far from the ship. This way!"

"That was so awesome!" Schiff cheered.

"Agreed, but we're not out of the thick of it yet," the captain proclaimed. "Hurry up!"

Precious minutes had passed while Kel regained her vigor. "Come on Red. Grab the prince and let's go. We've been here too long."

"Very well, Commander," replied the robot, hefting Jym into its arms.

"Anything around?"

"The patrols are near," Red informed. "But they are not pacing in our vicinity. They are two streets over."

"Let's make a run for it." Kel slid out of hiding, keeping a vigil for the persistent patrols. The group crept forward, stealthily moving through the crowds that bustled in the busy boulevards.

The Explorer's docking bay was close, only a few more blocks away. Kel became so focused on their destination that in the moment she didn't look where she was going.

"Oof!" She slammed into another passerby, both crumpling from the impact. Kel rose, ready for action until she saw the victim of her unintentional collision. "Captain! Boy are you a sight for sore eyes!"

"Commander," the captain greeted her. "You might not think that when you see the villains we have in tow."

"Uh, we may have a posse or two after us as well," Kel admitted. "Apparently some Gnarf named Boxie wants to capture us."

"It was a Gnarf that gave away our position at the casino," mentioned Schiff. "But we did manage to get the cloaking device!"

"So, the Gnarfs of Vortex are allied against us," Nado mused.

"I suspect Lord Hex hired them," said Kel.

"The Boxies are still only two streets away," Red reminded.

"Then we can figure everything out later." Captain Nado looked about, spying between the nearby buildings. "For now, we need to get off this station before we're spotted."

Having given their pursuers the slip, the reunited crew rushed for the docking bay. Their terminus in sight, the crew darted around the sharp curve that led into the airlock room. Taking a chance to glance behind, Schiff twittered, "Good thing we have a clear run to the ship!"

They rounded the corner into the terminal only to discover a horrific scene awaiting them. There stood a full contingent of Gnarf Boxies, the lady ambassador at their head! A vicious grin spread across her warty face, the gold bands on her tusks gleaming in the lights.

"You had to say it," Kel stewed at Schiff. "You just had to say it."

Boxie issued her ultimatum. "People of the sky-beast Explorer 2000, the Hex-man has ordered your arrest. So, by the hand of Ambassador Boxie the Beautiful, I hereby declare that you are to be remanded into my custody!"

Then, without warning, the airlock bulkheads of the Explorer hissed and whirred, lowering like a drawbridge. As the cargo bay doors slowly declined, they revealed a solitary person standing therein. Princess Mara raised her arms towards Boxie and her henchmen, uttering a single sentence. "Not today. Today you eat dirt."

"No one speaks to Boxie the Beaut – ," Boxie started. But her words were cut short by Mara's swift actions. The petite princess yanked her arms inward, pulling every Gnarf Boxie, including the malevolent malefactor herself, straight to the floor facedown! In the chaos, Captain Nado led the crew in leaping over their downed foes and boarding the vessel.

Upon using her abilities, Mara fainted to the floor of the cargo bay. Kel pointed it out, ordering Red to grab her and get the kids to their bunking quarters. With everyone on board, the doctor fired up the engines.

Boxie and her bloated band tossed and rolled, eventually managing to right themselves. In a fit of rage, she screamed, "Go!

Out of the airlock chamber you idiots!" Then into a communicator tuned to the station frequency, "Someone get to our sky-beasts and disable that Explorer!"

Every Gnarf scurried from the bay as the station's airlock doors began to close. Obeying their leader's orders, multiple Boxies had scrambled for their own docking compartments, boarding the crafts within. As the Explorer 2000 launched from Vortex, so did several Gnarf Boxies in fighters.

As Captain Nado and Commander Kel entered the bridge, the doctor called out, "We've got at least one bogey, inbound at our lower starboard flank!"

"Excellent work doc," Nado thanked him. "You are relieved of the bridge. Check on the kids, I'm afraid they've overdone it."

"Aye captain." Rox retreated to the galley, grabbing Schiff to assist.

Nado and Kel were joined on the bridge by Red. The captain turned to the robot. "Red, take the helm. Kel, you and I are on the laser turrets."

Kel saluted. "Aye captain."

As Red took control of the pilot's seat, the officers vaulted the chairs of the gunnery commands, landing in them harshly and causing them to squeak under the pressure. Before anyone had a chance to get fully situated though, a dull boom indicated an impact on the Explorer's starboard side.

"What was that?" Kel hollered.

"We've taken a hit," Red mildly reported. "Slight damage to the exterior hull, some internal systems have been affected."

"What systems?" demanded the captain.

"Unknown at this time, Captain," the robot coolly returned. "I would need to interface with the Explorer's onboard computers to find out."

"We'll handle that when we're in the clear. Ready the lasers, Commander Kel! Red, take evasive action!"

Control panels beeped and blipped as Red responded. "Employing tactical piloting protocols. Shall I activate the magnetic shielding, Captain?"

"Yes, do it!"

The robot flipped a few switches, and a hum exuded from the walls. Outside, tiny solenoids dotting the hull swiveled outward from underneath their protective plating. An electric charge pumped through them, generating an electromagnetic field surrounding the ship. Beneath the solenoids, minuscule emitters excreted plasma into the field, creating an energy barrier around the vessel.

From the outside, the Explorer was suddenly enveloped in a translucent bluish forcefield, capable of stopping almost any attack. Their visibility dropped to zero, seeing nothing but wraith-like blackness from within, as the plasma coated the entirety of the sloop. View ports were thankfully not needed as the targeting systems for the lasers, as well as the bridge controls, did not require line of sight.

More booms were heard in rapid succession. Captain Nado shook his head. "He's testing the shield for weaknesses. Get ready to return fire."

"Captain, we'll have to lower the forcefield for that," Kel pointed out.

"I know. It'll take precision timing, but we can do it." The captain stared incessantly at his control panel. "He's making an about turn. Now's our chance. Red, on my mark give us one tick to port, then lower the shield. Commander, when I give the order, we fire the lasers." He watched the readouts on his panel, the tension in the atmosphere increasing. "On my mark...steady...Red, now!"

The eerie darkness outside the windows instantly gave way to the stars and asteroids around Vortex. The shield was down. The hiss of the air jets notified the crew that the ship had shifted towards the port side. Captain Nado still didn't look up, barking the next command. "Kel, fire!"

Near-white laser beams appeared to tether the two vessels together momentarily as Kel and Nado discharged the shipboard weapons. The Gnarf fighter was disabled, floating away in a slow spin. The captain and commander gave a cheerful whoop, but their reverie was short lived, as Red interrupted the celebration. "We have two more bogeys inbound. They will be in attack range in less than one minute."

"Understood," acknowledged Captain Nado. "Red, plot a course for open space. Engage the warp drive."

In a flash, the Explorer was gone, leaving the Boxies flummoxed and furious.

Things had calmed quite a bit on the Explorer after their flight from the Vortex space station. The crew settled in for a dinnertime meal, joined by Jym and Mara, now fully recovered and rested. Rox gave them a clean bill of health after a quick examination, and they all relaxed in the comfortable old galley chairs, reminiscing and swapping tales of their adventures on the station.

"I have got to know a few things, Schiff," Captain Nado declared. "First, how do you know so much about the seedy underbelly of the universe? Second, how did you beat Vin at his own game? And third, what in the galaxy did you shift into that horrified all those people?"

Schiff glanced around, looking a bit embarrassed. "Okay, first, I grew up on the streets, and ran with a couple of gangs. Thankfully, I got out of that life...mostly. Secondly, I cheated at the game."

"No way!" Mara blurted.

"Yep. But that's okay, Vin was cheating too. I just cheated better!"

"How?" asked Jym.

"I'm a 'shifter!" Schiff responded. "I shapeshifted my hand to make it look like it was on the electric pad. I never touched the thing!" Everyone let out a hearty laugh. Schiff continued, "As for your third question, Cap, you don't want to know."

"Really?" voiced the captain.

"Let's just say the word 'eldritch' should sum it up, and leave it at that," Schiff replied. "I'm just glad we got that cloaking device!"

"We'll get that installed shortly," Kel told the captain. "Then we'll be ready to take on the Hexagon."

"All in due time," Nado assured her. "I've been wondering if maybe we should warp to another sector for a while, lay low until the

Gnarfs stop hunting us. If what Boxie said is true, then the entirety of the Gnarf fleet is at Lord Hex's beck and call."

"Begging your pardon Captain," interjected Red, calling from the bridge. "This unit has been in communication with the onboard computers and has made a discovery."

The captain swiveled to face the bridge. "Report. What are your findings?"

"The damage taken to the Explorer 2000 in the battle with the Gnarf fighter extended to some of the inner workings of the Casimir drive, as well as the navigational systems."

"What effect will that have?" Nado questioned.

Red gave a sobering answer. "It means that the warp drive cannot be utilized to rapid transit from this region, or we risk landing inside a star or planet. We can use it within the bounds of this sector, but for now we are unable to travel anywhere beyond."

"So you're saying we're trapped," Kel summated. "Wandering blind with an army of Hex's minions on our trail."

"Indeed."

"Can we repair any of it?" Nado wanted to know.

"Not with the resources on board," said Red. "It would require a planetary landing port with access to the correct components and materials."

A somber mood fell upon the party. If that was the case, they were in bigger trouble than they thought. An army of Gnarfs breathed down their necks, and their greatest adversary lay between them and their current goal. Looking around the galley, however, each mind had one encouraging thought, as long as they had each other, not all hope was lost in Taldish Sector.

Chapter 9

"Bumbling buffoons!" Boxie the Beautiful berated her pack of patrols. "Not one of you could have caught them?!"

One Gnarf, nursing a nasty knot on his noggin, nervously noted, "The boy, he had unnatural powers and strength. He took down my entire troop by himself!"

"Bah!" spat Boxie. "You were weak and stupid! Prepare my own sky-beast, useless fools! I will give pursuit myself."

As the Gnarf throng commenced hefting their bulk back to work, another group advanced. Boxie observed as a Lorian man stomped toward the now empty airlock docking chamber that had housed the Explorer. He was incredibly fashionably dressed, accompanied by a quartet of Fangorian mercenary bodyguards, their dark fur bristling on approach. They bared their fangs, the feature for which they had been named, at the Gnarfs.

Their Lorian leader yelled above the still hammering music, "Where are they? This was their docking bay, yes? Where are Captain Burnay Nado and that shapeshifter?" He addressed Boxie. "Did you see them? Did you help them escape, Gnarf?"

She was taken aback. "Help them?! We were here to catch them! And you should take a moment to realize to whom you are speaking! I am Ambassador Boxie the Beautiful, representative of Urkasak and the Gnarf people in this star kingdom! Use my proper title from now on, child!"

"Excuse me?" Now it was the Lorian's turn to be insulted. "Don't you know who I am?"

"Should I?"

"I am Vin Trell," huffed Vin, "master gambler, and son of Gren Trell, the crime lord. So make sure you show me the proper respect as well!"

For a minute, the two enacted a silent power struggle, each attempting to stare the other down. Boxie knew better than to waste time here though. She eased into a tusked smile. "Master Vin, why fight? It seems we share a common enemy. The Explorer 2000 has caused quite a mess here for both of us. Let us retire to a place where we can plot their downfall together."

"That...is agreeable," Vin complied. "I have a comfy apartment two floors up. Let's meet there."

They traversed the short distance to Vin's abode where Boxie made herself at home. Vin prepared some beverages, but just as they were getting settled one of the Fangorian mercs poked his muzzle through the doorway. "Sir, sorry to interrupt, but you have visitors."

"This can't wait?" fussed Vin.

"They are here for a loan repayment, meant for your father," informed the merc.

At that, Vin softened. "My father, you say? Heh, heh, better let them in." The hired muscle welcomed two Kritons into the room. Vin greeted them. "Ah, Shtrepp and Schlaar, two of my favorite customers! You have a loan payment?"

"Not a payment," corrected Shtrepp. "We are ready to pay back the full amount."

This surprised Vin. "Really? Where did you get that kind of money all at once?"

"We sssold a ssspecial ssskull to Ickshen," Schlaar answered. "He wash willing to pay a hefty sssum for it."

"A skull?" queried Vin.

"Yesh, a primordial Fangorian ssskull."

"Where did you get something like that?"

Shtrepp was all too excited to share their tale. "A ssspace exploration crew we were initially hired to capture, ended up paying ush the ssskull to help them inssstead."

Having sat mostly uninterested, Boxie's curiosity was now piqued. "What was the name of their sky-beast?" she asked.

"Sssky-beasht?" Schlaar was confused. "Oh, you mean their ship. It wash the Explorer 2000. They sssought to help ush even though we were their enemiesss."

"Enemies...," pondered Boxie. "You would say then that they wanted a peaceful solution?"

"Yesh," said Shtrepp. "They gave ush the ssskull to avoid a fight."

"Thank you for being so forthcoming," Boxie snickered. "I have no more questions."

Collecting the funds, Vin too dismissed the Kritons. "What was that interrogation all about?"

Boxie rubbed her portly paws together. "It was all too important. I now know the weakness of the Explorer 2000. Thank you for your time, Vin Trell, I no longer require access to your domicile."

"Hold on a minute! I agreed to help you, and without me, you never would have figured out this information. I want my own retribution as well." Vin crossed to other side of the parlor, swirling his drink. "The captain of that cursed ship and his shapeshifting comrade made a mockery of me and stole a very valuable device meant for my father. I can equip you with an experimental paralyzing gas that you can use to render them completely inert.

"It is meant for my father as well, but I'm willing to gift it to you. In exchange for this hospitality, I want to make sure you retrieve an item from them, a cloaking device. That is what they stole." He then ambled to the opposite side of the room, pulling open a cabinet and wrapping his fingers around the neck of a long bottle. He brought it to her. Boxie grabbed for it, but Vin snapped it back out of her reach.

"Ah, ah, ah!" he lectured, waving his finger. "First, you have to agree to my terms."

"I accept," snorted Boxie. Her eyes flashed like lightning as the poisonous bottle was slipped into her waiting grip. "Time to set a trap!"

Secluded in his cabin, Captain Nado looked through the porthole that gave a rather commanding view of the expanse of space. At least, by comparison to the other tiny viewports. Stars twinkled in brilliant blues and reds, a blooming purplish nebula barely visible in the far distance. Probably the edge of one of the solar systems of Taldish. He hadn't yet studied the navigation charts to find out exactly where they were.

The wonders of space were a glorious thing. Mysteries abounded in the cold darkness, waiting to be explored and uncovered. Dangers were in no short supply either, however, clearly evidenced by their current predicament. But there were other hazards bedsides the inhabitants of the galaxies. There were black holes, supernovas, the constant risk of running out of supplies or oxygen, and many more.

"That's why the explorers of old were some of the greatest heroes," the captain murmured to himself. "I hope I can live up to their legacy."

He took the time to peruse over the remaining trinkets fastened to his humble desk. The pink crystal and the lock of shimmering golden hair looked lonely without the primordial skull sitting between them. Though worth an incredible amount of bits, Kel and Rox had never asked him to sell it for fuel or rations. It was a reminder of their adventure together, a piece of their history as friends, tangible proof that he wasn't a failure, a nobody.

Tears formed in the corners of Nado's eyes. In that moment he mourned his losses. Not the skull, that was only an object, but seeing it absent brought out a deep sense of nostalgia that washed over him like a cascading waterfall. He missed his dad, gone for many years now, having succumbed to disease. He missed his mom.

She had survived their father, but Captain Nado hadn't seen her for quite some time. He missed his brother too. "Graylon, why did you leave us?" he mused aloud. The captain even missed the old life of the Explorer crew, fighting for ferry charters and struggling for funds.

For years they had striven for and struggled toward an opportunity like this, and now they finally had it. It wasn't exactly what Nado had imagined and had already cost him a piece of a memory. "All the more reason to forge ahead." He smiled broadly. "We're making new memories, bigger and bolder. And our little crew is growing. Yes, it is a grand adventure!"

Feeling rejuvenated, Nado egressed from his cabin to find Kel and Rox at the galley table. "Captain," the commander greeted him. "I just finished a rest cycle. I'm ready to get that cloaking device installed as soon as you are."

Nado nodded and replied, "Let's do it, Kel."

"I'll probably have to remove some of our radar wiring temporarily to install the device and get it hardwired in," supposed Kel. "It would mean we'd be in the dark for a bit, but no Gnarfs are in the area right now."

"If they do show up, though," Rox chimed in, "can we not just use the shielding again?"

"We can," affirmed Nado, "but it has limited uses. Every time the magnetic field is deactivated, the plasma gases are released. We can't get them back. We get around ten uses for every recharge. An engineering fault of the older Explorer models, I'm afraid."

"Hm. I was unaware of that." Rox rubbed at his jawline.

"No worries," Kel comforted. "There's a lot we haven't discussed concerning the tactical capabilities of the ship. We've never had to before."

"Well, let's not waste any more time," the captain said bluntly. "If we'll be radar blind while you're installing the device, I want the task done as fast, and as soon, as possible."

They dismissed and saw to their duties. Commander Kel picked up the cloaking device from its carefully packaged parcel, turning it over in her hand. It would take some doing, but the strange piece of technology could be made compatible with older ships. The item was tubular in shape and small enough to be held in one hand. She could tell the cloaking device was clearly designed to run concurrently with a shipboard radar system, emitting a radio frequency through the ship's own transmitter that was in opposition to the frequencies used by other craft, making them practically invisible to radar technology. Anyone looking out a view port would still see them, but targeting and tracking systems would be virtually useless.

It was quite well-made as far as Kel could tell, being able to transmit its own opposing radio waves in tandem with the detection waves the radar normally used. Therefore, it would not contend with the Explorer's ability to utilize radar capabilities while employing the cloaking mechanism. If installed properly, the shipboard computers could also differentiate between the frequencies, causing no confusion for the receiver dish.

This could work, Kel thought. *This could be the thing we need to accomplish our goal!*

She slipped down the ladder into the cargo bay to grab her tools. But as she slid, her descent decelerated, her duster and hair suspended in the air momentarily. As quickly as the phenomenon had occurred, it vanished, and she plopped to the bay floor below. Reaching for her own communicator, she hailed the captain. "Nado, did you feel that?"

"Sure did," his voice crackled back.

"It felt like the artificial gravity failed!"

"Sure did," he crackled again, the nervous energy in his inflections intensifying.

In moments, they had all gathered in the engine room to uncover the cause of the mysterious singularity. Red indicated a section of the warp drive. "The issue is beneath this panel. That is where the damage was inflicted. This unit did not detect the issue prior. Perhaps there is a fault in the ship's computers."

"Perhaps there's a fault in your own computers," Kel snapped back. She looked at Nado. "If this thing is going to randomly cut out on us, we can't stay in space. A lack of gravity, even artificial, will eventually make us all sick. We have to get this repaired now."

"Agreed," said Nado. "One task at a time though. Get that cloaking device installed first, then we can safely travel to a location where repairs can be made."

"I can't complete the install if there's no gravity. We have no tethering system to keep my tools from floating around, or hold the device in place while I work on it." Nado only stared at her with raised eyebrows. Kel sighed, acquiescing, "I'm on it, captain." She grabbed her toolbox and clambered up to the bridge. The panel to access the radar system's inner workings was easily removed, and she quickly set herself to the job at hand, Schiff accompanying as an assistant.

At the same time, Nado looked at the warp drive with Red and the kids. Princess Mara closed her eyes and held out a hand, saying, "I can feel where the dark energy manipulation is failing. It isn't circuitry or wiring or anything the computers might have detected. That's why Red couldn't find it." She opened her eyes. "There's a crack in the housing of the artificial gravity machine. That's the reason it can't maintain manipulation of the energy field."

"A crack," muttered the captain. "Cracks typically only spread over time. Kel's right, we have to get this taken care of immediately."

"Are the services of this unit no longer required for this endeavor?" queried Red.

Nado waved the robot off. "You're dismissed, Red. Head back to the bridge and keep a watch while the commander works."

"This unit will comply." As Red's gear-driven gait carried it to the ladder, the artificial gravity fluctuated again. The robot seemed unfazed, however, maintaining its mechanical march.

Nado and the kids on the other hand stared hard at one another, then at the warp drive. This could be a major issue if not dealt with swiftly. Unfortunately, the captain barely had time to think about it before Red's voice could be heard via the intercom from the bridge.

"Captain, we are receiving a hail on the radio," it relayed. "The message is coming from another nearby vessel."

"Blast!" Nado fussed. "Who could that be?" He yanked himself up the ladder rapidly using all four arms and leapt onto the bridge. "Patch them through, Red."

A low, thick accent emanated from the radio. "You are the Explorer 2000," it said. "Allow me to introduce myself. I am Flogg, grand vizier to the High King of Urkasak, King Bë-Konn. By order of the Hex-man, we are tasked with your capture and incarceration. Surrender. Remand yourselves to my custody. I can promise that none of you will be harmed in the process."

"Another one?" moaned Kel. "I thought we'd lost those Boxies!"

"Boxies, oh no! I assure you, we are not of that uncouth faction," droned Flogg. "I answer to the High King himself, and desire not to suffer the indignities of combat. Nevertheless, I have with me a full squadron of sky-beasts, manned by my priests, who are highly adept at that sort of thing when necessary. Please, do not make it necessary."

Captain Nado muted the radio so as not to be heard. "They must have found us by accident, out on a standard patrol or something."

"Regardless, they found us," Kel groused. "What are we going to do about it?"

"Is the cloaking device ready?"

"Not yet. It's going to take some time."

The radio speakers garbled again. "Well, captain?" Flogg pushed. "Will you surrender to my forces? That would be the easiest course."

Rather than responding to Flogg's boastful blabbering, Captain Nado began alerting the crew of their assignments. "Schiff, I need you to join me on the guns. Grab the port laser controls. Red, as soon as we fire the opening volley, bring up those shields again." Into his communicator he barked, "Doctor, we're about to be assaulted. You and the kids strap in back there!"

"What's going on Captain?" the doctor asked.

"More Gnarfs, a different group. They must have been scanning for our radar frequency."

Kel sat up. "Captain, don't you want me on the guns?"

"No," answered Nado. "I need you to get that cloaking device activated as swiftly as you can."

As they all took their battle stations, the gravity fluxed again. In the main hold, Mara and Jym exchanged a concerned look. They had both felt it coming, but there was nothing that could be done to stop it. Or was there?

"Jym," Mara started, "they need our help. The crew can't carry out their duties if the warp drive keeps messing up like this. We have to...I don't know...help it somehow."

"What are you thinking?" Jym questioned.

"We both sensed when the dark energy manipulation element was going to fail," the princess explained. "That means we know when the artificial gravity is going to do that blurb thing that it's been doing."

Jym lit up. "We can manipulate the field when the machine fails." Then his countenance darkened. "But won't that take a lot of exertion from us?"

"I think we'll be okay as long as we only use our abilities if the energy field warbles. We don't have to maintain the gravity forever..."

"Just whenever the machine can't," finished Jym. "I'm in. Let's go."

The siblings unstrapped and bolted for the bay hatch. Peering through the open med-bay door, Rox saw them leave. "Mara, Jym! Where are you going? You need to stay buckled in one of the seats!" The pair clearly had no intention of listening to him. "Oh, bother!" The doctor quickly unbuckled and chased after them.

On the bridge, Schiff and Nado had seated themselves in the gunner's chairs. "Get ready to fire," instructed the zealous Zennian.

"You know I've never done this, right?" Schiff anxiously said.

"The directional pad will swivel the turret," Nado gently taught. "Push the red button to fire. I will handle everything else." He checked his readouts, giving orders. "Two ticks upward...three to the left." Schiff followed his directives to the letter. The captain's gaze never budged from his panels. "Schiff, get ready. Red, prep the shields and patch me through to this Flogg character."

"Complying," Red responded. "They are now receiving our transmission."

"Flogg!" called Nado. "Can you hear me?"

"Yes, Captain," came the reply of Flogg's wide-sounding vocal patterns. "Have you an answer for me?"

"I have it right here," retorted Captain Nado. "Fire!"

Brilliantly, the laser beams extended through space, connecting with the Gnarf spacecraft ahead of them! They could hear Flogg's grunts and snorts through the radio, followed by his angry response. "I see you have chosen the evils of combat. So be it. We will pummel you with sky-beast breath until your own is completely disabled!"

The Explorer's forcefield activated just in time to repel the blasts from the enemy craft. They heard the dull rumbles of impact, but the ship remained unharmed. Nado knew they couldn't stay like this indefinitely though, eventually the forcefield would have to be deactivated to conserve power. The electrical charge of the solenoids would, in time, deplete the reserves of even the uninterrupted power supply batteries. Shields were meant for short term protection, not long term usage.

"Think Burnay, think," he muttered. "I need new plan." Aloud, he shouted to Kel, "Commander, is that cloaking device in yet?"

"Not yet!" she yelled back. "I need more time!"

Flogg's voice rang out on the bridge. "Captain, this bombardment can cease, if only you will surrender to me. You cannot hold out under pressure forever."

Down in the cargo hold, Jym and Mara took up positions near the engine room doorway, standing next to each other just outside the smaller chamber. They steadied themselves, taking wide stances and holding their arms in the direction of the warp drive. Clattering on the ladder clued them that someone was following them.

"What are you kids doing?" Dr. Rox demanded.

"We're helping," Mara stated plainly.

"You can't be down here!" railed Rox. "We're in the middle of a battle, it isn't safe! Come on, let's get you top-deck and get strapped back into our seats."

"The artificial gravity is failing," Jym tried to explain. "If we lose it, Kel won't get the cloaking thing fixed, and no one will be able to move around the ship to other stations. We could lose the fight!"

Rox insisted, "You two need to be kept safe!"

"We are safe!" snapped Mara. She calmed herself. "Thanks to all of you, we are safe. Let us help now. None of us will be safe if the gravity fails."

As if to emphasize her point, another fluctuation pulsed through the vessel. Everything in the cargo bay hung in the air for a moment, then returned with a thud to the floor. Jym motioned to the warp drive. "See?" he said. "We have to stop that."

The doctor did see. He also heard. Nado's thundering voice could be easily perceived from the bridge above, shouting, "Another blasted gravity flux! If we don't do something about that, it's going to knock one of us silly in a minute!"

Rox stared hard into Jym and Mara's eyes, reading the integrity and resolve therein. "Okay, but I'm staying right here with you in case something goes wrong. I'm really worried about you two overexerting yourselves."

With a smirking chuckle, Mara quipped, "Us too."

They waited, hands at the ready, poised to stop the next undulation. A quick peripheral glance and they both knew the other had sensed the same thing. "Here it comes," the princess primed. With a motion that looked like they were swatting tiny insectoids with both hands, the siblings brought their arms down with tremendous force. A gonging echoed in the bay, but the artificial gravity never changed. It worked!

Mara felt at her nose, as did Jym. There was no blood. "I guess with the machine doing the heavy lifting, we're not having to manipulate as much of the field," the girl surmised.

"Yeah," stated Jym, smugly. "I could do this all day."

"Let's not push our luck," Rox cautioned with a smile. "Remember, the artificial gravity generator is only a part of the warp drive. The field gets a lot denser once the warp function is engaged."

"Thanks, Rox." Mara returned his warm expression. "Hopefully we'll be out of here before that happens."

"Disengage the shields," Nado ordered at Red. "They'll sap too much power. Red, evasive maneuvers."

The forcefield dissipated, giving them visibility through the cockpit-style forward view ports again. A small fleet of seven hodgepodge warships were arrayed against them. One stayed behind the rest, slightly larger and more impressive than the other six. It was also decorated with a violet emblem that resembled a circlet of feathers.

Furiously flying across the control panel, Red's automatic appendages gave the Explorer a series of commands, engaging the thrusters and air jets. The ship moved and dodged the incoming enemy laser fire like a well-choreographed dance. The captain had to fight to keep up with Red's movements, his eyes glued to his targeting console.

"Schiff, four ticks to the left...fire! Uh, I have two ticks to...no, make that five ticks now...uh, Schiff, three ticks down and two ticks to the right...wait!" Nado flashed an angry glare at the robot. "Red, I can't get a shot off!"

"This unit can discontinue evasive action," Red replied. "However, that would undoubtedly result in a direct hit from the enemy forces."

Frustrated, Nado finally gave up. "Schiff, aim the stupid turret however you like and fire away! I'm going to do the same, maybe by a miracle we'll manage to hit something!"

Lasers careened through the expanse, whipping a whirling around one another as the Gnarf ships desperately tried to aim their own turrets to catch up to the robot pilot's deft maneuvers. The Explorer's own laser beams joined the strange light show, everything missing its mark and spilling into deep space. Continuous use of the fuel and air jets like this though would also quickly exhaust their fuel and oxygen supply.

"Kel, any luck?" Captain Nado checked in.

"Still working on it," answered Kel. "My tools keep getting scattered by the anti-gravity waves."

"Those seem to have stopped for now. How much longer?"

"Got to rewire a couple more components."

Nado wiped the sweat from his brow. "Something has got to change, or we're in serious trouble."

Something did change. Out of the void, an enormous battleship warped into the fray. The lasers ceased instantly, as all the Gnarf ships were overtaken by the much larger vessel. Similarly to Flogg's ships, this one also had an odd makeshift look to it. As the battle took a reprieve, Red called out again. "Captain, we are receiving another hail."

Staring out the viewport, Nado replied, "Patch them through."

The speakers crackled to life. "This is General Hämm, representing High King Bë-Konn of the Gnarfs. We are here to apprehend the Explorer 2000!"

Chapter 10

Galaxies are vast places, and hunting for a lone sky-beast amidst this endless black sea would have been impossible. Further, Boxie the Beautiful's concise convoy consisted only of a handful of fighters, a single gunnery craft, and her own transport frigate, meant more for comfort in transit than any kind of combat. Hopefully battle could be avoided though. Boxie pondered this as she played with the poisonous potion in her possession.

Unlike her fellow Gnarfs, Boxie had seen firsthand the nature of schemes and plots. She knew better than to assume that she could roam the heavens indefinitely, hoping to run across her quarry by chance. The roughed-up port-master from the Explorer's airlock chamber had been more than willing to provide additional information regarding the sky-beast. The station's onboard radar computers had captured the warp heading of the Explorer. While it was technically illegal to share such information with anyone other than the station's own law enforcement, the Gnarf Boxies could be quite persuasive.

The few fighters attached themselves to the larger craft and they were set to embark. Her own sky-beasts followed the heading, warping into the dark tapestry of open space. Following the heading wasn't an easy task, as even with that advantage they were still largely on a blind search of a vast region. But it was a start, and radar pings were the next step. Her Boxies on the communication apparatus also scanned the radio waves for any frequencies that might be in use.

Amid static and interference, a voice burst through, "...Hämm, representing High...Gnarfs. We are...Explorer 2000!"

"Tune in on that frequency!" instructed the lady ambassador. "Readjust the radar consoles!" Her minions carried out her bidding. "Anything yet?"

"We have a ping!" the radar operator answered. He fed the information to the navigators, who buzzed about feeding their own findings to the pilots. Within minutes, they were on the hunt in earnest, Boxie's fingers tapping together in a trepidatious twitter.

His ultimatum delivered, General Hämm fell silent. Captain Nado ran to the fore of the fuselage, craning to spy the newly arrived Gnarf forces. General Hämm had apparently brought the entirety of the Gnarf armada with him. No less than a hundred fighters, dozens of support frigates, approximately fifty gunnery schooners, and that one immense carrier flagship. Engaging Flogg's seven vessels was already a handful, a force of that size would have been impossible! A new strategy was needed, and fast. For now, protection was at the top of the list.

"Red, prepare to activate the shields," ordered Nado.

"Shields at the ready, Captain," the automaton assassin replied.

Captain Nado prepared to belt more commands to the crew, but someone else cut him off. The radio crackled, and Flogg's voice carried through. "General, you are a bit late to this encounter. The Explorer sky-beast has already submitted to me."

"Did they forget to stop broadcasting to our frequency?" whispered Kel. "They can't be that dumb and disorganized."

"Well, they are Gnarfs," Schiff quietly shrugged. "They aren't exactly famous for their intelligence."

"No need for secrecy," stated Red. "Our end is muted. They cannot hear you."

Schiff happily declared the obvious. "But we can hear them."

"Yes, we can," Nado butted in. "Let's be quiet and listen to what they have to say."

General Hämm was delivering his response. "Stand down, seer! This is not your mission to complete. The high king entrusted this hunt to me, so you will step aside."

"The high king also gave me leave to seize the Hex-man's enemies," retorted Flogg. "I am here with his blessing."

"You lie! His majesty would never stoop to allowing a dishonest madman to join in this, a warrior's job! I know your ploy. You still seek access to the throne of the high king!"

"Dishonest? Madman? How can you, a sword-wielding simpleton, make such a judgment of one such as I?"

"Simpleton, you say? Ha! At least I do not perform fool's errands. You would ritualistically starve yourself just to pretend that you are receiving visions!"

"Pretend?" Flogg's usually confident tonality wavered at this. "I see oracles that you could never comprehend."

Hämm snuffed so loudly it created feedback. "You and I both know that your powers faded long ago, vizier. You have not seen a true vision in years, yet still you and your priests persist in your ceremonies, fasting day and night, while my soldiers and I feast on godflesh regularly! And you say I am a simpleton."

"Because you are," Flogg fired back. "You try to solve every problem with force and might, leaving no room for politics and diplomacy. The Gnarf people cannot rely on you as a leader. They need someone who can see beyond the veil and provide a vision for the future."

There was a lull in the exchange, so Nado unmuted the Explorer's radio, chiming, "Good general, we the crew of the Explorer 2000, were in fact about to surrender to Flogg's fleet." He waited to see what response he might get.

"Are you nuts?" Kel scolded. "What if you get us killed?"

"Hold on," grinned Nado, with a mischievous glint in one eye and a wink with the other. "I think their own pride could be our ticket out of this madness."

Also listening in on the conversation, Boxie's tiny troop of sky-beasts stayed out of the mix for now. Her gunner seemed a bit impatient though. "Should we not attack and seize them now?"

"Nitwit!" she fumed. "We cannot hope to deal with even the forces of Flogg in our state. No, let the two continue their ranting and raving. We will wait for a more opportune moment."

"Are you sure, my liege? You do not want the Explorer sky-beast to escape, correct?" She glared at him. He realized his mistake and hastily added, "Oh, truly tremendous one."

"There is no need yet that we should get involved," Boxie soothed. "Patience, my Boxies. If Hämm and Flogg distract each other with this heated debate, so much the better for us. Let us see first where this conflict leads, then we will pick up the pieces after..."

Wave after wave of weightlessness would have flooded the vessel had Mara and Jym not been there to counteract the fluxing of the artificial gravity field. They were on the fifth one, by the princess' count, with a sixth on the way. Still, the pressure hadn't caused any strain on their bodies, though both were beginning to feel a bit fatigued.

Fluctuation number six rolled in, the kids once more stemming the tide before it could even begin. Something was different this time, though, the anti-gravity wave didn't end. The machine fully failed! Clenching their fists, the two held the energy field in place, hoping they could hold it long enough for Kel to finish installing the cloaking mechanism...

"WHAT?!!" roared General Hämm, causing massive squealing from the radio this time. "You would hand yourselves over to him?"

"Well, he was here first," Nado pointed out, taking care to only unmute himself when absolutely necessary.

"That does not matter!" the general pronounced. "All that matters is who is strongest, who can take you by force!"

"I understand your anger," soothed Flogg. "But the captain is correct. They are in my possession now."

"Captain, this shriveled creature speaks untruth to you," Hämm coerced. "He is a liar and cannot be trusted."

"I suppose that is accurate," agreed Nado. "I mean, I was only going along with him because he had promised us sanctuary, but you saw when you arrived that we had not really conceded. We were in combat!"

"There you see!" grunted a satisfied Hämm. "Flogg not only lied to me, but convinced you to lie as well, using another lie as enticement. He will not give you sanctuary!"

"Then I suppose we'll go with you," Nado bluffed.

"Of course you will!"

"That would be most unwise, Captain," Flogg interjected. "Hämm is a cruel monster and will mistreat you as soon as you are on board. He will not offer anything but pain and suffering, but I can provide you with comfort and food. You will be a guest on board our sky-beasts."

"That sounds pretty good." The crafty captain continued his con. "Alright Flogg, we will surrender to you."

"No!" protested General Hämm. "You already said you would come with me!"

"Flogg's offer sounds appealing. Can you do better?"

Hämm growled irately. "I will provide you with private bunking quarters and regular meals, just like my men."

Flogg countered, "Paltry offer, General. Why would they dine and sleep like common soldiers, when they could be in complete luxury in my own cabin?"

"I do like luxury," Nado pressed, hoping Hämm would keep taking the bait.

But the gritty general had heard too much. "ENOUGH!!! No more bartering, no more bidding, no more negotiating! Captain Nado, you will...you will...what was the Hex-man's phrasing? Oh, yes! You will reprimand yourselves to our custodian!"

"Ugh," moaned Flogg, still on the radio waves. "The phrase was 'remand yourselves to our custody,' brainless, brawling boob."

"That does it!" proclaimed Hämm. "I have suffered your insults too long vizier! Perhaps this will silence your forked tongue!"

The crew stared in awe as a humongous laser originated from the carrier. It struck the vizier's purple-adorned spacecraft smack on the prow. Flogg's ship was launched backward by the blast, having to use its own thrusters and air jets to regain position. A huge hole had been burned into the forward hull, certainly damaging some of their systems. As soon as they had righted themselves, Flogg answered back.

"You would dare such treason, Hämm?" the villainous vizier jeered. "Then you give me no choice but to declare self-defense."

A hatch on the underside of Flogg's main craft opened, mechanical arms lowering an ugly missile, covered in touch-sensitive spikes, into position. Thrusters on the rear of the missile ignited, sending it zipping through the arena towards the carrier! They heard Hämm's voice again, continuing to broadcast via radio waves.

"Flogg, what have you done?! Shields up!"

But his order wasn't fast enough. The missile found its target, the carrier being too big to fully evade the wicked warhead. A large but silent burst of fire quickly died in the vacuum, along with hundreds of Gnarf soldiers that were sent spiraling into the abyss. The impact of the missile was obvious, having blown a gaping hole in a portion of Hämm's carrier, that section imploding rapidly from the lack of pressure in the void around them.

"You pompous, arrogant, self-righteous, double-crossing s'wik!" Hämm blasted into the transmitter. "I'll see you blown to bits for this!!"

Lasers! Torpedoes! Warheads! It was a full-blown battle of colossal proportions! Hämm's fighters swarmed Flogg's forces, outnumbering them. But their foe had shielding, where the smaller craft did not. At least a dozen single-manned triangular Gnarf fighter shuttles fell to the vizier's warships. Two of those warships were disabled by the general's schooners, launching devastating remote-controlled explosives straight into the warship thrusters. Caught in the middle of the action, the Explorer 2000 floated alone in a veritable ocean of chaos and carnage.

"Well, the plan sort of worked," Nado offered with a sheepish shrug. "Red, let's get those shields up! I don't want to get hit by a wayward attack."

"This unit recommends repositioning the Explorer outside the line of fire," said Red.

"Not yet," warned the captain. "We move now, and we make ourselves a target. Let's sit tight for the moment."

"Let go!" Dr. Rox shouted at the kids. "It'll kill you, just let go!"

"We can't," grunted Jym. "The fluctuations keep building up."

"What does that even mean?"

Mara groaned in pain. "It means if we release the field now it could send a shockwave through the ship. We need a powerful surge to complete the counteraction."

Rox thought for a second. "Like the manipulation element in the warp drive when it would reactivate after a failure."

"Yeah," panted Jym. "That's what it was doing before it completely died."

"So, what could we use now?" The doctor wracked his brain. "How about the warp drive's bubble effect? Would that work?"

"Probably," said Mara between labored breaths. "Don't know for sure. But we'd need to know exactly when it was going to happen…so we could untether from the field…before the big surge."

"If you didn't untether in time, what would happen?"

"I have no idea!" fumed Mara.

Jym spoke more calmly as blood began to trickle from his nose. "We might die."

Though the battle raged on, the Explorer's plasma shields made viewing it impossible. The cloaking device was still a work in progress, so they were radar dark as well. Beads of sweat snaked down Kel's face. She knew at this point it was all riding on her success. Her engineer's mind focused on the task, solder those wires here, connect that set of switches there, bypass a coupling, splice a cable. One careful step after another.

The radio sprang to life again. "Wait! Wait! STOP!!" Hämm's guttural voice made the speaker pop this time. "Cease fire! All Gnarfs, cease fire! What are we doing?"

"Defending ourselves from your barbarism," replied Flogg.

"We are slaughtering Gnarfs!" yelled Hämm. "That is what we are doing! Killing our own kind!"

"You started the attack," mentioned Flogg.

"Shut up! That tricksy captain started this fight! He used the oldest military tactic known, divide and conquer. Don't you see? He pitted us against each other."

"What would you suggest we do?"

A sinister tone took over Hämm's speech. "All ships, target the Explorer sky-beast. Disable it and the fighters can attach tow lines. We will drag them back to Urkasak in chains!"

"And who claims the glory?" Flogg persisted.

"All of Urkasak! The high king! And us!"

Brief silence came from the other side. Then Flogg said, "You can disable them, but my war-beasts will do the towing."

"That is unacceptable! Your sky-beasts do not possess tow lines, you cannot perform the task."

"Then we will disable them, and you will tow."

"We have the greater firepower, our beasts will do both!"

"Ah, but what guarantee do we have that you will not then try to claim all the glory for yourself, dear general?"

"Infuriating ingrate!" yelled Hämm.

The argument went on in the background as Nado turned down the volume on the radio speakers. "Kel, we're running out of time. How's it coming?"

"Almost, Captain," she responded. "It was a tougher job than I anticipated. I'm close though. Good thing those Gnarfs are glory hounds."

"And morons," added Schiff.

"Such is the state of most fleshy blob brains," Red inserted.

That brought a bit of levity to the situation, but it was short-lived. The radio brought ill news. Hämm and Flogg could be heard ceasing their disagreement. The captain rushed to the radio control panel and cranked the volume back up.

"Fine," they heard Flogg saying. "That, I suppose, is preferable to fighting amongst ourselves like wild animals. Very well, we shall all target the Explorer beast, and my war-beasts will fly at the head of the formation upon our return."

"While my sky-beasts tow it," finished Hämm. "All Gnarfs, on my mark, prepare to fire!"

The captain looked nervously at Kel. "Commander?"

"Almost got it...," she replied.

Hämm began his countdown. "Five!"

"Kel?" questioned Nado.

"I said almost..." Kel spliced two wires.

"Four!" bellowed the general.

"Kel! Hurry up!" Nado yelled.

"Not quite...," the commander shot back.

"Three!" Hämm's death knell continued.

"Almost..."

"Two!"

"Got it!" Kel thrust her hand from under the radar panel and flipped a switch. A hum exuded from the device.

"One!"

Nado gulped. "Did it work?"

"I said one! Fire, curse you, fire!" Hämm's tirade went silent for a moment. "What do you mean you cannot target them?" A cheer erupted from the bridge of the Explorer! But Hämm wasn't finished. "Then try to hit them manually! I don't care how long it takes!"

"That's it," Captain Nado announced proudly. "They can't track us now. Red, warp us somewhere safe."

"That is not a navigable parameter, Captain." The robot only stared at him. "This unit requires more specificity than that."

"We haven't time to chart a proper course, just take us somewhere safe!" barked Nado. "Initiate the warp drive now!"

"This unit will comply."

Strain was etched on the kids' faces as they struggled to maintain control. Rox felt helpless, watching them writhe and squirm. But the field had to be maintained. The blood trails seeping from their nostrils gave him heartburn, so he dashed for the ladder. He hadn't dared leave the kids alone, but this was too much. He had to tell the command crew what was happening.

Reaching the base of the ladder, Rox overheard Nado's voice from above, shouting, "Initiate the warp drive now!"

The doctor's head whipped back toward the kids, still grappling with the dark energy field, fighting to maintain the precarious balance of the mounting gravitational shockwave. In a nigh dreamlike state, he heard the robot's clinical response. The Casimir thrummed and hummed.

Fear gripping his very soul, Dr. Rox yelled up the ladder at the top of his lungs, "Not yet! Don't warp yet!"

But it was too late. He felt the blurring and bending of space around him, the warp bubble wrapping itself around the ship. The kids themselves seemed to stretch and twist before his very eyes. The same gonging as before resounded in the cargo bay, this time much more intense. Everything went black.

Rox wasn't entirely sure how much time had elapsed when he awoke. The ship was dark, only emergency auxiliary lighting functioning. He was aware that he was floating. The Explorer was completely devoid of artificial gravity. Containers of supplies also wafted about in the weightless environment.

Kicking off the wall, the doctor swam through the air toward the kids, unconsciously drifting in the bay. He pulled them close to the floor in case anything automatically reactivated. It was then he noticed that, though they were weightless and should have been no trouble to move, the action put him out of breath.

The oxygen supply! Surely life support hadn't failed them. Hopefully not, but he couldn't be positive. Rox knew his breathing was difficult, so that was a bad sign. He didn't hear any noise from the upper deck, and that was another bad sign. More bad news, the kids were in a coma-like state, with who knows what level of internal trauma? Even the robot seemed to have been affected, as there appeared to be no activity whatsoever on the Explorer.

The doctor felt a wetness at his nose. He touched his upper lip, then looked at his hand. Blood. It trailed from his own nose as well. Did that mean he was suffering whatever the kids dealt with? If so, how? He wasn't even tethered to the field like they were.

As the feeling of woe began to overwhelm him, Dr. Rox's mind was flooded with a million questions at once. Rationalizing was typically his forte, though now he was having trouble maintaining sequential thoughts. That was worrisome. That meant the oxygen was low and he was beginning to suffer from cerebral hypoxia. And that meant... His ruminations trailed off again and he gradually lost consciousness, slipping into a nightmarish blackness...

Chapter 11

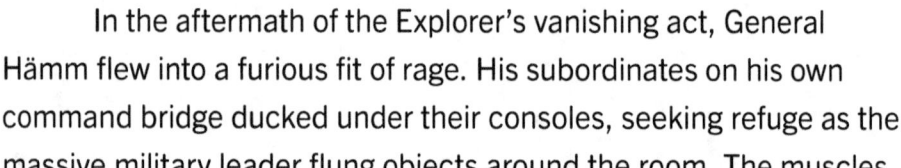

In the aftermath of the Explorer's vanishing act, General Hämm flew into a furious fit of rage. His subordinates on his own command bridge ducked under their consoles, seeking refuge as the massive military leader flung objects around the room. The muscles on Hämm's arms flexed and bulged, veins nearly popping from his burly body.

At last, the general's ire dissipated into a surly sulk. "Hail Flogg on the radio," he growled. "I would speak to him again."

"You are patched through," the radio operator said, quickly obeying.

"Flogg!"

"Yes, general?" Just hearing Flogg's vocal inflections threatened to send Hämm into another tyrannical tirade.

He managed his fury under a façade of meekness. "I am shuttling to your sky-beast. We need to have a conference about what has just occurred and lay out a plan to fix this mess before word gets back to Bë-Konn, or worse, the Hex-man."

"I will ready the airlock tether to receive you, general," Flogg replied.

"Good man," the warrior said through clenched teeth. "I will be there in a few minutes." The radio was turned off, and General Hämm addressed his men. "Prepare the shuttle. The grand vizier is about to receive me and receive the thrashing of his life!"

With an entourage of a half dozen soldiers in tow, Hämm stomped from the bridge, making his way down to the hangars of the fighter craft. He boarded one of the short-range shuttles and they began the journey to Flogg's warship. It took approximately thirty minutes to make to trip and for the priests to prepare the airlock tether for the shuttle. During that time, Hämm's anger only rose. The more he thought about the uncanny escape of the Explorer beast, the more he seethed. *Flogg would pay dearly for his insurrection!*

The airlock at last opened, an extended hallway made of reinforced plasti-steel allowing pressurized entry into the warship. Hämm wasted no time in striding to the bridge, where Flogg awaited him. The vizier was decked in his most outlandish accouterments, complete with flowing purple trappings and his most decadent feathered circlet. Apparently Flogg had delusions of making a superb display when the Explorer's occupants had been apprehended.

The display that was in store for him would be superb, of that Hämm was certain. He bellowed at Flogg's priestly crew, "Clear the bridge!"

They did. Alone with the twisted traitor, Hämm's face distorted into a gnarled, gnashing, animalistic grimace. His eyes went wild, his nostrils flared, his breathing grew heavy and strong. The mighty menace charged!

———◦○◦———

Outside the warship bridge, another priest jogged from the lower decks, a missive in his hand. He showed it to the bridge commanders, allowing them time to review the document. They confusedly shrugged at one another before granting permission to the lesser priest. Someone else had asked for authorization to come aboard, Ambassador Boxie the Beautiful, of Vortex.

Several minutes later, Boxie's bulgy build was at the sealed door, seeking entrance to the chamber beyond. "Do I have consent to enter the command center?" she requested.

"I guess so," answered one of the priests. "General Hämm is in there with Flogg in...private conference. Enter at your own risk."

"To see that sight, I will risk it," laughed Boxie.

Whirring and moaning, the doors slid open. Boxie stepped through, and the priests wasted no time in securing the portal behind her. A sensational scene awaited her, as Hämm chased the much smaller Flogg around the control room, dodging consoles and leaping chairs. The advisor fearfully flitted about, as much as any Gnarf can, desperately attempting to keep out of the warpath of the wrathful general!

"Imbecile!" Hämm shouted. "Idiot! Ignorant undoing of our people!"

At once, Hämm's meaty mitt managed to grab hold of Flogg's fleshy hide, yanking him from his escape attempt mid-jump. The vizier's feet never touched the floor as he was swung around and thrown vehemently against the far wall. Stunned, Flogg flumped to the floor, but had only just slid down the surface when Hämm grabbed him again! No tossing this time, as instead the general began slamming Flogg into various consoles and furnishings around the room.

It seemed for a moment that Hämm was done, having gotten all his rage out of his system. But, rather foolishly, his opponent opened his mouth. "You have made your point, general," Flogg mumbled. "You will choose might over mentality every time. And that is why you forever fail!"

Spurred on by anger once again, Hämm yelled incoherently, abusing Flogg even further. Rather than utilizing him as a battering ram though, the mountainous Gnarf commander smacked the vizier against the wall again, sliding his hefty hand under Flogg's chin. It found the throat, proceeding to squeeze. But Hämm was not satisfied with choking his victim, no, he wanted something more visceral.

"YOU! USELESS! WASTE! OF! FLESH!!" he roared, slamming Flogg's head against the wall with every word. "If it hadn't been for your arguing and selfish ambitions, the Explorer would be in our grasp at this moment! But you had to debate and fuss over your 'glory' and 'image'. Argh!" One final slam marked the end of Hämm's assault. He finally let Flogg drop to the floor.

At this point, Boxie had likely seen the full spectacle that she was going to see. The grand vizier had been part of the conspiracy against her, having reported her to the high king when she was caught "stealing" his jewels. Observing the literal bashing of one of her bitter foes was indeed rewarding. Knowing that both he and Hämm had been bested by Captain Nado, just as she had been, was also a nice touch. But there was business to attend to now.

"General," she announced herself. "Grand Vizier? How goes your hunt?"

Hämm looked up, only just realizing that another was in the room. "Boxie? What are you doing here, banished one?"

"I prefer to be addressed by my full title," quipped the ex-queen. "I am Ambassador Boxie the Beautiful, representative of – "

"Silence!" ordered the general. "You are a banished thief, and I am a famed god-killer. I will call you what I wish."

Boxie hurtfully huffed, "Fine."

"You have not answered my question. What are you doing here?"

"I have a proposition," Boxie offered.

Hämm only glared. "I'm listening."

"For both of you." She pointed at Flogg, who still lay slumped upon the deck.

Snorting, General Hämm lifted the limp oracle to his feet, plopping him into a chair. Flogg brushed the general's hands aside, scowling and snarling in his direction. Hämm then indicated for Boxie to continue.

"I too encountered the Explorer 2000 on Vortex," she began weaving her tale. "They eluded my Gnarf Boxies, but I followed them here." She paused, feigning a pout, "Unfortunately, I was too late to assist in the battle. However, I have uncovered a means of catching them."

Now both Hämm and Flogg perked up. The sundered soothsayer was the first to speak. "You have? What is it?"

"When you want to catch vermin, what do you do?" she rhetorically asked. "You cannot chase them, for they will simply keep running away and hiding. You must set a trap."

"What kind of trap do you have in mind?" Hämm wanted to know.

"Between my sky-beasts, yours, and what is left of Flogg's forces, we have enough here to cover a large portion of the sector. We send the sky-beasts to wait in the heavens, creating a dragnet."

"And then we will be able to find them wherever they are and blast them!" finished Hämm, assuming he knew her plan.

"No," Boxie stated simply.

"It figures a fool like you would not understand the complexity of this strategy," Flogg insulted.

"Need I bounce your skull off the wall again?" growled the general.

"Stop!" Boxie halted them. "We do not wish to attack them in open space, they will use their cloaking device again and warp away. No, what we need to do is lure them onto my vessel with bait."

"What kind of bait would you propose we use?" Hämm pointedly interrogated.

"Bait is always something that plays upon the pest's weakness," said the audacious ambassador. "Therefore, I will be the bait."

"Ha!" thundered Hämm. "What weakness have you perceived in the Explorer beast that makes you think you would be good bait?"

"Compassion."

Light shone from an indeterminate location, illuminating the expanse around Captain Nado. He scanned the area, suddenly aware that he was floating, weightless and airy. In every direction he saw bright prismatic stars, shining yellow nebulae, distant galaxies filled with celestial bodies. It was a beautiful sight! He was in ecstasy at the wonder and awesome majesty of the universe.

Then a sudden realization set in, Nado was not in the ship! He wasn't in anything, just wafting in space. Yet, his breathing had not been hampered, had it? No sooner did he think it than things took a turn for the worst. Pain began crushing his chest, the cold freezing his skin. He struggled for breath, but there was no air to breathe. The light dissipated, leaving him in the dark emptiness. Swirling into the blackness, Nado clawed and clutched, suffocating in the icy vacuum.

The Captain convulsed and jerked, striving to break through the starless void. He suddenly sat up, banging his head against smooth metal. Gradually, his eyes adjusted, and the med-bay of the Explorer 2000 started to take shape. He was laying in one of the medical bay sleep pods, the surface above him too close to sit fully upright.

"Welcome back to the world of the living, Captain," he heard the voice of Dr. Rox say.

The room was darkened, only lit by the auxiliary lighting, running off the backup batteries. Struggling to shake the grogginess from his mind, Captain Nado swiveled to let his feet touch the floor. He put two hands on his knees for support, the other two holding his head. It throbbed from the pain of a migraine, making his thoughts feel like a soupy mess.

"What happened?" slurred the Captain.

"Some kind of energy field interference," Rox said. "I don't think I could explain it, but...I should have said something far earlier."

"About what?"

Rox sighed, "The kids. They came into the hold during the fight. They were trying to mitigate the undulations from the artificial gravity element. I came to keep an eye on them, thinking I was doing my job. Even after the element completely failed, I let them maintain their hold on the energy field, but the energy was building up. The activation of the warp drive, combined with the buildup of dark energy in the hold..." He paused. "I should've notified you sooner."

Nado put a hand on the doctor's shoulder, but not to console him, only to stop him from spiraling. "What's done is done. Do you know where we are?"

"I was hoping you could answer that."

"Get me up to the bridge," said Nado, struggling to stand. "We'll see if Red can provide any answers." Something occurred to the captain. "Wait, I thought you said the artificial gravity had failed? How are we standing here?"

"Wherever we are, we've already landed," replied Rox. "The oxygen vents are open, so the planet has a breathable atmosphere."

"Where's everybody else?"

"Red's on the bridge, awaiting orders. Must've had an automatic reboot command set up in its central processor. Kel and Schiff are sleeping off the effects, the robot and I moved them to their bunking compartments. You had a pretty big bump on your head, so I moved you to med-bay for observation."

"And the kids?"

The doctor couldn't meet Nado's gaze. "They're in their compartment too. They've slipped into a coma-like state. I don't have the means to treat them on the ship."

"I see," muttered Captain Nado. "Let's reconvene with Red, see if it can tell us where we are. Then we'll go from there."

They quietly traversed the short distance, Rox assisting Nado the whole way. Closer to the doctor's face now, Nado saw the dried blood on his mustache. "What happened to your nose? Looks like you lost some blood too."

"Oh, that. Don't know exactly." Rox shrugged with a heavy sigh. "I suspect that whatever trauma the dark energy manipulation inflicts on the kids must have occurred to me as well, as I was at the epicenter of the event. But so far, that's the only effect I've suffered. I was the first to awaken, so it seems I'm fine."

Quiet and calm, the bridge was a far more serene scene than the last time Nado had been here. Most of the controls were deactivated, their consoles and panels dark. Red sat in the pilot's seat, swiveling to greet them as they approached.

"Greetings, Captain," it saluted. "This unit notes that your injury was not a serious one. That is preferable, as you are the most educated gunner aboard."

"Thanks for the compliment, I think," Nado quipped. "Red, where are we?"

"In a safe place, just as you requested."

"But what planet are we on?"

Red looked out the forward viewports. "It is uncharted."

"Then how did you know to come here?" Rox asked.

"It is programmed into this unit's navigational parameters."

"Then it can't be uncharted." Nado shook his head. "That makes no sense. Someone had to know about it, or it couldn't be in your programming. I'll check the nav binders."

"This unit has already studied the binders. There is no record of a habitable planet of this size within this solar system."

The captain now peered out the windows as well. "I suppose the only way to figure this out would be to explore the planet."

"You think that's a wise idea?" questioned Rox. "We have no clue what might be out there."

"It's worth a look. Let's wake Schiff and the commander."

Rox held up his hands. "Better to let them sleep off whatever effects they're dealing with. It should pass soon enough. Then you can do your exploring. I'll stay on the ship with the kids." The captain started to leave, but Rox stopped him. "Captain? I'm sorry...for my lack of communication. Maybe this wouldn't have happened. Are you angry with me?"

At first, the captain had no response. Then he finally confessed, "Yes. But I also know you couldn't have anticipated this. You are forgiven." The doctor started to speak again but Nado interrupted. "Let's not discuss this any further. I'm going to rest in my cabin until the ladies awaken. Have Commander Kel retrieve me when they are ready to disembark."

A few standard hours later, the commander and Schiff were back on their feet as well, shaking off the odd sensations of the involuntary insentience. They received the doctor's retelling of the sequence of events, Schiff trying to comfort him, while Kel had little to say on the matter. She wasn't sure how to handle it. On the one hand, Rox had done what any of them would have done. But on the other hand, he really should have told somebody what was going on. Of all the times for him to be reckless, it had to be the worst possible timing.

For now, though, she would keep her opinions to herself. If things were tense between Rox and the captain, she dared not muddy the waters further by trying to add her own two bits to the situation. Let it be, focus on the task at hand. She gathered Nado and his supplies, and they headed for the airlock bulkheads with Schiff and Red.

Armed and ready, they watched and waited as the doors lowered, revealing a sandy beach with a tropical forest at its far edge.

Brown mountains rose above the tree line in the distance, accented by smoky, swirling fog at their peaks. The sky shone a bright, pacific blue, and they could hear the sound of ocean water lapping at the shore, a warm and gentle breeze tussling their hair. Sensing a great calm, everyone holstered their firearms, except Red.

"I think we're good, Red," Kel told the robot. "This place seems pretty peaceful."

"Protocols dictate that an assassin's weapon should always be at the ready," responded Red. Kel just shook her head.

They proceeded from the bay onto the beach, the white sand squishing and crunching as they disembarked. Tiny creatures with hardened shells camouflaged as sparkling rocks skittered aside at their approach. Schiff bent to touch one, and it hunkered inside its protective carapace, hissing and spitting seawater out.

"Well, excuse me!" Schiff recoiled. "I was going to say you were cute, but you ruined that sentiment, buster!" The animal scurried along with its fellows. Schiff relented, "Alright, you guys are still pretty cute."

"Red, are your internal scanners picking up any other life forms?" the captain asked.

"Negative." Red's head turned from side to side. "However, it would be prudent to point out that this unit's detection systems offer a severely limited range. Life forms may be present further into the forest." It stopped for a moment. "Detecting energy signatures coming from the tree line."

"How many?" Kel checked.

"Twelve separate signatures. They appear to emit an energy signature identical to that of – " The robot was halted when a dozen quadrupedal creatures leapt from the shrubbery! Their shining metallic surfaces and glowing ocular sensors were fairly unmistakable. "Robots," finished Red.

Equipped with mechanical jaws and spiked teeth, the gear grinding guards raced at the crew, snapping and biting! They emitted a terrible sound from their vocalizers resembling a gruff yap. Two were armed with laser emitters on their topsides which nearly burned a hole through Schiff's chest had Kel not pulled her to safety.

Quickly firing a precise shot to the right, Red quipped, "As you can see, the dictation of protocols and programming is quite – "

"Oh, give it a rest!" piped Kel.

In swift succession, Red fired off another shot, immediately switching the carbine to its other hand. Two more shots, and Red had dispatched four of the attackers. Meanwhile, Kel led Schiff to cover behind the lowered bulkhead door, hiding on the backside of the ramp. She aimed for the two in the back, their heated lasers threatening to blast the crew into mist.

With the laser-bots focused on Kel, two others charged at Nado. The first bit at his right leg, which he rapidly retracted. The automaton missed its attack, allowing Nado to bring that same booted foot down on the thing's head, crushing it beneath his weight. Its partner leaped at the captain's chest, but Nado had drawn his pistols and planted a bolt from each into the belly of the beryllium beast, knocking it from the air. Plasma from the bolts burned through the surface plating, destroying the circuitry within.

For Kel, lining up the shot was difficult, as she was pinned down from the laser fire. Further, three more of the mechanical monsters had swarmed their position. One snapped at Kel's feet, but she was able to yank them out of the way in the nick of time, blasting a hole in the robotic sentry before it could attack again.

Schiff, on the other hand, was having a tough time escaping the two that chased her around the Explorer's landing gear. After a minute, she was able to create enough space between them to give herself a brief respite. Schiff dashed behind a landing strut on one side, then another silvery sentinel came out on the other. The deception was just enough to trick the robots' ocular sensors before they utilized their scanners, giving Schiff an opportunity to get close and kick both of them into the tide, the seawater instantly ruining their electronics.

Seeing that Schiff was safe, the commander whirled to face Red. "Red! Take out the ones with the lasers!" She then proceeded to poke out of hiding and lay down suppressive fire on the laser-bots, offering a distraction.

Having destroyed the four it was initially targeting, Red rolled from its own cover to blast the two, putting burn holes in each with perfectly placed plasma bolts. But one had crept around, attacking Red from the back, and sinking its trap-like incisors into Red's plating. Kel took steady aim, sniping the thing from her robot compatriot's flank. The final combatant leapt at Red's head, but the automated assassin caught its adversary by what seemed to be its neck, smashing it to the ground. Red then tore the thing in half, finishing the fight.

"Utterly unsophisticated," quipped Red.

Captain Nado looked at the scene. "What were those things?"

"Robots, Captain," answered Red, a hint of cynicism in its voice. "This unit was quite clear before."

"I know they're robots," said Nado, oblivious to Red's simulated attitude. "What I meant is why are they here? Who built them? Where did they come from?"

"That is not what you vocalized, Captain."

"Red!" ordered Kel. "Knock it off."

She and Schiff slowly emerged from their cover under the ship, also surveilling the area. Nothing else moved, except the large leaves of the tropical trees in the breeze. Everything had gone completely silent again. This time, however, it was not serene, but eerie. After the battle with the robot guards, everyone was on edge, wondering what might happen next. Weapons drawn, the captain and commander inched toward the forest.

"Do you think there are more of them?" queried Kel.

"Not sure," the captain replied. "But better to be safe than sorry, right? What about you? Any ideas why they might have been here?"

"Nope. You said Red mentioned that this planet was uncharted, correct?"

"Yep."

Pistol still drawn and pointed, Kel stroked her chin with her empty hand. "Then someone must have been here first, and just never recorded the planet."

"All the more reason for the Explorer Initiative program to have remained available and alive," Nado snipped. "Aronites... always think they know what's best for the entire universe."

Schiff chimed in, saying in overdramatic tones, "Or maybe, those weren't real. Maybe, it was a hallucination! Maybe we're all in a weird, conjoined dream, and are actually lying on the beach right now, face down in the sand..."

After a few seconds, Kel stated, "Probably not."

Silence enveloped the group as they crossed the tree line into the dense tropical forest. There were no paths, not even natural ones, to indicate where the robots had come from. There were tracks in the dirt, but they did not match the tapered, pointed feet of the computerized quadrupeds. They looked a lot more like...

"Humans!" exclaimed Kel. "Those came from human feet, I'm sure of it."

"But how can you be positive?" asked Schiff.

Again, after several seconds, Kel stated. "Because I'm Human, and they look like mine."

"Ah, good deduction!" congratulated Schiff.

Kel just rubbed her forehead and kept their slow and steady pace. It was then that Red emitted a report. "Captain, commander, life forms detected by this unit, on the periphery of the scanners."

"Everyone be ready," warned Nado. "Red, how many? Where are they located?"

"Hard to get a solid read, Captain. The life forms are in constant movement."

Something whizzed through the trees, flying straight into Commander Kel's shoulder! She cried out in pain, falling to the ground, an arrow sticking out of her left arm. Suddenly, several more arrows whistled past, barely missing the crew.

"Hit the dirt!" shouted Nado, dropping to the forest floor. Schiff followed suit, leaving Red the only one still standing. Following its programming, the deadly android primed its weapon, seeking for a clear shot.

"Red, hold your fire!" Kel commanded.

"Protocols dictate that – "

"Cram your protocols! Don't shoot!"

Nado confusedly exclaimed, "Commander, they shot you!"

"With a blunted practice arrow." She showed them. The arrow was tipped with a rounded arrowhead, coated in a sticky substance. "It's okay, probably just a warning shot. Besides, if they really are Human, I don't want to hurt them."

"Understood." Bravely, Captain Nado stood to address the stealthy archers. "Friends, we come in peace!" His large frame was immediately pelted with sticky arrows. Nado looked down at his arrow-covered chest and bellowed, "Alright, that does it! Everyone, stay low and get those people! I want these troublesome… troublemakers dealt with!" More arrows landed against his shoulders and arms.

"Captain, life forms are retreating further into the forests," advised Red.

"Keep them on your scanners! Crew let's go! I want answers!"

Tearing through the forest's foliage and flora, the crew of the Explorer 2000 gave chase!

Chapter 12

Branch after branch whipped past their faces as the crew crashed their way through the thick forest leaves. Roots seemed to reach up with a mind of their own to trip them up and hamper their pursuit of the mysterious natives. Red's long, treading gait led the crew further and further, deeper into the forest. Twists and turns kept them in a strange pattern of movement, and it became difficult for Kel to determine how far they'd gone from the beach, or even which direction it was from their location.

Onward and forward their quarry eluded them, continuing to stay just on the edge of Red's scanner range. Frustratingly constantly out of reach, the enigmatic inhabitants jumped and bounded through the underbrush, over small trees, and around muddy pits. But with Red at the forefront of the group, many obstacles were cleared by its metal frame, unaffected by the laborious leafage that desired to harry their hastened hunt.

The path created by Red's destructive charge allowed the crew to maintain a manageable distance between themselves and the natives, the latter never quite able to escape. Faster and fleeter the chase surged onward, until at last the forest gave way to a large clearing. Now in the open, the natives whirled to face their pursuers, bows drawn and arrows nocked! The crew unholstered their own weapons, Red readying its carbine, Nado drawing his dual pistols, Kel removing hers, and Schiff entering a martial stance.

With the greenery finally out of their faces, Commander Kel took a moment to take in the scene around them. She finally got a good look at the natives, clad in outfits made of woven grass and leaves, sticks bound together with homemade twine acting as armor. Their faces were veiled by wooden masks, painted with various colors and designs.

The clearing was filled with a village of primitive log huts topped by thatch roofing. Many more natives milled about, carrying out their various daily routines. Some cooked over open fires, others ported water from the wells, children darted here and there engaged in a juvenile game. The villagers were not adorned as the scouts, lacking the wooden armor and armaments. Everyone stopped and stared at the intruders.

And the crew stared at them, especially Schiff. The villagers all possessed features that betrayed their race. Though chiefly humanoid, upon their heads were mops of pastel hair, colored in blue, green, pink, and purple. Nado and Kel both exchanged a brief expression, one that informed each that the other had the same thought.

Schiff voiced the thought aloud. "They're all 'shifters, like me…"

At that moment, a figure emerged form the largest hut that sat near the base of a gentle waterfall. "Hold!" it shouted. "Hold your fire please! We are a peaceful people!"

The woman to whom the voice belonged was slender and lithe, built similarly to Schiff, and also bore a thick mop of hair, hers teal in coloration. However, this woman was not dressed as the other natives but rather more like a researcher, with a simple dress, white laboratory coat, and thick lensed glasses. She practically tiptoed down the planked ramp that led to the large shelter, her bare feet avoiding more of the shelled creatures from the beach that scuttled in the sand underfoot.

"You're a 'shifter too," uttered Schiff.

"Yes, I am," the woman replied. "I am called Mother Anise."

"Is this, is this," Schiff stuttered, "is this the shapeshifter homeworld?"

Echoes of heavy footfalls reverberated throughout the dark corridors on the unfinished construction site. Open space could be seen betwixt the thick metal beams and rafters, as large pieces of plating were slowly floated into position to be riveted and welded together by the vast work force that operated in the colossal construction. Shuttles ferried parts and supplies from the planet below, bringing the spacesuit clad laborers more materials and tools for the nearly completed manufacturing project.

Satellites sporting enormous luxonite solar panels drifted alongside the structure, long cables providing power to the UPS batteries and artificial gravity generators inside. They also powered the oxygen recycling units, as well as an incredibly powerful plasma forcefield that created a breathable atmosphere within the bounds of the mammoth metallic monstrosity.

Lord Hex trekked down a hallway, his long cape billowing behind him. Clearly on a mission, nothing stopped his long and purposeful strides as he stomped ahead. Older model H-7 robot sentries armed with shock staffs stood at attention, saluting as he passed. The bridge of the creation was intact, the controls and consoles having been finished recently. But that was little consolation to Hex, as his pet project was several standard months behind schedule.

Entering the bridge, Hex scanned the room for the foreman, a scrawny Sorogan named Zuugs. There he was, leisurely sipping a hot beverage and laughing at some pointless joke while an army of hired hands made gradual progress. Hex flexed his fists, imagining them pummeling this pompous punk to a pulp. The masterful marquis could have punted this runt across the length of the site or slung him by his eyestalks into the void of space itself. Deep breaths soothed his lordship, his volcanic temper restrained...for now.

The grouping of managers and team leads surrounding Zuugs immediately quieted upon seeing Lord Hex's advance. Realizing something was up, the foreman himself turned, only to find his skinny neck stump in his lordship's powerful grip, strong hands squeezing hard. Hex lofted the Sorogan man into the air, letting his three toed feet wriggle and kick, meeting the foreman's frightened gaze with his own dark and cruel glare.

His presence established, Lord Hex released the much smaller Zuugs, allowing his tiny form to plummet to the flooring. The foreman landed with an "ugh!", his body squishing and squelching on impact. Almost afraid to do so, Zuugs rose to his feet and bowed his head in reverence to the Marquis du Hex.

"Milord," he stuttered, "we did not expect your arrival so soon. As you can see, the project is well underway, we have – "

Hex leaned close and uttered in low tones, "Be silent." He stood to his full height, surveying the command chamber. "How is it, Zuugs, that you were paid in advance, given nearly unlimited resources, granted a generous timeline, pampered with regular meals and free beverages, and yet…this is still INCOMPLETE?!!!"

His thunderous roar sent the miniscule manager tumbling again. This time, Zuugs stayed on the floor, kowtowing obsequiously. "Milord, my men work tirelessly to achieve your vision, but the task takes many materials. The fabrication process takes time."

"You had time in abundance," Hex retorted. "Now the project is overdue, well in arrears from my perspective. Were I in your position, I'd be in quite the hustle. So tell me, why do I find you lazily lapping and flapping your lips, when you should be in a dizzying tizzy to finish your work?!"

"It was a short break," explained a very confused Zuugs, "mandated by our contract. It's all in writing!"

"Contract?" the marquis chuckled. "You dare not mention 'contracts' as an excuse. You are in breach of contract, as the product is not completed according to the very benevolent schedule you were provided."

"My apologies, milord," groveled the foreman. "It will not happen again."

"No it will not. As you have failed to uphold your end of the bargain, I see no reason why I should do so either."

"Are we being fired?"

Lord Hex laughed out loud this time. "No, my silly little stooge, your services are not being terminated. They are being expedited."

"Sir? I don't understand..."

"No more breaks!" yelled Hex. "From now on, you will work non-stop until all is in readiness. Meals will be rationed according to logged hours, water will be withheld unless progress can be visibly pointed out, and the bunking quarters will be locked until your laborers fulfill a triple quota of their individual tasks. You have three standard cycles to get the project completed."

"Milord, that is impossible!"

"Silence!" spat his lordship. "If it is not completed within the new specified timeframe, you will be terminated. And not in the employment sense of the word, dear Zuugs."

Stunned, a solemn Zuugs replied, "Yes, milord."

In roguish fashion, the marquis turned to leave. "Oh, and Zuugs?"

"Yes, milord?"

"Don't make the mistake of thinking that if I am not present, you will not be held accountable." Hex's gloved hand indicated a series of security cameras. "I am watching. I am always watching."

"Yes, milord." Zuugs started to stand, but Lord Hex snapped his own wrist, forming a swift fist, and the Sorogan fell to the floor again, seeming to be tripped by nothing!

"That is but a taste of my power," the warden of the Hexagon murmured. "Do not fail me, or you will suffer far worse than this." Lord Hex appeared to rub at his face under his shadowy hood, his glove returning with drops of blood. He then turned to a nearby H-7. "Ensure that my orders are carried out to the letter."

It saluted again, vocalizing in a nigh monotone pitch. "This unit will comply, milord. This unit also has a message for you."

"Which is?"

"A visitor awaits you in your private quarters, milord."

Hex nodded. "Very well. I shall meet them there."

It was fortunate for Zuugs that his lordship's private chambers were also a completed section of the construction zone and had been made quite comfortable. Separated into two areas, a study and a waiting room, the spacious compartments offered cushioned seating, beverage cabinets, and unobtrusive lighting of a dim orange hue. The waiting room was styled simply, but the study bore a unique design. A broad iron-colored desk dominated the room, with a matching high-backed chair positioned behind it. The chair rose to a triangular peak, able to swivel in a complete circumference.

A secondary entrance allowed Lord Hex access straight to the study, bypassing his guest in the waiting room outside. He perched in his throne, taking care to ensure he held a commanding presence in the chamber. He flung his cape aside theatrically, allowing it to rest over one arm of the chair.

"Are you ready for your visitor?" queried a robotic aide at the door.

"One moment." Hex adjusted a few items on the desk, thought better of it and stashed them all in a drawer. Tapping his fingers against his chest, the marquis retrieved two items back from the drawer, an ornamental dagger and an onyx gemstone, and placed them strategically back onto the surface before him. "Ready. Wait not yet!" The melodramatic marquis swiveled to face away from the waiting room entrance. "Now I'm ready. Bring in my guest."

The magnetic door swished open, the aide greeting the guest with, "Lord Hex, your visitor."

Still facing away, Hex stated, "Welcome, esteemed guest of the Marquis du Hex, warden of the Hexagon worlds." He twirled garishly. "What can his lordship do for you, dear petitioner?" Lord Hex was caught off guard. This was a presence he did not expect. Before him stood a shifty looking Kriton with white scales, adorned in reinforced black leathers, with a scar across one marled eye.

"I must confess," the marquis began, "I did not anticipate the Pale Pillager, leader of the Darna-ké, and former war-chief of the Khanakhat tribe. It is an honor to meet you, Gnash."

The albino Kriton spoke gruffly and plainly. "I am not Gnash. He ish dead. I am hish brood-mate, Klensh."

"I see. It is still a pleasure to make your acquaintance. To what do I owe this pleasure?"

"I passssed through Vortex recently and heard tell that you are hunting the elusssive crew of the Explorer 2000."

"You're not wrong," Hex replied. "But what is your interest?"

"I too hunt thossse murderersss," hissed Klensh. "They are the onesss ressponssssible for my brood-mate'sss death!"

"Hmmm," rumbled his lordship, proceeding to muse, "They killed a crime lord? Very brazen of you Captain Burnay Nado." To Klensh he said, "So, what is it exactly that you want from me?"

"It ish not what I want, but what you want. I believe I can help you in your quesht."

Lord Hex relaxed in his throne. "In what way? I already have the entire Gnarf armada scouring the sector, acting on my orders."

"Gnarfsss? Their brainsss are muddied by their foolish religionsss. They will do you no good."

"I suppose it has been a while since I heard any reports from King Bë-Konn," agreed Hex. "But what can you offer that they cannot?"

"I have connectionsss with the prishon keepersss at Black Hole Penitentiary. You want an army of sssuper-powered, highly motivated, nasssty ssscoundrelsss? I can arrange that." A fanged grin stretched across Klensh's elongated snout.

Things slowly returned to normal in the village as the scouts lowered their bows and arrows, the crew following suit. The tense atmosphere calmed and settled into a more relaxed state, the children returning to their games and play. One of the scouts whispered to Mother Anise in an unintelligible language. She only shook her head gently and placed a hand on the warrior's bow. The welcoming party resumed their duties as village guards, while Anise brought the crew into the sanctuary beneath the falls.

Once they were all offered fresh water and fruits, Schiff asked again, "So, was I right? Is this the 'shifters world? Is this where we came from?"

"While I appreciate your enthusiasm," answered Mother Anise with a soft smile, "this is unfortunately not the shapeshifter home planet. I'm afraid it is still true that we haven't got a home. Merely nomads and pilgrims are we."

"Oh." Schiff became quite crestfallen. "I thought we'd managed to stumble into it, seeing as this is supposedly an uncharted planet."

"It is uncharted, true, but it was not always that way," explained Anise. "I removed it from the Galactic Community database that I might seek refuge here."

"Then how did our robot know to come here?" interrogated Kel.

"I thought that might have been his doing," Mother Anise ruminated. She then addressed Red. "Hello H-8-RED."

The robot's head turned, its ocular sensors lighting up. "Greetings."

"You don't recognize me, do you?"

"Negative," returned Red. "This unit is unable to identify your features."

"I thought not." Mother Anise sipped her freshly squeezed juice. "Still, it appears I did accidentally leave something behind."

"Did you construct H-8-RED?" Nado queried.

Anise bounced her head from side to side and replied, "Not entirely. I assisted in the programming though. I gave him his navigational and piloting protocols."

"Then you must know who programmed his assassination protocols," said Kel. "Tell me who so I can shoot them!"

"I don't know who else was working in Lord Hex's labs," the elder shapeshifter responded.

"Lord Hex?" exclaimed the captain. "You worked for him?"

"Oh, yes. Why do you ask?"

"Because he's currently after us," answered Nado. "He sent Red to kill us, but the commander here reprogrammed its IFF parameters."

"But why is Lord Hex trying to kill you?" Mother Anise was clearly bewildered by that.

Commander Kel took the time to explain. "It isn't us he's specifically after. It's the two kids we're escorting. They're monarchs of an unknown origin."

"I see," stammered Anise. "I certainly wouldn't want children to suffer at Lord Hex's hands. I'll gladly share what I know if you think it will help. I was a researcher and robotics programming specialist in his private laboratories on Yawin."

"I've heard stories of Yawin," Captain Nado excitedly mused. "Tell me, is the world of industry as magnificent as the tales say?"

"Magnificent?" questioned Anise. "I don't know about that. It is true that the entire world is dotted with massive cities primarily consisting of factories and labs, commercial headquarters, and warehouses. But the stories don't tell you that the atmosphere has turned a sickly yellow from the smog, the surface is plagued by lightning storms and sandstorms because the ecosystem is out of balance, nor do they tell of the corporate bondservant contracts, that basically allow the corporations to – to rule over their laborers like slave-masters!" Anise's rant subsided, and she relaxed herself. "Sorry. I get very impassioned when it comes to Yawin."

"We could tell," noted Kel.

Schiff interjected, "Why are they allowed to do this?"

"Because the planetary government was paid off by the big corps long ago." Mother Anise shrugged. "Now the government seats are all filled with the big CEO's and their lackeys. They ran off the smaller, independent businesses, anyone that might threaten their profit margin, so now only the biggest and cruelest occupy Yawin."

"I thought Yawin was supposed to be 'the world of building a better tomorrow'," muttered Nado, quoting the old slogan.

"Only a better tomorrow for their own pocketbooks," Anise quipped. "Innovation and invention gave way to corporate greed and marketing strategies."

"Back to the matter at hand though," Kel said. "What's going on with Red, and this world, and those other shapeshifters? How do you factor in with Lord Hex?"

"Of course," granted Mother Anise. "As I said, I was a researcher in his labs, as well as a robotics programmer. Lord Hex is a wicked force, ruling his corporate interests with an iron grip. I thought it was just a job, but when I found out he was planning to amass an army of assassination robots, I took all my research and robotic components and ran. I thought I had covered my tracks well, but apparently I left a clue in the navigational memory files."

"An army of these things?" Kel worriedly repeated.

Mother Anise raised a hand in comfort. "Don't worry about that. This H-8 is a unique prototype. There was a power failure at the plant, and we lost a lot of the base code for their programming. And with what I stole, Lord Hex should be far behind in completing the other H-8s."

"You robbed Lord Hex?" Schiff was impressed.

"A few crates of robotics components," admitted Anise.

"Is that where the sentries on the beach came from?" asked Kel.

"Crude, but it was all I had," shrugged Mother Anise. "But there's more, he wasn't just working on robots. I also found a large quantity of cloning pods, hooked up to stereo-neural cranial implants."

The captain perked up. "That's brainwashing technology."

"You are correct. Lord Hex was trying to build a legion of assassin robots coupled with an army of clones. Not just any clones either...shapeshifters."

"I don't understand," murmured Schiff.

"He wanted the shapeshifters' powers under his own command," Anise continued. "They were to be fully grown in the pods with their brains pre-programmed, then released as adults ready to help carry out whatever dark deeds Lord Hex had planned. He was concocting the perfect spy, thief, and double agent. With the shapeshifters and the robots combined..."

"He'd be unstoppable," finished Kel.

"That's why I also liberated the shapeshifters," explained Mother Anise. "Unfortunately, they were still children when I opened their cases, and the stereo-neural implants hadn't completed forming their minds. That is why they may seem a bit primitive to you. I thought it best when we escaped and ended up here that I let them grow and mature as naturally as possible."

"That explains how you got here," Schiff piped up. "But why does Lord Hex want all these things?"

"I overheard much when I was employed," replied Anise. "I don't know everything, but I can tell you that he spoke with another subordinate about the Galactic Community government. He specifically said, 'bring them to their knees', but that was all I could make out."

"But Lord Hex is a representative of the Galactic Community here in Taldish Sector," pondered Captain Nado. "Why would he jeopardize his position by assaulting the GC?"

"I don't know the answer to that," Anise responded. "However, I do know that he has one more secret project, something I only caught a glimpse of. I was asked for my navigational expertise in quoting any variants with warp travel when using a large vessel. I asked for clarification on the word 'large' and they told me something bigger than had ever been built before. They showed me only a part of the blueprints, but it was a spacecraft so incredibly enormous that it could sheer other ships in half just by brushing into them!"

"I thought craft of that class were only theoretical," the Captain mentioned. "The only models I've ever seen were for virtual experiments."

"What class of craft?" Schiff wanted to know.

The officers looked at her with grim expressions. Almost at the same time, Kel and Nado both gave a fearful answer. "Dreadnaughts."

"Ever since I was a boy, stories were told of how the Humans wanted to build a spacecraft that was so powerful it could be the end of a war before it even started," Nado said. "With the already massive size of the ships in their flotilla, it seemed they might be able to accomplish it."

"But Humans originated from another part of the universe, far from here," added Kel. "We had no home planet from which to garner adequate materials. Even partnering with the Aronites, Gonians, and Baldins of the Octagon wouldn't yield enough raw components to fulfill the requirements of the outer hull."

"The idea was abandoned," finished the captain. "If the Humans, the most technologically advanced race in the known universe, couldn't accomplish this feat, then more than likely no one could."

"Three hundred years my people have been trapped here, unable to get back to our actual home planet," Kel stated. "If we couldn't figure out dreadnaughts in that amount of time, I don't know who could. The largest ships in the flotilla are the habitation modules, and even those were pushing the boundaries of warp travel capabilities based on vessel size. And they would be less than half the size of a dreadnaught."

"But I thought the Casimir drives only affected open space," Schiff wondered.

"They do," clarified Nado, "but they do have an effect on what's inside the craft as well. That's why they're designed to protect the ship with a warp bubble."

"If a dreadnaught is all that difficult then, why would anybody want one?"

"There's only one reason to want a craft of that magnitude," replied Kel.

Captain Nado jumped in. "Most spacecraft weaponry is designed for ship-to-ship battles, but something that large could potentially house enough generators to power up an orbital laser."

"Oh, no," cried Mother Anise, who had fallen silent in the recent exchange. "Not an orbital laser. Tell me I didn't help create one of those."

"What does an orbital laser do?" Schiff asked nervously.

"Again, theoretically, an orbital laser would be fired from a spacecraft in flight," answered Kel. "It would have enough firepower to break through the upper atmosphere of a planet to strike the surface below. The gases in the atmosphere would transform the laser into a beam of super-heated plasma, capable of destroying entire cities in a single blast."

"It gets worse," Anise murmured. "If a laser like that were used multiple times on the same planet, it could rip holes in the atmospheric layers, or create a ripple effect, either one causing the destruction of the entire globe."

Standing and staring out the window, Captain Nado solemnly said, "With a ship like that, Lord Hex could have the power to glass an entire planet."

"That's what we're up against?!" shouted Schiff, leaping from her seat. Starting to hyperventilate, she promptly fainted.

Chapter 13

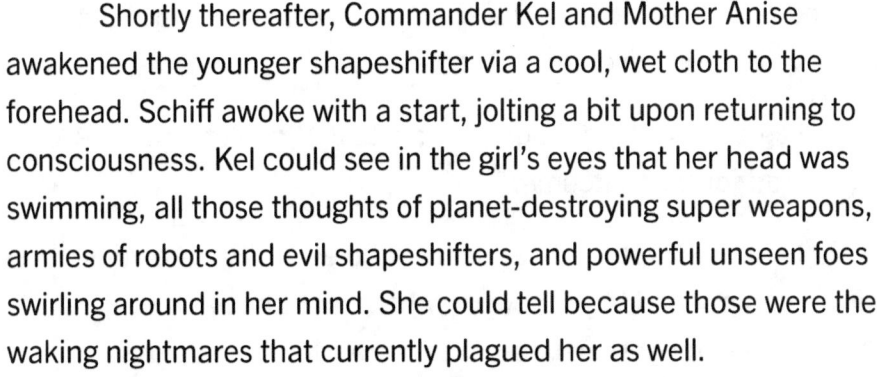

Shortly thereafter, Commander Kel and Mother Anise awakened the younger shapeshifter via a cool, wet cloth to the forehead. Schiff awoke with a start, jolting a bit upon returning to consciousness. Kel could see in the girl's eyes that her head was swimming, all those thoughts of planet-destroying super weapons, armies of robots and evil shapeshifters, and powerful unseen foes swirling around in her mind. She could tell because those were the waking nightmares that currently plagued her as well.

A gentle rushing from the waterfall just to the rear of the hut became one of the only audible noises within the walls of the structure, as the conversation had come to an abrupt halt. Birdsong and rustling leaves from the forest accompanied the cascade in perfect harmony. The whole atmosphere felt compelling and inviting, in stark contrast to the rampaging maelstrom inside Kel's brain.

The captain, on the other hand, betrayed no sign that he was experiencing the same, instead staring intently out the window, by all appearances utterly detached. *An unusual state for him*, thought

Kel. *He's typically antsy and excited about things like this.* She approached him. "Hey, Captain?"

He jumped a bit at her salutation, performing a rote about face. "Yes, Commander Kel?"

"A bit for your thoughts?" returned the commander.

After a moment to think, Captain Nado replied, "Ever since we met that Gonian man and picked up the kids, we've been leaping from one crummy scenario to another. Then we accidentally wind up in this place and gain some intel on our enemy, only to then discover that he is well out of our league." He paused. "But I want to help Mara and Jym. I want to find their parents, reunite them with family. They deserve that...everyone deserves that."

"I agree," Kel said. "But sometimes that can't be done. Are we prepared for that outcome?"

"I am." Nado looked her dead in the eyes. "But are you? After what happened to your own mother and father, and your siblings, I wouldn't dare ask you of all people to continue this crusade, especially now that we know more about Lord Hex and his capabilities."

A deep sigh escaped the commander, her shoulders drooping from the burden of those heavy memories. She shook them off. "You know I'm with you to the end, Captain."

"I was hoping you'd say that," Nado admitted. A broad smile spread across his face like a sunrise. "Help me get Rox and the kids moved to the village. It's time to get recuperation and then...we take the fight straight to Lord Hex's doorstep!"

It didn't take more than a couple of hours to transport the children, along with the apparatuses to which they were connected, to the large hut. Mother Anise and Schiff primed the homey hutch to make it as comfortable and accommodating as possible. Two separate straw beds piled with homemade quilts made cozy nests for Mara and Jym to rest upon, while the rest of the room was cleared to make way for the plethora of medical supplies that Dr. Rox brought with them.

Each was hooked up to intravenous tubing, one providing a saline solution for hydration and electrolyte balance, another delivering a more viscous liquid compound of proteins, carbohydrates, fats, vitamins, minerals, essential amino acids, and essential fatty acids for sustenance. Additionally, Rox had them covered in sensors to monitor their oxygen levels, heart rates, and blood pressure.

The prince and princess appeared peaceful in their current state, though all were aware of the dangerous nature of their conditions. It could be only a short matter of time before they reawakened, or it could be more long term. Or worse, it could be never. Rox busied himself with the task of seeing to the kids, avoiding eye contact with the rest of the crew. Noticing this, Kel sensed that he was still punishing himself in his mind. She decided to try and lift his spirit.

"For what it's worth," she began, slowly sidling to the doctor's workspace, "I think you're doing a great job taking care of the kids."

"I appreciate the sentiment," responded Rox, "but they wouldn't be in this mess if it hadn't been for my indecisiveness in the battle. I should have communicated our position to the bridge."

"You're not a combatant," Kel offered. "You don't have the same kind of training that Nado and I went through."

"Which is why I should have stuck to what I knew was right. I should have kept the kids belted into the galley chairs where it was safe."

"If they hadn't helped when they did, we'd be Gnarf fodder right now! There's no way I'd have gotten that cloaking device installed without the artificial gravity engaged."

Dr. Rox vehemently disagreed. "Who's to say that their involvement isn't what led to the complete failure of the machine itself? Perhaps the manipulation element would have stayed in its failing state rather a failed state! Then we never would've reached the catastrophic levels of energy buildup that occurred."

"If they hadn't been there to help, and you hadn't been there to watch them, I think the element would have failed anyway," fussed Kel, growing perturbed with Rox's stubbornness. "And you being at the center of the event allowed us to know what had happened afterward. How would we have figured any of it out if you hadn't witnessed it?"

"A witness is only as good as their credibility," Rox groused. "And I think I've proven that I'm not as reliable as we'd all thought. Including myself."

"Oh my gosh!" blurted Kel, her anger getting the better of her. "Stop with the pity party!"

Rox whirled at that. "Pity party? Pity party?! I have the weight of the lives of the entire crew resting in my hands! I am tasked with your health, well-being, and safety, and I failed in every aspect."

Several moments of silence ensued. Eventually, the commander calmly asked, "We're all alive, aren't we?"

"Yes," replied Rox. "But that was not my doing."

Unsure what else to say or do and feeling the heat of irritation burning hotter with every passing word from the doctor, Commander Kel abandoned her effort. It was all too evident that he was going to keep living in his self-loathing until it had run its course. Fine, if he wanted to sulk and pout, that was not her problem. *Let him deal with it himself if that's what he wants!* Though the moment that thought crossed her mind, she immediately regretted it. They were friends, had been for a long time.

Ambling through the village, the bustling of the shapeshifters becoming blurred in the background, Kel ruminated about their time at GCCA. The Galactic Community Collegiate Academy had been a prestigious school, only available to the highest-ranking societal members within the GC. There they trained the future elite, the councilmen and women, the nobility, the diplomats, and politicians. Only the Aronites and Humans were eligible to enroll, and even then, many of those races were barred based on social background.

But in the two years leading up to her high school graduation, the new council voted to open the floodgates of the collegiate academy to allow anyone to attend. It was there she met Nado and Rox. The three became fast friends over a classic schoolyard bullying incident, wherein Nado was getting pushed around by some of the Aronite and Human students. Thinking herself alone, Kel stood up to the juvenile jeering, telling those immature imbeciles right where they could shove their insolence! They had turned on her, but almost out of nowhere Rox stepped in and backed her up. A trip to the local café turned into a long conversation in which they made plans to stick together through their schooling, and after graduation make plans to start an enterprise with one another.

Since then, they had been inseparable. Nothing could or would ever tear the trustworthy trio apart. Oh, they fought and bickered, their quarrels sometimes lasting for days. But families do that, and though they weren't related, Kel knew in her soul that something deeper than blood ran between them, loyalty, integrity, faithfulness, and hope. *It binds us tighter than the duct tape and bubblegum that hold the Explorer together.* The commander chuckled aloud at that musing.

Graduation from the collegiate academy had led to the foundation of their ferrying business, but first they needed a ship. Nado's dream was to captain an Explorer model, but they had all been decommissioned by that point. Closure of the Explorer Initiative program immediately followed the opening of the academy. Though never proven, it was still rumored that the reason behind this closure was related to the desegregation of the school.

Whether by luck or happenstance, Kel couldn't be sure which, they managed to search the one junkyard that still had one Explorer model ship left, registry number 2000. Using every bit they had left in their savings, the trio bribed the junkman at the site to allow them to purchase the vessel. His workers had just put the Explorer into the dissemination chamber when the paperwork was signed. The Explorer 2000 had escaped destruction, and the three owners now had their ship.

Years had passed before they had been able to scrounge up enough coinage to get the ferrying off the ground, a business that Nado always saw as a means to an end. His ultimate goal was to reach the stars, explore the universe, find new galaxies and uncharted worlds. Kel and Rox, both having little to return to on the flotilla, conformed their own ambitions to Nado's, all of them hoping to one day leave the Octagon system.

For Kel, she had been perfectly happy to let Nado dream away while she worked on the ship, piloting ferry charters to and from the various Octo moons. The money was the primary reason she performed the trivial tasks, gradually growing more and more despondent when it came to hopes and aspirations. The bits took the place of the dream, simple monetary gain being the only aim for a time.

Then that Gonian man showed up with those kids. Those kids who reminded her so much of…no. She couldn't think about that right now. Kel couldn't think of that until she was confident that Mara and Jym would pull through. Then there was the matter of finding their parents, reuniting them all. Only then could she feel those old emotions again.

Still fretting over the perilous predicament that the young monarchs were in, Dr. Rox flitted from one to the other, constantly checking on one monitor or another. Mother Anise read the consternation on his exhausted expression and stated, "You should rest as well. You're their caregiver, you'll need it."

"What I need is some way to scan for cerebral edemas," Rox snipped. "Or intracerebral hemorrhages, or aneurysms, or any other form of brain trauma that they might have undergone!"

Anise fiddled with her glasses. "I might have a way we could do that."

"Do you have that level of tech here?"

"Unfortunately, there was nothing regarding healthcare technology in what I stole from Lord Hex," Anise lamented. "But here on the island there are medicinal herbs that grow throughout the forest."

"I don't need to treat surface wounds, though," mentioned Rox.

"These aren't for that," Anise corrected him. "When mixed into the proper poultice, their fumes can be inhaled. Exhalation of this poultice's fumes will produce colored gases that indicate the status of a person's brain, and whether there is trauma present!"

Dr. Rox, true to his normal fashion, rubbed at his jawline. "I studied a little of homeopathic remedies, but I've never heard of anything like that."

"They are native to this planet," explained the shapeshifter. "Possibly only native to this island. I've used them to treat our hunters when they suffered head injuries."

"Will that even work on Vampyrials? I've done my best to treat them as best I know how, but they've been considered a dead race for over a century. The academy's school of medicine didn't train much on treating Vampyrials."

"Oh, I'm sure it will – ," Anise began, then stopped herself. "Wait, did you say, Vampyrials? As in Prime Executor Mantis type of Vampyrials?"

"Yes," Rox nervously answered. "But they're just kids. They don't want to hurt anyone. Don't tell me you're after them too."

Mother Anise shuddered. "Of course not. We seek only peace here. I just remembered something else about Lord Hex's labs..."

"What is it?"

"I'll explain while we gather the herbs. Come, we must move quickly." On her way out the door, Anise grabbed Schiff and Nado to assist, talking quickly as they traversed the island. "I recall Lord Hex speaking about Vampyrials. He was looking for some, and thought he had a way to track them down. I never gave it much thought, I mean, as you said yourself doctor, the Vampyrials were all exterminated a century ago.

"But something about Hex's speech sounded as though he was certain that there were more Vampyrials alive somewhere, and he was positive that the archives on Hexagon II held the answers he needed to track them down!"

"All the more reason for us to go to the Hex worlds," declared Captain Nado. "If those archives can tell where to find Vampyrials, we have to beat him to it!"

"That's assuming he hasn't already found it," countered Rox. "If he has, that would explain how he knows about the kids. It could also explain why their mom and dad are missing."

Nado addressed Anise. "How long ago did you overhear this?"

"Right before I ran away," she replied. "It's been several standard GC years."

"Blast!" exclaimed Nado, his excitement growing by the second. "So he could have accessed the archives by now."

"Maybe, but his indication was that he was a long way from being able to accomplish that, and he never spoke of knowing the whereabouts of any Vampyrials as far as I know."

"Then maybe we stand a chance!" cheered Schiff. "Maybe he hasn't found the archives, and he knew about the kids another way. They were connected with someone in the community council, right?"

"You're right," the captain agreed. "The Gonian man carried with him the badge of a high-ranking council member. Lord Hex is their representative, he could've heard about the kids through the council!"

"Seems like we'd be expecting a miracle if that's the case," interjected Rox. "We know Hex has unfettered access to the Hexagon worlds, and the capability to guard those secrets from everyone else. Plus, he's had time on his side to prepare and equip himself for all of this."

"But it's possible!" Schiff gleefully argued.

"Perhaps, but not plausible."

"But it's possible!" Schiff's joyful attitude increased with every word.

"I get that, but – " Rox noted the generous grin on Schiff's face. "Alright," he relented, "it is entirely possible that we could beat Lord Hex at his own game."

"Yay!"

Mother Anise quieted them. "Ssh. We're here. The herbs are in the next clearing."

Everyone quieted and calmed as they scaled a small butte to reach the plateau that Anise had indicated. Beyond the tree line the forest opened into another clearing, smaller than the village clearing by far, but sizable enough. Here the sun shone down like heavenly beams, highlighting the glittery haze that hung in the air.

A tiny pond commanded one end of the clearing where it butted up against the cliff wall of a much taller, rockier mountain above. The pond was filled by a spring that trickled from the mountain's side, feeding a winding stream weaving its way through the clearing and emptying into a larger body of water below.

All around them grew the herbs, the source of the particulates that amalgamated into the glistening mist. Anise directed them in collecting only exactly what they needed, no more, no less. Upon completing their task, they headed back down to the village.

Agitated and growling incessantly, General Hämm paced furiously across the lavishly carpeted chambers aboard Boxie the Beautiful's sky-beast. "This will take too long!" he fumed. "Why must we wait for the Explorer beast to come to us?"

"Because you will only scare them further away," retorted Flogg, lounging lazily in a large armchair.

"Cease your arguing!" spat Boxie. "Such behavior will only lead to more trouble. If we are to succeed, we Gnarfs must band together."

"Banding together would be easier if it weren't for the fact that I am forced to work with a liar and a traitor," Hämm complained.

One of the Gnarf Boxies entered the chamber. "Excuse me, Boxie the Beautiful, but you have a hail on the radio. It was relayed here by the dragnet."

"What is the message?" she drawled.

"It is for your ears only, milady," the Gnarf Boxie replied.

Ungracefully heaving herself from the pallet of thick blankets and throw pillows that she had idly sprawled upon, Boxie flipped and flopped to her feet, her gross girth bouncing and jiggling all the time. She excised herself from her unpleasant company and followed her subordinate to the private radio room. The Gnarf Boxie regressed, leaving the lady ambassador alone with the controls. She played the recorded message.

"Hello, Ambassador Boxie the Beautiful," a lilting voice exuded from the speaker. "This is Vin Trell, reaching out for a very specific purpose. I know in our last meeting, we concluded rather abruptly, and I was unable to confer with my father before sending you on your way. I have now had that conference via similar long distance radio communication, and he confirmed a desire to have the captain and shapeshifter placed into my custody at Vortex.

"If you have instructions to the contrary, my father said to inform you that you will be handsomely repaid for the two individuals, and any difficulties that you encounter with your own superiors he will gladly deal with. He is a man of considerable wealth and influence, and we can be quite valuable allies. The captain's audacity, and that of his shapeshifter friend, needs to be reprimanded, so a clear message can be heard by anyone who dares oppose the Trell family, those who do so are bound to be punished.

"He is on route to Vortex, expected to arrive in two standard weeks. So, once you trap those scum, be sure to send them along to us. Keep the rest, but the captain and shapeshifter are mine!"

The message terminated after that last ultimatum. Boxie thought long and hard about that additional payment. Could she get away with that? Certain "complications" could arise making it impossible to deal with the captain and the 'shifter. Such issues could potentially lead to their supposed deaths, allowing her to ship them off to Vin without any backlash.

But was it worth upsetting Hämm and Flogg? What about Bë-Konn? Or the Hex-man? Carefully considering and weighing all the pros and cons, Boxie the Beautiful picked up the transmitter to record her own private message back to Vin Trell. Soft and sinister, she practically whispered into the radio.

"Consider it done."

Gathered around the makeshift operating room, the crew of the Explorer 2000 stood on edge. Nado and Kel observed from the main doorway, while Schiff took up residence on the far wall near the window that overlooked the waterfall. Red stood at attention just outside, while Dr. Rox and Mother Anise administered the herbal concoction to Mara and Jym.

The inhalation process took a few minutes to get just right, trying to ensure that the mixture went up their nostrils correctly. They also had to ensure that enough of the poultice got inhaled in the first place. After several minutes of attempts, Rox managed to get Jym to breathe the herbal remedy just right. Hearts pounded in every chest as the mixture swirled inside his lungs. The exhalation finally came, the resulting haze of the poultice coming out as a combination of amethyst and sapphire coloration. Rox looked to Anise for advice.

"He's clean," she reported. "No cerebral trauma."

A sigh of relief echoed around the room but was short-lived as now it was Mara's turn. Anise performed the same motions as Rox, though hers were definitely more refined. Kel could tell she'd done this several times before. Mara's exhale produced a steady stream of amethyst and sapphire as well!

"They're alright," concluded Nado. "They're going to be alright."

"We just need to wait for them to wake up, I guess," Dr. Rox sighed.

"I didn't want to say anything before," inserted Mother Anise, "but there is another remedy I use these herbs for, a secondary poultice."

"What does it do?" Schiff queried.

"As stated, it is secondary to the first one. If they exhibit no signs of trauma, we can use the next poultice to wake them up. I was afraid of getting anyone's hopes up prior to the utilization of the first mixture."

"They're okay for the second poultice though, right?" Captain Nado questioned.

"Oh, yes," answered Anise. "With the results of the first poultice clean and clear, we can administer the second one and get the kids back on their feet."

"Okay," said Rox. "Let's get that second poultice made."

"Already done." Mother Anise revealed the concoction, pulling it from her coat. "I whipped it up concurrently with the first poultice. I've done this a few times, it has become second nature to me."

Impatiently, Captain Nado insisted, "Then why are we standing around? Come on, we've got kids to save!"

"Alright," laughed Mother Anise. "Dr. Rox, can you assist me?"

Without a word, the doctor resumed his duties alongside Anise. Together they gently wafted the powders of the poultice under the nose of Princess Mara. Her coma-like sleep gradually began to fade, as her eyes fluttered open, her lips parted, and she started trying to form words.

"Where are we?" the young girl weakly asked.

"Somewhere safe," Rox assured her. "Somewhere safe."

"Where is Jym?"

"He's here. We're taking care of him next."

Now it was Prince Jym's turn. In the same manner as before, the mixture was waved under his deeply breathing nostrils. He coughed and sputtered a bit before coming to, his breathing accelerating at first, but then coming back under control with a long sigh. He too looked up with a dreary expression, words playing across his lips and tongue.

"What was that?" Rox leaned closer. "Say it again."

Grabbing hold of the doctor's jacket and pulling himself closer, Jym whispered only two words, "I'm hungry."

The whole room chuckled in relief.

Chapter 14

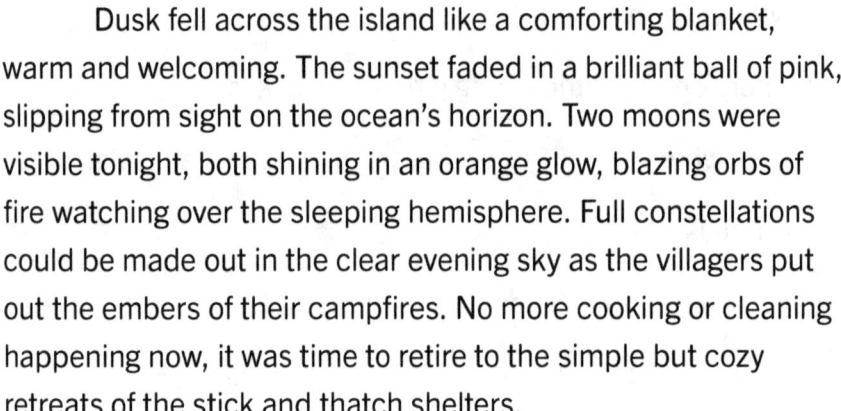

Dusk fell across the island like a comforting blanket, warm and welcoming. The sunset faded in a brilliant ball of pink, slipping from sight on the ocean's horizon. Two moons were visible tonight, both shining in an orange glow, blazing orbs of fire watching over the sleeping hemisphere. Full constellations could be made out in the clear evening sky as the villagers put out the embers of their campfires. No more cooking or cleaning happening now, it was time to retire to the simple but cozy retreats of the stick and thatch shelters.

Tables were lit by lanterns filled to the brim with tiny luminous insectoids, bright enough to light an entire room. Everything was set for the evening meal, which consisted of an assortment of flavorful fruits, salty seafood meats, and all natural juices diluted slightly with clean water from the falls. Though the people of the island led modest and humble lives, the fresh food set before the crew seemed to be an extravagant gourmet buffet. After several standard cycles of dehydrated rations, this bountiful banquet left nothing to be desired. They filled their bellies, each secretly hoping that they wouldn't need to eat again for a week.

Jym ravenously devoured everything in sight. Dr. Rox reproached him. "Jym, slow down. I know you need to refill after your ordeal, but you must take it easy! I highly recommend that you and Mara both avoid using your abilities for a while, let your bodies recuperate."

"Okay, okay," the prince acquiesced.

Meanwhile, Mara only nibbled at her spread, her melancholy mood having obviously returned. Taking note of her reticence, Commander Kel gave the princess a gentle nudge. "Hey, what's wrong?"

Mara glanced up from chasing a chunk of fruit around her plate with a spoon. "Huh?"

"I asked what's wrong," reiterated Kel, following with a lighthearted jest. "You look like someone just told you that you were ugly and dressed funny."

"Just sad," Mara replied simply, ignoring Kel's awful attempt at humor.

Kel sighed, "Kiddo, if you won't tell us what's going on, how can anyone help?"

"I'm not sure anyone can help at this point," Mara bemoaned. "It's been, I don't know how many cycles, and we're still no closer to finding out anything about our mom and dad." Tears streaked down her cheeks. "I miss them."

"I know." Kel's heart broke again for the young monarchs. "I understand what it's like to miss family, believe me."

"What happened to them?" asked Jym.

The commander pursed her lips tightly. "Let's just say I lost them and leave it at that. It's not a subject I care to dwell on right now."

"Sorry," Jym apologized genuinely.

"It's alright," Kel responded with a soothing smile. "It's just a sensitive matter. Some wounds always hurt, no matter how much time has passed."

"What about the rest of you?" Mara voiced. "Tell us about your families. We know so little about you guys. I want to hear your stories."

The crew all exchanged looks of hesitation and confusion. After an awkward delay, Dr. Rox at last shrugged and broke the silence. "I guess I'll go first, after all there isn't much to tell anyway. I grew up on the flotilla, like most Humans, as an only child, but unlike many, my parents were…well, I suppose you could refer to them as Human nobility. Our family doesn't hold any feudal titles per se, but we were well off and enjoyed a lot of societal influence.

"My father had inherited his occupation from his father, a strange ancestral lineage having been applied to the position. He acted as the director and overseer of the largest stasis pod chamber in the entire flotilla, a job he wanted his son to take over one day as well. My mother and father planned out my whole life, even going so far as to tell me that I would only be allowed to attend the GCCA if I went into the medical wing of the school to study.

"Not desirous to be their surrogate, I left the flotilla and did attend the collegiate academy, even studying medicine. But when graduation day came, I opted not to return to the flotilla and the life my parents wanted for me. I chose my own path, joining forces with my two best friends, Nado and Kel. I decided I would be their ship's physician. And I haven't regretted that decision for a single moment." Rox paused and gave a second thought to that last phrase, a burdensome contemplation suddenly weighing upon his shoulders. "Well, I mostly have no regrets. Only one recently." The doctor quickly fell silent after that.

"Okay, my turn!" chirped Schiff. "I am not an only child, but 'shifter lives are so random and we have no home-world to grow up on, so we tend not to stay at home very long. We travel and see the universe, hoping to one day find our origins. I fell in with a couple of street gangs on Octo V, two bitter rivals actually. It was the Zorgs of the Gonians, and the Gorgs of the Baldins. Don't ask why the names rhyme, that story is childish and dumb.

"Anyway, I would regularly shift between Gonian form and Baldin form, playing both sides of the gangs, learning everything I could from both. Then both gangs asked me to kill the alternate version of myself, so I faked my death!" She halted, puzzled by the wording. "Deaths? Should that be plural? Oh well, moving on!

"I saw that there was a talent agency hiring for 'shifter entertainers, so I applied and got the job. And that's pretty much it." Schiff looked a bit forlorn. "Dang it, that was fast. I thought there'd be more to my story than that."

Heads progressively pivoted in Captain Nado's direction, the kids' ears anticipating whatever terrific tale awaited. They'd heard his stories of the universe told with such drama and flair throughout the journey, now they waited with bated breath to hear the saga of his own personal plot. Rather than his typical eager excitement, however, the captain's intense gaze appeared as though it would burn a hole through the long wooden table.

"When I was a boy," he began, "my older brother Graylon and I dreamt of nothing more than attending the Galactic Community Collegiate Academy when we came of age. We would graduate with honors, belauded by our peers as the pinnacle of scholastic students. Then we would enlist in the Explorer Initiative program, the inner circle for the most elite of intrepid outer space pioneers.

"But the day we went to enroll in the GCCA, only recently made available to the general populace, the Explorer Initiative program was disbanded. The Explorer model ships were to be decommissioned and slated for destruction. I strove to stay optimistic and complete my studies despite the council's decisions, but Graylon was infuriated. He vowed that he would speak to the council himself, change their minds, by force if necessary. I tried to convince him otherwise, but he refused to listen, stating that the universe could still be what we hoped for, that he would do anything and everything to make it so."

"What happened to Graylon?" Jym queried.

"I tried to keep in touch with him," continued the captain, "writing to his apartment over the years, but I never heard back. I found out after graduation that the address I had for him had been empty for a long time. My fearful suspicion was that Graylon had actually gone before the council and angered them enough that he'd been thrown into prison or something. I searched and searched, but I found no trace of him, not even on any prison records.

"Our father was a good man, but he had been sick for a very long time, mom struggling to keep up with expenses. He passed away while I attempted to locate my brother. I tried to send money to mom via courier as often as we had it to spare, hoping she would respond and tell me that Graylon had come home to take care of her. She was happy for me and my new ventures with Kel and Rox but missed her sons…and her husband.

"I still hope that one day I'll find out where Graylon went and what he's doing now. But until then my only knowledge of him is that he has thus far been unsuccessful in his goals. The Explorer Initiative remains on lockdown, so he hasn't accomplished the one thing he set out to do."

"Maybe when all this is over, we can all go see your mom," offered Princess Mara.

That old, broad smile returned and Nado's dark countenance brightened. "I believe she'd like that very much. And so would I."

"There's still one thing that has bothered me though," inserted Schiff. "I know Kel asked 'Uncle', or whatever his name was, the Gonian guy, but we've never gotten a straight answer about this from either you, Prince Jym, or you, Princess Mara."

"About what?" Jym questioned.

Schiff shook her hands at the ceiling. "Where did you guys get your titles? What are you a prince and princess of?!" she practically screamed in exasperation.

"Oh, that," dismissed Mara. "It was what we were listed as on the manifest of the derelict vessel that carried our stasis pods. The one the salvagers pulled us from. That's all we know."

Schiff stood utterly perplexed. "I thought there'd be more to that story too…"

Everyone relaxed as they laughed earnestly. The night sky waxed as they fellowshipped further, the warm evening breezes giving way to colder ocean winds. Hatches were battened, clutter cleared away, and comfy quilts laid out for the rest cycle.

While the kids, Schiff, and Dr. Rox slept peacefully, the captain and commander kept a steady vigil, knowing that soon they too would turn in. Even Red had shut down temporarily for a recharge. Nado's tall frame consumed the entryway, and Commander Kel could see that he held some object in his upper right hand. His upper left arm supported the right, keeping it positioned near his mouth.

Upon closer examination, Kel spied an ornately curved bell pipe in the captain's hand. "Are you taking up smoking, Captain?"

"Thinking about it," he replied. "What do you think? Does it make me look distinguished?"

"Uh, no."

"Blast." He chucked the pipe aside. "I thought perhaps it would give me a more seasoned appearance as a spacer."

She chuckled, "You want to know what I think? I think you don't need it. You already look the part as far as I'm concerned."

"Well, I appreciate the sentiment – " A noise of shuffling through sand caused him to hold his tongue. "Did you hear that?" the captain whispered.

"Sure did," answered Kel. "Let's check it out."

Scanning the area, both spotted a shadowy figure slipping through the darkened village, making its way toward the mountain's base. They quietly trailed the being, careful not to be caught themselves. Whoever they were following didn't seem to be concerned with hiding their presence, so the task of tailing them ended up being fairly simple.

Before long, they came to a crevice in the side of the mountain, a craggy cave that would barely fit a thin child turned sideways. The person squeezed inside, Kel and Nado observing at a distance. After waiting long enough to be sure they wouldn't be ambushed, the officers crept to the forgotten fissure and slipped between the cracks.

Captain Nado had a hard time navigating through the winding channels, Kel not faring much better. Their quarry must have been a smaller individual to slide so smoothly through this skinny slit. Eventually, the tight tunnels opened into a cavernous chamber, stalagmites and stalactites aplenty around the edges. A reflective pool dominated the northern portion, casting beams of moonlight, that shone in from a large gap in the rocks, throughout the chamber. The center of the cave, however, had been cleared to make way for an enormous structure of metal framing and wiring, tapering to a point at the top.

"That looks like…," Kel began.

"A radio transmitter," finished Nado.

"That's because it is." A third voice chimed in. They both started and jumped, whirling to the left to see Mother Anise highlighted in the dark cavern by the natural luminosity from the reflective waters.

"What is going on here?" Kel demanded.

"Nothing," assured Anise. "I swear to you, there is no need for suspicion. This is a pet project I've been working on. I had largely ceased my work, but seeing you all here with H-8-RED has convinced me now more than ever, I must finish this."

"What exactly is it?" Nado asked.

Approaching the tower, Anise explained, "I was working on a planetary cloaking mechanism, a radio tower powerful enough to transmit a signal whose wavelength covered the globe. It can be done here, as the mineral ore veins that run in this mountain range act as natural conductors for such an endeavor."

"You have a cloaking device that strong?" interjected a very excited Captain Nado.

"Not yet," Anise answered. "I have a lot of tech here that I stole, but not the one piece I need. They were hard to come by, I only knew of a couple in existence. I lack the necessary component to complete the construction, the actual radio frequency disruptor that functions as the cloaking device. I thought I could fabricate one myself, but that manufacturing capability has eluded me..." Anise trailed off for a moment. "I must protect my children. They don't know the outside universe, and I dare not risk being found by Lord Hex. If the H-8s' navigational programming still has this planet recorded, his retribution will be swift and merciless."

Parts and pieces clanked and echoed as Mother Anise commenced sorting through her vast variety of technical appliances. A knowing expression passed between the captain and commander, the former looking quite sympathetic, the latter with a much more hardened countenance. He nodded, she shook her head forcefully. He offered a smile, she returned with a scowl.

"It's the right thing to do," Nado said softly.

"But we need it," countered Kel. "Besides, we just got the thing and had to fight hard for it!"

"We have the means to defend ourselves," argued the captain. "They do not. Furthermore, I submit that…as crazy as this may sound…perhaps we gained the device for such a time as this."

Commander Kel still needed some convincing. "How will we get past Lord Hex and get to the Hexagon then?"

"We'll figure something out, I'm sure of it!"

"I wish I shared your optimism, Captain."

"It is still the best weapon in our arsenal," Nado offered.

Kel pondered for a minute, about to answer when another voice joined their hushed discussion. "Well, I suppose if we gave her the cloaking device, we could just stay here indefinitely, right?"

"Geez!" the commander exclaimed, jolting from fright yet again. Schiff stood next to them. Kel gave the shapeshifter a dirty glance. "What are you doing here?"

"You guys were talking, and it woke me up," Schiff replied. "I saw you chase after somebody and followed. I shifted into various forms so you wouldn't spot me. But what about my question? We give the device and just stay here, cloaked, on the planet? Doable, right?"

"Not if Hex has a way to track the kids in the Hex II archives," Captain Nado corrected.

"Oh, nuts, I forgot about that."

"If the kids stay here, even under the cloaking device, we run the risk that Lord Hex could still eventually find them," Kel laid out. "And then we put the entire village and Mother Anise at risk too."

"It's clearly a war room topic," declared Nado. "Let's get some sleep and the whole crew can triage in the morning."

He and Kel hurriedly egressed from the chamber, headed off for a rest cycle preceding what would be a very busy day. Schiff lingered, watching Mother Anise scurry about her work. The elder shapeshifter noticed the younger and paused her work to approach.

"Schiff?" Anise said, breathing deeply to build up courage. "You know, you could stay here with us, live among your own kind, on a world we could finally call our own. You would be more than welcome, and I would certainly appreciate having a friend to carry on conversations with."

Schiff, at once feeling conflicted and confused, could only answer in simplistic terms. "I'll have to think about that."

"Sleep on it then, and let me know in the morning."

Morning came as the sun crested over the mountains, the nighttime dispelled as though a curtain were lifted. Sunlight washed the village so instantaneously that it felt like the shadows were rapidly retreating from a fight. The crew of the Explorer 2000 arose and enjoyed a hearty breakfast, followed by long baths in the hot springs that were located about a two hour hike up the mountainside. Mother Anise was all too pleased to show them the way, indulging herself as well.

In the hours that followed, Nado and Schiff sifted through the myriad of technological apparatuses that Anise had liberated from Lord Hex's labs, retrieving anything they felt might be of use to repair the ship. Meanwhile, Kel and Red tag-teamed the reconstruction and repair of the island sentinels, getting the robotic sentries fixed and reprogrammed. Taking the kids, Dr. Rox began the tedious task of removing the medical machinery from the large hut and transporting it back to the Explorer.

It was a busy morning, but once they were all gathered on the ship, Nado called the war room meeting to order. "Last night, Commander Kel and I discovered that Mother Anise has a dire need. The 'shifters will be in grave danger unless two things happen. Firstly, we need to take the kids away from here. If Lord Hex has a way to track Vampyrials, then it'll only be a matter of time before he finds them here. Secondly, they need a way to cloak the entire planet. I know that sounds unfeasible, but with the ore veins that run through the mountains, they act as a natural enhancement to the radio waves needed for the cloaking to work.

"That brings me to my point. She has most of the tech necessary to pull off this feat, however, she lacks a crucial component, the cloaking device itself. She has a transmitter for the opposing frequency, but nothing to generate that frequency. We do have that technology right here on the Explorer. Though I am captain, I am not the only one affected by this decision, so I put it to my faithful crew, do we want to leave Anise and the 'shifters with our cloaking device for their safety or keep it ourselves? I put it to a vote. All in favor of gifting the cloaking device to Anise, raise your hand."

Captain Nado expected some resistance and debate from both Kel and Rox, but surprisingly neither of them opposed. Every hand at the table was raised in support of the captain's vote. It was unanimous. The emotional manifestation on the faces of the doctor and commander was indeed one of resignation, but not defeated or deflated. Nado had known them long enough that he could read the "you were right, and we were not" faces that they made.

Beaming from ear to ear, Captain Nado proclaimed, "Then it is agreed. Commander Kel, can you remove the cloaking device?"

"I'm on it, Captain," the commander said, heading off to grab her tools.

"We have a lot of work to do yet, crew," Nado ordered. "There are repairs to be made, supplies to inventory, a water reservoir to fill, engines to be maintained, and a gift to be offered to our kind hosts."

Setting themselves to the tasks at hand, the crew bustled from the ship to the village, village to ship, back and forth, porting provisions, securing supplies, and affecting the much-needed repairs. Once everyone had reached a good stopping point, Nado gathered them together once more at the settlement's center. Commander Kel carried a wrapped parcel, which she presented to Mother Anise.

"For your hospitality," commenced the captain, in his most epic, booming inflections, "we, the crew of the Explorer 2000, would like to offer this humble gift."

The parcel was handed over, Mother Anise twisting it around and around in her hands. "You didn't have to grant us anything." She cautiously unwrapped the petite package, revealing the cloaking device. "Oh, my," she gasped. "No, no, we can't accept this. You need this."

"You need it more," affirmed Kel.

"But where did you get it?"

"We won it by gambling," stated an oblivious Schiff.

Mother Anise seemed baffled. "Gambling?"

"It doesn't matter where it came from," Kel covered quickly. "All that matters is that it's yours now, and the 'shifters can be kept safe and undiscoverable."

"I don't know what to say," blubbered Anise, tears of joy welling in her eyes. "You've saved all of us." She spontaneously began bouncing with excitement. "Oh, wait, I do know what to do! Wait here!" Impulsively, Anise bolted from the sandy clearing, returning several minutes later with her own parcel. She placed it in Kel's hands. "Here, take this. It's experimental tech, a one-of-a-kind prototype. It is a warp drive decelerator. I can help you install it."

"I've never heard of that," confessed Kel. "What does it do?"

"The decelerator is meant to be utilized to slow the warp effect at the last moment to allow warping almost directly to a planet's atmosphere," Anise informed. "Like I said, it's a prototype, so it may be finicky."

"Something like that could be used to revolutionize space warfare," noted Nado. "Ships could virtually warp past radar defenses straight into an orbital attack position."

"Another piece of technology best kept out of Lord Hex's hands," mentioned Anise. "But I believe it will be put to good usage in your possession."

"With this, we could make Princess Mara's plan more of a reality," mused Kel. "She wouldn't have nearly as much strain to deal with when she stops the ship if we utilize the decelerator."

"I don't think the kids should be using their abilities at all for a long time," Dr. Rox interjected. "I worry about their health where that's concerned. We got very lucky on this last wild undertaking."

"I can do it," Mara quietly said.

"I know you can, sweetheart," assured the doctor. "I question whether or not you should."

"We can discuss that at a later time," Nado stopped them. "For now, I want to thank you, Mother Anise, for everything you've done for us. We will not forget the kindnesses of you and your people."

Captain Nado dismissed the crew, sending them back to their work. As Schiff started to go, Anise softly stilled her exit. "Schiff?"

The young shapeshifter halted. "Yes?"

"Have you thought any more about my offer? To stay here with your own people?"

"I have," answered Schiff. "And while I am grateful, I think I've found my people, my home."

Mother Anise nodded knowingly. "I understand. They're a fine family to choose. You've done better than many other shapeshifters. I hope we meet again someday."

"Probably," said Schiff, airily. "I mean, we do have a spacecraft and we do know where your planet is, and we know where your island is, so chances are we'll be back at some point."

Anise only laughed, taking Schiff's hands as a mother would a daughter, clasping them tightly and releasing them as she told the young girl, "Forge your path among the stars little 'shifter. Should you ever return, know that you will have a place here as well."

Two more standard cycles passed before the repairs were fully complete, new hardware installed, thrusters refueled, and the spacecraft ready for launch. At last, the Explorer 2000 was ready once more to take on the hazards of the universe. The shapeshifters bid a fond farewell to the crew, waving and watching as the bulkheads closed completely.

As soon as they were sure that all civilians were clear of the craft, the captain gave the command, "Commander Kel, ignite the lower thrusters."

It took a few minutes before Kel had a report. "We are at takeoff elevation, Captain."

"Red, take us away!" Captain Nado elatedly exclaimed.

The rear thrusters blasted and boomed, sending the Explorer zooming into the skies. Soaring past the clouds and upper atmospheric layers, the vessel shook and rattled, but never faltered. The vapors and mists dissipated, leaving nothing but the open expanse of space in the viewports ahead.

Chapter 15

Dull groanings of creaking metal filled the room as Zuugs stepped through the doorway into the auburn glow of Lord Hex's study. The malicious marquis faced away, sitting in his high-backed chair, but revealed himself gradually with an exaggerated spin. His lordship's features remained an eerie enigma, the hooded cape still draped across his firm and fit frame.

"Milord," stammered the Sorogan foreman. "The project is complete, as you requested. We have managed to fit it into the timeline specified."

"Congratulations, Zuugs," Hex rumbled in response. "You have preserved the lives of you and your labor force."

"Only somewhat," reported Zuugs. "Many were lost to starvation, dehydration, and sleep deprivation. But the contract is fulfilled."

"Yes, it is."

"We are done, milord. What remains of my union is packing to leave the site."

"Not yet," Lord Hex growled. "First there is the matter of a... test run."

"A test run, milord? That was not stipulated by our contract – "

"I am altering the contract." Fluidly, Hex rose from his chair. "You will see it through, or I will alter it further."

Zuugs quaked with fear as he attempted a debate. "But milord, we are not slaves, we are independent contractors. We upheld your demands, so we must be released from the work order."

"What kind of laborer does not wait to see if his project functions as intended?" jeered the marquis. "Are you sure you want to deal with the fallout of my raging wrath if this weaponized wonder fails to work properly? Then I would be forced to hunt you and your construction crew to the ends of the universe, my vengeful volatility burning hotter every cycle that I cannot locate you."

Envisioning the Marquis du Hex's formidable grasp once more at his throat, Zuugs obediently bowed his head, lowering his eyestalks in fearful reverence. "We will accompany the vessel to a suitable test site, where his lordship may conduct whatever analysis his heart desires."

"A wise decision," commended Hex. "Assemble your union in the main corridor. Assign them duties for the activation, piloting, and engineering of the ship. I will have the H-7 navigators set a heading for Hex IV, whereupon we shall test the weaponry. After a successful test, you and your laborers shall be discharged." Lord Hex finished with a wave of his hand, dismissing the scrawny Sorogan.

As soon as he was certain to be out of earshot, Zuugs grumbled to himself, "This contract keeps getting worse all the time..."

Now clear of Mother Anise's uncharted planet, the Explorer 2000 could access its newly repaired and fully functional warp drive. "Red, chart a course for Hexagon II," Captain Nado requested.

"This unit would comply," replied their copper plated pilot, "but first, protocol dictates that the captain must be informed of all incoming radio hails."

"Who would be hailing us out here?" wondered Kel. "There's no one else nearby, is there?"

"The broadcast is meant for the Explorer," Red answered. "However, it is not a direct hail. It is a general call, possibly a pre-recorded message."

"Patch it through," ordered the captain.

Red did as instructed, and the radio crackled with Boxie the Beautiful's screechy, scratchy speech. "Hello, crew of the Explorer beast. It is I, Ambassador Boxie the Beautiful of the sky kingdom Vortex. I am sending you this message to apologize for our encounter on Vortex and to inform you that I only attacked because I am an outcast of my people and wished to regain my place among them.

"Regardless, I have seen the error of my ways. I will never be allowed to rejoin the Gnarfs of Urkasak, and so I have reached out to ask you to assist me. I can give you information concerning the locations of all the Gnarf sky-beasts in Taldish Sector, as well as how to avoid them. I dare not share it over the radio waves in case they intercept this broadcast and simply deviate from their current courses. We must discuss it in person.

"As for my repayment for this assistance, I require only that you meet with me and take a letter I have written to the Galactic Community. I am asking for asylum and protection, as I will surely need it after I have betrayed the Gnarfs. My coordinates are encoded into the numerical sequence that follows."

Succeeding Boxie's voice, several taps could be heard, as if someone were playing the transmitter like a percussion instrument. Commander Kel recognized the sounds almost immediately. "That's a variation of morse code."

"Quick, capture those taps before they end!" Nado called.

"The tapping has been recorded, Captain," reported Red. "Analyzing and decoding. This unit now possesses the coordinates of Boxie's vessel. Uploading coordinates to the navigation systems now."

"Excellent work, Red," the captain stated. "Shall we set a course?"

"Whoa Captain," cautioned Kel. "This has 'trap' written all over it in big, bold, flashing neon lights! We'd be nuts to follow a missive like that."

"Don't be so certain, Commander Kel," Nado argued. "If a Gnarf is willing to go so far as to betray their own, and then seek sanctuary from the GC, that's an incredibly out-of-character thing for them to do. Sounds pretty genuine to me."

The commander addressed their robotic ally. "Red, what do your protocols dictate? Please inform the captain that this is suicide!"

"Anything to advise, Red?" asked Nado.

"This unit is not qualified to dissect the nuances of safety versus uncertainty in this particular situation," it responded coolly.

"Oh, now your tactical protocols don't want to chime in!" Kel fussed. "After all those times you so willingly gave it without being asked, now I ask for it and you won't give it! Hapless hunk of hardware!" The robot remained silent, further enraging the commander. "Well, don't you have any clever quips, or puns you'd like to fling at me? Anything?"

"This unit is not inclined to engage in a battle of wits…," Red paused, ocular sensors trained on Commander Kel, "with an unarmed opponent."

"That does it, I'm going to melt you down into slag!"

"Only if your fleshy blob brain can comprehend the process to do so."

Nado regained control of the swiftly escalating conversation. "Perhaps we'll ask the others, put it to a vote like last time?"

"Fine by me," Kel sulked, shooting fiery darts at Red with her eyes.

Utilizing the onboard intercom, Captain Nado called for a quick briefing in the "war room" again. Everyone assumed their usual seats and before long the scenario had been relayed to the remainder of the crew. For a while, no one spoke. They all sat in stunned silence, no one quite sure what to make of Boxie's offer.

At last, Dr. Rox piped up. "I'm with Kel on this one. Sounds too good to be true. It's got to be a trap."

"You agree with me?" the commander kidded. "The universe might be coming to an end after all."

"Hey, I agree with you on plenty of things!" retorted Rox.

"Not that often..."

"My opinion of the matter," Nado interrupted, "is that we have a rare and valuable opportunity. If Boxie is telling the truth, this could help us avoid entangling with any more of Lord Hex's Gnarf minions, allowing us freer passage to the Hexagon. If she is lying, there is still intel that we could gather on the status of her own forces."

"Seems like there's a bit of a rift between the Gnarf leadership," mentioned Schiff. "There was that general guy, plus the Flogg guy, and then there's Boxie. None of them seemed to be working with each other, they were all their own separate groups."

"And I think that still gives us an advantage," said Nado. "At the very worst, Boxie is playing us for fools, trying to create her own capture and gain notoriety. If that is the case, maybe we can use that for our own purposes like we did with Flogg and Hämm."

It was a good point that the captain made. Commander Kel thought long and hard about it. If Boxie was earnest in her plea, they had a unique chance to do the one thing they hadn't been able to do from the start of this whole mess, get ahead of their enigmatic enemy. But the price if they were wrong…

The table was still stirring with conversation. Now Nado had moved to asking the kids their thoughts on the situation. "Princess Mara, Prince Jym, what do you think?"

"Something feels wrong about it," Mara replied.

Almost at the same time, Jym stated, "I say go for it!"

This spawned an argument between the two, as the princess debated, "No, something is off. I can't explain it, but I can just sense the lies."

"We can't judge Boxie just because she tried to hurt us before," countered Jym. "We were given a second chance. It only makes sense that we should offer her one too."

Turning to Kel and Rox, the captain made another entreaty. "Come on, see? A second chance! Everyone needs a second chance. It worked with Schlaar and Shtrepp."

"That's got to be your weakest argument," Kel muttered.

Though she intended to say more, her next phrase never formulated as her thoughts were suddenly turned to syrup by the doctor's interjection, "Captain, you're right. I change my vote. I agree with you."

"Wait, what gives?" blurted the commander. "Just a few seconds ago you were on my side!"

"That settles it!" Nado exclaimed. "It's a vote of four to two. Majority says that we board Boxie's ship and see what it is she truly has to offer us."

"With a caveat," added the doctor. "We go armed to the teeth."

At least he suggested that, thought Kel, though she was still very peeved at his rapid and uncharacteristic turnaround.

"Agreed," Nado confirmed to Rox. "I never had any intention of going on board a Gnarf vessel without the proper arsenal to do so." He then addressed the room. "Alright crew, to your posts! Let's get ready to enter the lair of a former enemy."

As the meeting was dismissed, Kel sought out the doctor. He had already slipped back into the medical bay to secure his equipment and new collection of herbal remedies from Mother Anise. The brash commander marched straight to him and demanded, "What is going on with you? You are the most rational, cautious, safe-treading person I've ever met, and you decide to go with Nado's impetuous plan to convene with the very individual who chased us all over Vortex trying to capture and possibly kill us?"

Not meeting her cold stare, the doctor sighed, "I had to agree with him. I have to relieve the tension on this ship somehow."

Kel was confused. "Tension? What tension?"

"You've felt it," he replied. "The other night, when I shared the story of my upbringing, the captain never acknowledged me once. Even when I was telling of our collegiate experiences, not once did he even look at me. He's still angry with me."

"Did he tell you that?"

"No, I just…get the feeling."

"He said he forgave you, right?"

"Yes, but that was in the moment, and he was still pretty upset at that time. He never said he wasn't mad anymore."

"The only tension on the Explorer is your own," dismissed Kel. "Get your head screwed back on correctly. I need the old doctor back."

At that, she turned and exited the bay, leaving Dr. Rox alone with his "tension". There was too much at stake for him to be wallowing in self-pity and self-aggrandizement. Their captain was not the type to hold a long grudge, the doctor should know that by now. Captain Nado was much more the type to disremember and dopily space out. If he were going to maintain any frustration or anger with a crew member, especially an officer, the captain simply would've asked Rox to vacate the ship and remain behind.

Both she and the captain had made stupid mistakes in the past, and neither held it against the other. Why would he hold this one mistake against Rox? It was an imbecilic notion to think that Captain Nado of all people would stay that upset with someone he considered to be a close friend and ally. Did the doctor goof up in the middle of a rather tense battle? Sure. But that was well past them at this point. Time to move on.

Or was it? If Dr. Rox was picking up on something, it could be that she was unaware of the situation. Unlikely though, as Kel was typically the more perceptive of the trio of officers. There was a chance, however, that it was a "man thing" and she was ill-equipped to deal with that sort of matter. The callous commander wasn't usually one to involve herself in that sort of situation, but if a peacemaker was called for to mediate between Rox and Nado, she would obligatorily assist.

The hum of the warp drive distracted Kel from these critical cogitations, pulling her mind back to the present moment. Red and the captain waited on the bridge for their navigator, while Schiff and the kids were safely ensconced in the galley chairs. Dr. Rox had his own seating in med-bay, similar to that of the galley but hanging via retractable arm from the ceiling so it could be easily removed in the event of an extreme emergency.

As she bounded the short set of steps into the command center of the Explorer, Captain Nado gave the commander her orders. "Commander Kel, if you would be so kind, set our course for the coordinates provided by Boxie."

"Aye captain." Practically punching the controls on her station, Kel began inputting the necessary course headings into her navigational computers. She took that time to voice a question to her commanding officer. "Captain, are you angry with Dr. Rox?"

"Why would I be?" a puzzled Nado returned.

"You apparently told him you were angry with him," she reminded.

"I did?"

"A few cycles ago, when we first landed on Mother Anise's island…"

A series of perplexed expressions passed over the captain's face, followed at last by one of realization. "Oh, yes!" He shrugged. "I'm over that now."

"Have you told the doctor you're over it?" hinted Kel.

"No. But he knows I'm not mad anymore."

"You might want to talk to him."

"Are you serious?" queried Nado. He then jested, "You mean, you want us to talk about our feelings? Kel, I know you're a woman and all – "

"Don't you dare finish that thought!" she yelled back. "I swear I'll throw my boot at you!"

Captain Nado guffawed as he said, "Have you finished plotting the course?"

"Yes."

"Good," the captain acknowledged. "Red, activate the warp drive."

In excellent fashion, the once finicky drive whirred and rumbled, indicating that all the repair work had been completed to perfection. The wispy warp bubble enveloped the ship again, blurring the galaxy outside as the space in front of them seemed to collapse on itself, being simultaneously expanded at their stern. Mere seconds later, the warp was successfully accomplished, leaving the crew peering through the viewports into the vastness of the vacuum. A lone vessel drifted here, identifiable as a Gnarf ship by its cobbled together appearance.

"Why do all their ships look like that?" a youthful voice asked from the bridge entryway. Prince Jym had unbuckled himself and rushed to see out the forward windows.

"Gnarfs have no real innovators or engineers," answered Captain Nado. "They rely instead on pilfering and pillaging whatever tech they can accumulate, assimilating it with other vessels and structures. They weld and solder until they have a ship like that, pieced together with parts and components from various sources."

"Cool," the boy uttered.

Attached to the side of Boxie's spacecraft they could make out an airlock tether already in place and awaiting them. Captain Nado indicated for Red to begin the process of carefully bringing the Explorer 2000 to a complete halt. The small transport shuttle inside the cargo bay, endearingly referred to by the officers as the "puddle jumper" would need to be utilized to connect to the tether.

"We won't all fit in the puddle jumper, Captain," Kel pointed out.

"We'll have to squeeze," the captain replied. "We should all go together. We'll just leave Red behind to guard the ship. They may be able to overpower one, or even three, of us, but they can't take down all of us at once."

"Fair point," agreed Kel. "What's the old proverb? 'A three-strand cord is not easily broken', right?" As they commenced arming themselves for the trek, she mumbled, "I sure hope this works…"

Greatly anticipating the arrival of her gullible guests, Boxie the Beautiful gathered her girth in her enormous lounge, her bare feet swaying back and forth. The radar operator had already stopped by to inform her that the Explorer beast had shown up for the rendezvous. Then the radio operator came in to tell her that the people of the Explorer beast were on their way to meet with her. Her Gnarf Boxies had also apprised her that the crew carried with them a small arsenal's worth of weaponry. That was fine with Boxie though. Let them come with their guns and shields and knives. She would have them all in chains soon enough, her victory sealed and glory restored.

Boxie's fingers twitched impatiently, fiddling with the miniscule remote control hidden within her robes. The trap was set, the bait was impeccable, now all that remained was to get her prey into the perfect position. They were on their way, being led by her minions down the wide corridors to her private and luxurious chambers. Much like the embassy on Vortex, silken draperies hung from the ceiling and walls, creating a dreamy atmosphere. Cushions and pillows littered the floor, a multitude of them mounded into a heaping hill on one side of the room atop a chez lounge. That was her shipboard throne, not as comfortable as the embassy's furnishings, but just as intimidating.

A whir and a whoosh signified that the magnetic doors had opened. Escorted by no less than a dozen of her Boxie warriors, in waltzed the entire crew of the Explorer beast. There was the captain, a four-armed Zennian with shock white hair. She recognized the first mate, whose shoulders seemed rather broad and stout for a Human woman of her height. Boxie observed the shapeshifter's purple hair bouncing along to her perky gait, trailed by the powerful little boy covered in natural black tattoos. A girl who resembled the young boy sauntered behind him, looking more than a bit frightened, and then another Human man she did not recall.

Spreading her arms wide, Boxie welcomed her visitors. "People of the Explorer beast, I, Ambassador Boxie the Beautiful, warmly greet you. Please, come in and make yourselves comfortable."

"We'll come in," responded the big Zennian captain, "but comfort in this particular scenario is...unlikely."

"That is to be expected," Boxie said with mock understanding. "Just join me here by the lounge that we may speak of the matters pertaining to the Gnarf armada's whereabouts and my subsequent flight to the Galactic Community for sanctuary."

The crew slowly inched forward. The captain had his hands on his plasma pistols, the commander's fingers tapping at a pistol of her own. A long-range ballistic rifle had been slung across her back. The shapeshifter bore no weapons, but held her palms aloft in a martial style, while the Human man rested his left hand on a derringer and his right on an operating scalpel. Of the two children, the only one that bore any weaponry was the boy, brandishing a makeshift metal sword.

Meeting Boxie's gaze, the Captain mentioned, "I see you're aware of our armaments. We have no desire to use them, but we will if we find ourselves in a pinch."

"Of course, Captain, of course," croaked Boxie. "You will not need those instruments, I assure you."

Unexpectedly, the girl chimed in. "She's lying. I can feel it."

It took nothing more than that. Weapons were at once in every hand of the Explorer crew, aimed in Boxie's vicinity! Waving her hands innocently, Boxie the Beautiful tried to dissuade them from this course of action.

"Please, please," she urged, slowly folding her arms as if to scold a child. "As I said, you will not need those weapons...," Boxie stealthily pressed the activation button on the remote control, "because you will be incapable of doing so!" She sniggered a rotten, retching, repulsive little laugh as greenish-yellow fumes started pouring into the room from the vents. It moved quickly, filling the room with the sickly mist with unparalleled speed for a gaseous substance.

Before anyone could pull a trigger or swing a sword, everyone in the chamber was choking and hacking on the poisonous fog. Even Boxie herself was affected, finding herself completely paralyzed, limp and lifeless. Aside from breathing, all other motor functions had been stripped from every occupant of the room. The crew collapsed to the floor, eyes wide with terror and fear.

She'd done it! She'd tricked them! And now no one could ever belittle or berate her ever again! All of Urkasak would know the great deeds of Boxie the Beautiful, who apprehended the Explorer 2000 beast without ushering in a battle, without even firing a single shot. She would be the triumphant hero, returning to reclaim her place and title. King Bë-Konn would be deposed once the Hex-man saw her value and strength.

All at once, the room was cleansed of the fog, just as she had planned. An aide in an oxygen mask entered and approached Boxie. With only a nod, he administered an antidote to his mistress, freeing her from the petrifying poison. Once able to move again, Boxie addressed her captive audience.

"Well, well, well," she jeered. "It appears that the people of the Explorer beast are no match for the guile and wits of Ambassador Boxie the Beautiful!"

"Shall we inform the armada?" asked the aide.

"What?!" screamed Boxie. "Of course not! I alone will bring these as tribute to the high king and the Hex-man."

"What of their sky-beast?"

"Was anyone left on board?"

The aide shook his head. "No milady. We scanned for energy signatures, and there was nothing left on board. The cloaking device also appears to have been discarded as far as we can tell."

Boxie leered a sinister smile. "Leave their sky-beast for the general and vizier to discover. It will delay them long enough for me to reconnoiter with Vin Trell and his men at Vortex. We will drop off the captain and shapeshifter with them and then continue to our ultimate destination, Urkasak!"

"You do not wish to tow the Explorer beast back with us?" the aide inquired. "It could make for a grand entrance."

Her grin dropped instantly, a sour scowl taking its place. "I will make a grand entrance. My return to the home-world will be superb and victorious! Let Flogg and Hämm duke it out over petty scraps, while I claim the true prize." Boxie's glare grew hard and determined. "No one will be able to dispute my greatness again. Now get back to your post and instruct the rest of my Gnarf Boxies that we are going home!"

Spluttering, spittle-launching laughter exploded from her lumpy lips, all at once dispelling the frown. Shrieking a war-cry of sky splintering volume, Ambassador Boxie the Beautiful cheered her minions onward. If outer space were not a vacuum devoid of sound waves, their whoops and hollers would have been heard across the galaxy.

Chapter 16

Anxiously pacing across the lavishly carpeted flooring of his auspicious apartment, Vin Trell had nearly worn a hole in the finely woven fibers. A drink in his right hand, he roamed the room, walking from the peephole at the door, then to the window that overlooked a portion of the bustling city streets of Vortex, then back to the cabinet to refresh his beverage. So on it went until one of his Fangorians poked his head into the parlor.

"They're here," was all the mercenary had to say.

"Have them bring the prisoners directly to my father's room," instructed Vin. "They can await his arrival there. Come around the back way, I'll open it up for you."

As soon as the merc was gone, Vin trotted to the drink cabinet, his anxious energy now transformed into giddiness. Boxie's trap had been a roaring success! Now he had the hoodlums in his power. They would be at his mercy. Oh, the fun he could have while waiting for Father to arrive! He'd get them nice and loosened up for the old man, ready to spew forth whatever information he might require of them.

Upon securing his drink for later, the gaudy gambler crossed to the rear of the apartment, opening a pantry door. The inside was filled with canned goods, pre-packaged foodstuffs, and cooking utensils. All were fake, of course, and hid the true nature of the tiny thoroughfare. Pulling one of the serving spoons slightly to the left, Vin opened a secret passage located on the back wall of the pantry. It swung wide to reveal a dimly lit chamber beyond.

Therein could be found a dusty old room, leftovers from the Star Guard offices that used to dominate this structure. The garish young man remembered the history of the station. The Guard had been run off years ago, unable to establish a decent hold in the region. They were replaced by a mercenary force, the Vardens, who were paid and armed by the guild that more or less operated at the highest levels of Vortex, a group referred to as the Yildi. No one ever saw or spoke to the Yildi...unless they owed a substantial amount to one of the upper casinos, of course.

The timeworn area itself had been an interrogation room under the Star Guard, but now it served a far different purpose. Should Vin or his father ever require it, this place now functioned as their own private torture chamber. Sound-dampening foam lined the walls, which were reinforced with quiet steel and soundproof glass. The only way for sound to get out of the room was via a microphone on the otherwise bare metal table, and it only broadcast to the observation area behind the soundproof two-way mirror.

At the far end of the hallway that led to Vin's apartment was a tremendous trash bin that rested upon remote controlled casters. These could be operated from within the chamber to cause the bin to roll aside, revealing the outdoor entrance to the secret torture room. A few payoffs to the complex superintendent meant that the Trells went virtually untouched in this building, able to conduct whatever business they might need.

Pressing the button on the panel in the observation room, Vin watched as his Fangorian guards, along with three Gnarf Boxies, unceremoniously shoved the captain and the shapeshifter into the torture room. The pair stumbled to the ground, already beaten and bruised, and clearly recovering from the paralytic poison gas. Boxie herself entered through the observation room doorway, looking quite proud, and even more puffed up than usual, if that was possible.

"I give you your prize," she announced theatrically. "Now where is mine?"

"First, the cloaking device," demanded Vin.

"It was not on the ship," Boxie said simply. "They must have gotten rid of it or stashed it somewhere."

"They'll tell us where it is in time," the Lorian sneered. "Your payment." Vin handed over a huge chunk of monetary notes, rolled thickly enough that one could actually choke on it. "Now, take your men and leave."

"What's the matter, Vin?" joked Boxie. "Do you tire of my company already?"

"I want none of your nonsense," he retorted. "My father will be here within the standard week. He won't want any outside involvement when he arrives. Secondly, you and your Gnarf Boxies attract too much attention. Attention that I don't need! And thirdly, you have your own dramatic entrance to make back on Urkasak, do you not? I'd hate for you to miss it."

"Quite right," Boxie agreed, "we do have a schedule to keep. I must stay ahead of those grubby grabbers, Flogg and Hämm." She turned to her cohorts. "Come my Boxies, we have much work left to do." Then to Vin, "A pleasure doing business with you Master Trell."

As the Gnarfs regressed from the chamber, Vin breathed as though he were surfacing for air after a long stint underwater. However, it was not due to emotional relief, but rather physical as Gnarfs were among the most repugnant creatures in the galaxy, their foul features surpassed only by their sickening stench. He was most pleased to see them leave.

"Besides," he murmured to himself, watching the captain and shapeshifter helping each other rise from the floor, "I have other toys to play with now..."

Scouring the sector via a dragnet, ultimately sitting on his hands, and waiting for a report to be delivered over the radio waves, was not General Hämm's idea of hunting for fugitives. A direct and involved approach would have been more suitable. Chasing his foes and firing indiscriminate lasers sounded much better to the general. Intimidating, overwhelming, and brutalizing his foes with the might of the Gnarf fleet made a far more interesting tale to share around the evening bonfires than "we waited for a radio signal" ever could.

As Hämm was bemusing, one of his command center officers entered. "Sir?"

"What is it?" huffed the general.

"The Explorer beast, sir. The dragnet has radioed a report.

They found it drifting in open space approximately one lightyear's distance from the Vortex sky kingdom."

"Do we have the coordinates?"

"Yes, sir."

"Then don't stand there prattling!" Hämm thundered. "Prepare the sky-beast for warp!"

"Right away sir." The officer bumbled from the chamber, leaving the general alone.

"Now we will see who will take home the prize," he grunted. "Flogg and Boxie can eat mud. I will show the high king that I am still his most worthy and trusted advisor."

Watching out of the commanding viewport in his quarters, General Hämm observed as the darkened bubble wrapped itself around his sky beast. The stars of the expanse blurred and stretched as the walls around him creaked and groaned. Within seconds, they had warped to the location that the coordinates had specified. Wanting to make a daunting display, Hämm adorned himself in his finest armor, the bronze breastplate gleaming like a heavenly light. His belt of shrunken heads and bone helmet completed the desired appearance of a woeful warrior, unyielding, unrelenting, and unmerciful in his assault.

General Hämm stormed to the bridge, finding his officers murmuring amongst themselves. No work was being done to tether the Explorer, nothing being accomplished to further their aims of capturing the tiny sky-beast. Seeing this inactivity, Hämm flew into an ear-splitting wrathful rage!

"You lazy louts! On your feet!" bellowed the belligerent brute. "Why are you sitting and chatting when you should be attacking and subduing this foe?!"

"Sir," answered one of the men, "the ship is without power, floating empty. We detected no energy coming from within."

Another clarified further. "There is no one on board."

"What?!" shouted Hämm. "How is there no one on board? They cannot abandon the vessel in this expanse!"

"General," said the radar technician, awaiting acknowledgment.

"What?" his superior growled.

"Another sky-beast is in the region. The radar says it is a Gnarf vessel."

"General?" the radio operator spoke up, also holding for affirmation.

"WHAT?!!" roared General Hämm.

"They are hailing us."

"Then patch them through!"

The speakers on the radio popped and buzzed with static. A voice began to sift through, low and droning. Recognizing the tonality at once, General Hämm's upturned, flaring nostrils started to twitch, shaking his nose ring fiercely.

"Greetings general," Flogg's voice rumbled. "It seems we are both late to the party. The Explorer beast has been vacated, presumably the occupants have fled in a new sky-beast."

"Vizier," returned the general, as coldly and gravely as he could manage. "Your presumption leaves much to be desired. They had a cloaking device, why would they drop their sky-beast now? There is more here than we can see. My prediction is that they have left it behind for some other reason, perhaps supplies or something of that nature. They will return to it when they have what they need. In the meantime, we should take the Explorer beast back to Urkasak. They will attempt to recover it, and we will then pounce upon them like the predators we are known to be."

"If that is the case," debated Flogg, "then we should wait here for them to return. Why potentially flaunt failure in front of King Bë-Konn? We could go through all the trouble of retrieving this sky-beast, only to discover that the crew is not coming to redeem it."

"No!" Hämm firmly stated. "I am done waiting for something to happen. We must take action! We will take the Explorer beast back to Urkasak, and in the safety of our own territory we will comb every corner of it until we are certain there is truly nothing aboard. If we must wait, then let us do it from the comfort of the home-world, and not out here in the open heavens."

"Very well," came the reply from Flogg. "Who will take the honor of towing the Explorer beast back to Urkasak?"

"I care not! At this point, I only want the Hex-man's task done and over, that we may resume our normal duties of raiding and looting."

"Then you will not mind if my own sky-beasts perform the job?"

"Just do it!" yelled Hämm. "I will recall the dragnet and we will all go home at least somewhat victorious."

"Can you then provide us with the means to tow the Explorer beast?" inquired Flogg. "Our own do not possess the tow lines necessary."

Snarling and sneering, General Hämm assigned men to assist the supercilious seer in securing the hardware to his own vessel. Outside the fuselage windows, the general could see Flogg's sky-beast spending much time in attaching the Explorer beast to itself. The minutes dragged into hours as he seriously considered blasting Flogg into dust.

But all would be made right as soon as they were home again. The Explorer beast was a prized possession of the crew, they would come for it, of that he was certain. It would make for far more enticing bait than that sorry sack of sordidness, Boxie. Whatever she was waiting for, she could continue to wait. General Hämm now had the Explorer beast. Their quarry would soon come to him.

Meanwhile, Flogg's priests struggled with the tow lines and tethering. Hämm rolled his eyes and grunted his disapproval. He couldn't watch this nonsense anymore. It was too irritating to observe. What a floundering buffoon this vizier could be!

"Notify me when Flogg and his idiots have completed the task," the general snorted. "I will be in my quarters. Then we will warp home."

Wildly spinning, the room gradually came into focus for Commander Kel. Her eyes stung, still blurry from the gas that Boxie had used to capture them. How could they have been so stupid and naïve? Unbelievably, the Gnarfs had managed to catch them in a trap. Now the captain and Schiff had been whisked away to Vortex, into the clutches of Vin Trell, and here she was with the kids and Dr. Rox, desperately attempting to right herself and find her bearings.

A miniscule portion of the Gnarf ship had been converted into a holding cell. Kel was able to make out the features of the cell as her vision adjusted to the low lighting. All around the compact containment hold were walls of solid grey metal, save one that consisted of thick, hardened bars, reminiscent of what one might find in a prison. Two very basic cots had been tossed inside, the kids resting thereupon.

In a corner on the floor sat Rox, reposed against the far wall with his knees pulled close. He rested his arms upon his legs, supporting his chin atop that. By all appearances he seemed like a lost child who had given up hope of getting found.

"Seems like you came to pretty quick," said Kel, mostly just trying to break the awful silence.

"I can't sleep much anymore," the doctor informed. "Side effect of whatever happened during our last encounter with the Gnarfs."

"How are the kiddos?"

"They'll be alright for now." Rox tightened his mouth, his lips disappearing behind his beard. "We really walked right into it. And once again, all because of me. If I had stuck to my gut and listened to you and Mara, we might not be in this mess."

"None of us could have suspected that Boxie, of all people, would have a paralytic gas," mentioned Kel. "Those aren't exactly produced in large quantities."

"I feel so stupid!" Rox berated himself. "But I'll make it up to all of you. I can distract the guards long enough for you and the kids to get away."

"Then what happens to you?"

"I don't know and I don't care. I have to make things right, earn back the crew's trust, no matter the cost to myself."

"Stop it," lectured Kel. "You didn't make a mistake here. We all waltzed into that snare that Boxie had set. Besides, earning back the crew's trust is not a requirement, ever. As strange as this may sound, especially coming from me, we're a family. You don't have to earn our forgiveness and trust. It comes freely."

"That's not how my family ever operated," sighed Rox. "They were very strict, and if you made one little misstep it was over. Privileges revoked, relationships cut off, punishments aplenty. And those things could only be resolved by working off your mistakes."

"The Explorer and her crew are nothing like that," the commander assured him. "That doesn't sound like true compassion and familial love to me. Now get your head out of that mire, and let's put our heads together to figure out a way to escape this catastrophe."

Dr. Rox nodded fervently. "Okay. I'm with you Commander."

Before they could begin to plot anything, however, the heavy magnetic doors leading to the exterior hall of the holding area slid open with a squeak and a swish. Half a dozen Gnarf Boxies stomped inside, bodyguards of their lady ambassador. Boxie the Beautiful's flabby flanks barely cleared the entrance as she strode into the room with a strange gait. Her most extravagant outfit had been stretched across her body, Boxie's wanton weight threatening to burst the seams at any second.

"Hello treasured guests," she cawed. "I thought you'd like to know that we have just entered orbit around Urkasak. Re-entry is imminent, so be sure you are all comfortable and secured for the bumpy ride. Sky-beasts are not known for smooth atmospheric transfer. Try not to get too damaged."

Her memorandum delivered, Boxie and her guards paraded from the chamber, leaving Rox and Kel scrambling to fortify the cell in preparation for re-entry. They woke the kids, still groggy from the poison, and positioned them alongside the rear wall, braced in the corner. The first cot was set in front of them, catty-cornered to create a triangular nest. The second cot was then used as a brace, being just long enough to reach from the opposing corner and still butt up against the back of the first cot. Both thin mattresses were removed, the crew utilizing them as padding for the walls and bracing cot. They pushed hard with their feet, forcing their backs tight to the wall, and held each other close for balance and support.

"Hold on tight," Kel instructed. "Here it comes."

Heavy rumblings pounded in their eardrums, as violent shaking felt as though it would rip them apart! The crew held fast, clinging to their makeshift protection and one another. After several minutes, everything faded, the noise, the intense vibrations, all had quieted and calmed, the vessel attaining balance and equilibrium. They all sensed when the ship had touched down, a jerking quake signifying that the landing gear had been deployed and set upon.

"Now what?" asked Jym.

"Now we wait to see how we can get out of this," Commander Kel replied.

"And if we can't?"

"We will. We have to."

The telltale noises of the hefty magnetic doors resounded throughout the hall once more, as again they were graced by the presence of Boxie the Beautiful. She and her slovenly entourage marched into the holding room, using a control panel on the wall opposite the cell to release its barred access. Sliding into the ceiling, the bars retracted, allowing the prisoners to egress. But Gnarf Boxies with electrified gauntlets prohibited any kind of aggressive action at this juncture.

"What are you going to do with us?" Kel demanded.

Boxie leaned close. "We will turn you over to the Hex-man, as he requested. But first, I have plans for you. It is time for my jubilant homecoming!" To her Boxies, she ordered, "Ready my procession. These four are to be stationed at the rear of my carriage, bound and gagged."

The gnarled Gnarf led her men, who roughly pushed and shoved the Explorer crew, out of the ship via a ramp, across a messy spaceport, and into a large livery. Therein, Boxie boarded a wide, flat wagon with enormous wheels, pulled by two gargantuan animals. As ordered, her captures were tied with coarse rope and their mouths stuffed with cloth. Kel looked around and couldn't help but let her hope dwindle. This was going to be a tough spot to get out of...

Newly returned from roving the deep heavens, General Hämm and Grand Vizier Flogg currently walked alongside King Bë-Konn, flanking the high king on either side. Tall, open, glassless windows provided a spectacular view of the sprawling cities and villages that spread from the base of Bë-Konn's luxurious palace, as well as the gigantic jungles rising beyond. The trio perambulated about the king's war room, which was decorated with all manner of Gnarf weaponry and armor, a humongous square table covered by a highly detailed quilted map dominating the center of the chamber.

"As you can see, my king," Flogg rambled, "the combined effort of the general, and primarily myself, has led to the discovery and subsequent appropriation of the Explorer beast. Now that we have it in our possession, we believe the elusive crew will come to us. A brilliant strategy if I do say so myself."

"You have done well enough, I suppose," harrumphed King Bë-Konn. "If we must wait for the crew to come then that is what we will do."

"It is the wisest thing to do, my king."

"And you are certain there was nothing else hiding aboard the Explorer beast?" the portly potentate questioned.

"Only a deactivated metal man," answered his wicked vizier. "It had no power that our instruments could detect."

"So then, are we set to notify the Hex-man?" the general impatiently asked. "I would that we be done with his deals and requests."

"Watch your tongue!" spluttered the high king. "We do not know if or when he will be listening. The Hex-man is a cruel and vicious trickster god. As of yet we have no way of conquering him without bringing his own curses upon ourselves. Patience my good general, we will see the end of the Hex-man's nagging tasks very soon."

Their conference was cut short by a loud horn piercing the tranquil morning. King Bë-Konn rushed to the nearest window and glanced at the cobblestone streets. "What is that?! Only visiting kings receive such a welcome!"

A screeching, scratchy voice echoed from far below. "All hail Ambassador Boxie the Beautiful! All hail the captor of the Explorer crew!!"

That voice was all too familiar to Flogg and Hämm, who exchanged a concerned look. The high king, on the other hand, gave them both an ugly, uninhibited grimace. "That better not be what I think it is," he snarled.

"It couldn't be," said a stunned Flogg.

General Hämm only quaked with fury, his anger boiling into a volcanic shout of, "NO!!!"

Parading to the base of King Bë-Konn's opulent pyramid was clearly making Boxie's day. Commander Kel, however, was not nearly as pleased. Gnarfs of all shape and size, caste and class, congregated at the edges of the avenue to watch the procession roll through town. The carriage came to a gradual halt right at the stairs of the royal palace. What she could only assume was the king stepped forth onto a protruding terrace that jutted from the left side of the stairway. He was joined by two others, one in a purple robe with a feathered headdress, the other arrayed in wartime regalia, complete with a helmet made of a giant skull.

"Welcome Boxie the...Beautiful," the king hesitantly huffed. "You have been victorious," the king paused to glare at his companions, "where all others have failed. You will be richly rewarded for your devotion to your king, to the Hex-man, and to all of Urkasak! You will return to the sky kingdom Vortex a wealthy woman!"

"If it pleases your majesty," crowed Boxie in response, "I desire no riches or lavish gifts. I have only one simple desire."

"What do you desire, Boxie?"

"To come home to Urkasak for good!" she proclaimed. "To have my banishment repealed, and all former charges against me dropped! Surely that is not too much to ask for the hero of the kingdom, the one who saved us all from the Hex-man's wrath!"

The crowd cheered. They were obviously on Boxie's side, an opportunity to avoid Lord Hex's retribution reason enough to support her cause. Once again, Kel noted the steaming hot anger the king felt for the pair that accompanied him.

"Very well, Boxie," the king acquiesced. "You shall have your request."

A deafening roar of approval erupted from the throng of Gnarfs. Motioning to the palace guards, the king waved for the prisoners to be taken to the dungeons. Yet again, Kel, Rox, Mara, and Jym were gruffly ushered along, yanked, bumped, punched, and elbowed all the way from the carriage to a side entrance at the base of the pyramid. Torches lit the hallways and stairwells of this dark and dank passage, winding downward a short way, then breaking right towards the rear of the sizable structure. Eventually, their eyes were blinded by the sun again as they were escorted across a courtyard and into an astounding arena. From there, the guards shoved them onward through the constantly curving halls of the colossal coliseum until they reached a series of stone cells that were gated by the same thick metal bars of the holding chamber on Boxie's craft. Not only were the doorways constructed in this manner, so were the roofs, allowing the elements to affect the prisoners incarcerated therein.

Shoved into these tiny and miserable dormitories, the crew had little choice but to obey their captors, waiting for a more opportune time to affect their escape. Perceiving the area around them, Kel saw next to nothing that could help them in their present state. The Gnarfs were on their home territory here. It would be very difficult to overcome their might.

"Halfwits! Moronic mud-eaters!" roared King Bë-Konn. "Now look what you made me do! Not only does that arrogant witch get to live on Urkasak again, but I must also regard her as one would a hero of our people! AAAAAGGGHHH!!!!!" He flung a vase across the room, smashing it against the far wall. That seemed to soothe the king's wrath for now.

"She tricked us," General Hämm concluded. "That crafty creature tricked us."

"Obviously," sneered Flogg.

"Do not start in on me, vizier," the general spat. "You were the one who initially agreed to her 'plan', not me!"

"If it weren't for your utter ineptitude – ," Flogg started to retort.

"SHUT UP!!" the high king blasted. "Both of you shut up! You both failed, miserably I might add, and were outdone by the worst of all Gnarfs."

"Your majesty, she is here," a guard interjected.

King Bë-Konn calmed the room and commanded, "General, vizier, take a seat and remain silent. I will deal with you two later. Guard, bring in Boxie the...Beautiful."

The door swung wide, and Boxie pranced, as best she could, into the king's grand hall. She bowed overdramatically as she gushed, "My king, it is a great honor to be welcomed back into your presence as a conquering hero. As you can see, I have gifted you the crew of the Explorer beast, as requested."

"Do you have them all?" interrogated the lumpy lord of the Gnarfs. "I only saw four. The Hex-man indicated that there were more. A captain, two children, and three of the god-race."

"Only two of the god-race," informed Boxie. "One was a shapeshifter. Alas, the captain and the shapeshifter did not survive the reaction to the paralytic poison I used to capture them. An unforeseen side effect of their alien bodies, more than likely."

"That is not good," mumbled Bë-Konn. "The Hex-man was clear that the captain was not to be harmed."

"The Hex-man does not need to know that it was our capture that did it," offered Boxie. "He could have been lost anywhere during their adventures."

"That is true. Very well, that is our story, and we will all stick to it." King Bë-Konn breathed deeply. "Boxie, I grant you the pleasure of relaying the message to our couriers. Tell them to send word to the Hex-man, we have his prize!"

Chapter 17

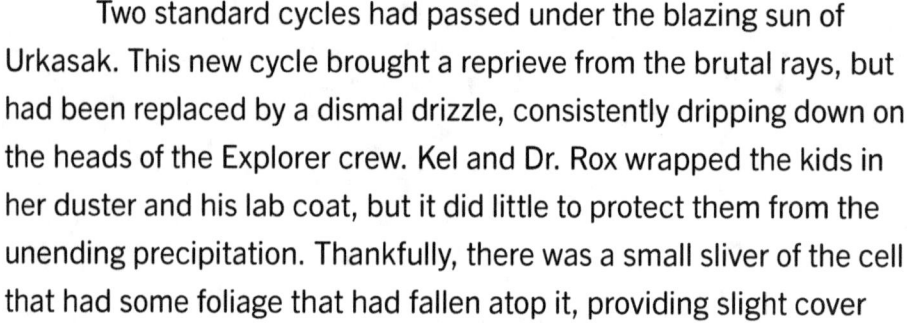

Two standard cycles had passed under the blazing sun of Urkasak. This new cycle brought a reprieve from the brutal rays, but had been replaced by a dismal drizzle, consistently dripping down on the heads of the Explorer crew. Kel and Dr. Rox wrapped the kids in her duster and his lab coat, but it did little to protect them from the unending precipitation. Thankfully, there was a small sliver of the cell that had some foliage that had fallen atop it, providing slight cover from the rain. But all in all, it was an abysmal situation.

"I might be able to move the bars," offered Mara, her teeth chattering as a bracing breeze swept through the cell. "The energy fields here are weak, but I could try."

"Last resort," the doctor said. "You and Jym need to preserve what little strength you have left. And we still don't know the full extent of what could happen to your bodies if you tried using your abilities."

The commander nodded in agreement, shivering from the cold, misting rainfall. Perhaps there was more that could be done, but their planning was interrupted by the sounds of plodding footfalls plopping through the puddles on the stone walkway outside. It was time for their daily rations, a slop of mushy meat and squashed vegetation that often made them feel sicker just by trying to eat it. Their usual server, however, was absent, replaced by the shorter Gnarf who had accompanied the king. He was still outfitted in his purple robes and feathered headdress, even in the pouring rain, carrying their platter in regal fashion.

"Your meal," he droned, in a low drawling voice, passing the platter through the bars.

"I know that voice," remarked Kel. "I'd recognize it anywhere. You're Flogg, the high king's grand vizier."

"I still currently hold that title, yes," Flogg replied despondently. "But as of right now I am tasked with the lowest of my order's duties, feeding the prisoners. I must atone for my failures until my penance is completed. Only then can I regain my place at King Bë-Konn's side."

"What are you planning to do with us?" Jym wanted to know.

"You and your sister are to be kept alive for the Hex-man's arrival," answered the downcast advisor. "I do not know why he hunts you. As for the two of the god-race, a feast is being prepared, at which they will be served...as the main course."

"You want to eat us?" Rox inquired.

"It is our way," mused Flogg. "Nearly two hundred years ago, the god-race came to Urkasak from the heavens aboard their metal sky-beasts. They brought with them their advancements and technology. They taught us their language, the use of their tools and weapons, and the functionality of the sky-beast itself. The gods taught us of their history, from which we gleaned the architecture and culture that the Gnarfs still employ to this day.

"Legends say that once the tribal chieftain Urko had learned all he needed, he turned on the gods and killed them, consuming their flesh and absorbing their souls. It was this process that granted him the power to unite the clans, giving the Gnarfs access to the stars above. There we continued to thrive and grow, capturing more sky-beasts and converting them to our own design. No one dare stand against the Gnarf armada anymore. These tales are why we are called the god-killers."

"What's your role in all of this?" asked Mara.

"I am the religious and spiritual advisor to the high king," Flogg replied. "And I am his oracle. Through many rituals and ceremonies, I see the future of our people, the fate of all the Gnarf kings. Over three hundred kingdoms span this world, but the high king, Bë-Konn, is king above the other kings, ruling them with his might and power."

Sniffling from an oncoming cold, and recalling the argument the general had engaged in with this odd character, Commander Kel queried, "When was the last time you had a vision?"

"It is true, my priests and I have been dry as of late," admitted Flogg. "But that is a temporary issue, soon to be remedied. While all the others feast on your flesh, we will not indulge, but will instead drink your blood. The future of the god-killers will be assured."

"Have there ever been any of the...god-race that you haven't overcome?" Jym questioned.

"Only the trickster gods have escaped our methods. We first met them over one hundred years ago, their powers and wickedness too great for us to safely consume. The Hex-man bears these same powers, and the same cruelty and malice. We dare not eat him, lest we be cursed by his dark and twisted evils."

"But what if you could?" Mara interjected. Kel locked eyes with the little princess, noticing the light of an idea forming within. The Vampyrial girl continued, "What if I told you there was a way to overcome the trickster gods?"

"That is impossible!" puffed the proud prophet. "They cannot be eaten. And what would you know of this anyway?"

"Because," said Mara, rising from their huddle, "I am one."

She closed her eyes and stretched forth her arm. A loose rock on the opposite side of the walkway began to shimmy and shake. As blood trickled from Mara's nose, she manipulated the energy around the object, causing it to fly several yards down the path. A frightened Flogg slowly rotated his gaze back to her. "You have his powers...," he murmured in awe. "Speak, trickster, how can we defeat the Hex-man?"

"There is but one way," the princess bluffed. "You must suppress the powers of the trickster gods by beating them in single combat first."

Flogg's frumpy feet began to dance clumsily underneath him. "I must inform the high king of this news at once!"

"Not yet," Mara stopped him. "There is more that you must know. But I will only reveal it if you agree to my terms."

"What terms?"

"The Humans are to be released, along with my brother. I alone will be turned over to the Hex-man."

Flogg thought for a bit. "I will confer with his eminence and see if these are acceptable terms for him first. Then we will see if your knowledge is worth having."

Flying from the forlorn and soaked scene, Flogg dashed from their presence in a tizzy. The doctor and Kel both turned to Mara. "What are you thinking?" Rox demanded. "I thought I said no abilities!"

"And what's this about going to face Lord Hex alone?" cried Kel. "You don't have to sacrifice yourself for the rest of us! This is not the greatest plan."

"Do any of you have a better one?" the princess retorted.

No one spoke, but they didn't have to. The sentiment of the group was fairly clear. No one spoke up because Mara was right, no one did have a better idea.

Every few hours, Vin Trell and his goons had tromped into the torture chamber to terrorize Captain Nado and Schiff with physical trauma delivered by their fists and feet. Nado knew he could take any beating they were capable of dishing out, but glancing at Schiff told him that she wouldn't hold out much longer. A getaway was needed, and fast. On this most recent visit, Vin lingered behind for a minute.

"You'll break soon enough," he gloated, "and then you will tell me what you have done with the cloaking device before Father gets here, so I can make him a very happy man. After that, we'll make an example of you. No one crosses the Trells. No one."

Following his over-enunciated ovation, Vin spun on his heels and departed in a dapper manner. The two captives were left with their hands cuffed, all four of Nado's bracketed to the wall, while Schiff had been plopped to the floor in a crumpled heap. For now, the only sounds in the room were from their own heavy, labored breathing.

Finally, Captain Nado commented, "I think they're done for the cycle. We can rest and regain some energy."

"They'll be back," moaned Schiff. "But when they do, they'll be in for a big surprise."

"What does that mean?"

"He said 'Father' was coming," she clarified. "That means Gren Trell, the head honcho himself, is on his way here."

"Again I ask, what do you mean?"

"You'll see."

Before Nado's eyes, once more Schiff commenced taking on a new shape...

Metallic moans echoed throughout Lord Hex's monstrous machine. The thick magnetic doors to his portentous study swooshed open, one of the H-7s making an appearance. It entered mechanically and spoke monotonously.

"Milord, you have two messages from the radio operator," it reported.

"Deliver them," rumbled his lordship. "I have many details to see to for the testing of the weapon systems."

"You have received a hail from Klensh," the robot continued. "He has formed his posse and is headed to Vortex to gather intel. The second hail is from the Gnarf couriers. Ambassador Boxie the Beautiful informs that the Explorer crew is in King Bë-Konn's custody on Urkasak."

"Surprising," Hex mused. "I was beginning to think that the Gnarfs had failed me. Perhaps their messages are simply slow due to the Rover Express striking because of the Titan/Exian conflict. I suppose Klensh's services will not be required. And it would seem that my weapons test will need to be put on hold for now. Set a new course for Urkasak."

"This unit will comply, milord. It will take at least two standard cycles to prepare the vessel for warp drive."

"Very well. As long as Bë-Konn doesn't do anything foolish, we should be fine..."

Vin Trell re-entered the torture room after several more hours had passed. Nearly a full standard cycle with no food and water should move things along. Time to see if his guests were ready to be more cooperative. The secret entrance swung aside, revealing mostly what he expected to see. There was the old table, the two-way mirror, the solitary spotlight fastened atop a short rolling post, the captain chained to the wall and –

"Father?" the younger Trell uttered.

In the center of the chamber, looking as suave and stern as ever, was Gren Trell. His wavy silvery hair was slicked back in a neat, smooth fashion, and his manicured goatee had been styled to match. He was dressed in some of his nicest finery, a slimming three-piece azure suit with a gold timepiece chain draped across the abdomen. Shined, tall, brown boots and a corresponding bronze-colored cape completed the appearance of a well-to-do entrepreneur.

Vin stammered, "I thought you weren't going to be here for a few more cycles?"

"I decided to move up my timetable," the elder Trell replied in an unflappable manner. "The numbers are up, there's little to worry about. And I wanted to retrieve my…cargo…that was left in your possession."

"The cloaking device, yes Father," stuttered Vin. "Well, you see – "

"I've already taken care of it." The gentleman crime lord was as cold as space itself.

"Of course, Father." The son suddenly thought the room seemed a bit off. "Father, where is the shapeshifter?"

"I've already dealt with her." Gren Trell played with his fingernails. "She broke before the big fellow, spilled everything. I had my own men take her remains out back. Now, unshackle the

Zennian. I want to hook him up to a new acquisition. I think he'll find the experience quite...electrifying."

"Right away, Father." Vin set himself to the task of undoing all of Captain Nado's restraints. The brawny Zennian collapsed upon release. Gren and Vin both stood over him ominously, until the younger looked at his father's face and recoiled. "Father, what happened to your scar?"

The elder Trell seem puzzled. "What scar?"

"The one under your right eye, from...Mother," Vin reminded. Then his eyes widened with horror. "Wait a minute. You crafty 'shifter!"

Gren Trell's voice then changed into a more cheerful chirp as he said, "Oh, I didn't know he had a scar. Oops."

"Guards!" called Vin.

Two Fangorians burst onto the scene, fangs bared and fur bristling. One sported a dark brown pelt, while the other a snow white. Before they could even make it a second step into the area, however, Brownie took two Zennian fists to the muzzle, while Whitey received the other two of the captain's barreling blows to the jaw! Vin moved to apprehend Schiff in Gren form, but she deftly dodged and implemented the same maneuver on him as before, a quick finger jab to the chest, another to the throat, and a final palm thrust to the diaphragm. The handsome young Lorian stood completely helpless.

"Not again," he mumbled through practically frozen lips and teeth.

Schiff toppled him with a light push. "One con artist to another, don't ever underestimate the power of the classics."

Hefting the metal table, Captain Nado swung it with all his remaining strength into the two-way mirror, shattering the glass. He reached through the jagged portal and smashed every button on the control panel until the hall access door slid aside. Scooping Schiff onto his left shoulder, Nado plowed into the apartment complex hallway.

"You know, I can run on my own legs," Schiff quipped somewhat weakly, having transformed back to her normal form.

"I've run with you while escaping Vortex once before," Nado rapidly returned. "We'll move faster like this, trust me."

"I would be insulted, but I'm getting a free ride," shrugged the shapeshifter as they careened toward the elevators to make their daring escape.

Under protection from the elemental forces that streamed from the clouds high overhead, King Bë-Konn, along with General Hämm and Boxie, trailed Flogg closely, following him to the holding cells of the arena. Though not torrential, the rain still sailed steadily downward, casting a dour, doom-like mood on the procession as they strove to fit all four fat figures under the single tent that acted as their umbrella. Gnarfs stationed at every corner held the tarp aloft, keeping their bloated sovereigns from getting wet and sour.

"I assure you, my king," Kel heard the vizier saying, "the girl has the powers of the trickster gods. Visions of our greatness overcoming the Hex-man have flooded my sight. She will show us the way to attain this victory."

"We will see," was all the high king had to grumble in response.

Upon reaching the cell of the Explorer crew, Flogg commanded, "Girl. Show him your abilities. If you do not, I will punish you so severely that you will wish for the Hex-man to claim you at once."

Princess Mara didn't hesitate. "Very well." Despite silent urgings from Dr. Rox not to use her gift, the princess flipped the small rock again, displaying her prowess. She proceeded once more to wipe the blood trail from her nose and upper lip.

"There, my king," Flogg gushed. "The girl has the same powers as the Hex-man. She is an evil god, like him. She has offered me wisdom in defeating the Hex-man, but only if you agree to the terms I mentioned."

The warty king approached the bars, leaning his wrinkled face close. "If this is not a farce, then I agree. Now little one, tell us the rest of the procedure to kill the tricksters."

"Once they are defeated in combat," Mara lied, "you must make sure to skin them, as the evil rests primarily on the surface. And avoid eating the heart, for it is from there that their wickedness stems."

"Is that all?"

"That is all."

"Ha!" Bë-Konn boisterously laughed. "Surely you realize how ridiculous that sounds."

"But if it could put an end to the Hex-man," wondered the general, "would it not be worth it to test the theory?"

"An excellent point," King Bë-Konn agreed, turning his attention to Mara. "Which is why tomorrow at first light, the arena will be filled with Gnarfs eager to see the first ever defeat of a trickster god. One of you will fight our champion to see if this experiment works."

"I will accept the challenge," the brave girl stated.

The high king's loud laughter shook the pillars. "Not you," he uttered. "Him." A pudgy finger pointed squarely at Prince Jym.

"That was not the deal," protested Mara. "I said they had to be let go. I'm the only one who has to stay!"

"Mara." Jym touched his sister's arm gently. "You've done enough. Maybe too much. I can handle this. Besides, of the two of us, I am the only one with training in swordplay." He addressed the king. "I will fight the champion."

"Shall I form the ranks and choose a fighter from among the high guard?" interrupted Hämm. "We have plenty of men trained in the art of pit fighting."

"No," replied the corpulent king. "I have punished Flogg already for his failures, but I have yet to address your own shortcomings, General. So you will be the champion of the Gnarfs who will face the trickster boy in the arena tomorrow."

"But my king, I – "

"Do not argue! I suggest you go and prepare for your match, Hämm. I'd hate to be disappointed again, and do not wish that you should be embarrassed by a child."

At that, both Boxie and Flogg grinned, their faces full of sadistic glee. The general only returned their looks with a cold stare. "As my king commands," he begrudgingly grunted. Appearing no longer concerned with the cold, wet moisture in the air, Hämm stamped back up the walkway, quickly out of sight.

"Good luck in the fight tomorrow," issued the obese King Bë-Konn. "If the fight goes well, we will honor the deal, and the Hex-man will trouble all of us no more."

Snorting cackles and chortles all the way, the terrible trio regressed toward the pyramid palace. Dr. Rox looked pleadingly at Kel. "Please tell me we have another plan."

"At the moment," she replied, "I've got nothing."

The doctor took Jym by the shoulders, facing him square. "Rest up and eat extra rations. You can have mine. You're going to need it. You're our last hope."

Everyone settled in for a long rest cycle, huddling under the slim cover and trying to keep warm. The night passed fitfully, dawn breaching the horizon all too soon. The brilliant rays of this solar system's sun chased the storm clouds from the sky, leaving it clear and blue. A contingent of Gnarf guards retrieved the crew from their quarters, separating Prince Jym from the rest. Commander Kel watched him as long as she could, feeling a knot in her stomach growing larger the further they grew apart.

War drums started beating a foreign rhythm, the chants of at least a thousand Gnarfs joining in overhead. The arena was already packed to the gills with onlookers, no doubt eager to see the great general oust the trickster boy. Kel shook her head. *There must be something else we can do!* she thought. But nothing came to mind. As they ascended a flight of stone stairs, the stadium opened up before them, a raucous, rambunctious, uproarious display overwhelming their senses. Gnarfs cheered and jeered, bellowed at, and belittled them, all calling for the same thing, blood. *We need a miracle.*

Inside the cargo bay of the Explorer 2000, two guards sat on duty, having the tedious task of guarding the single occupant, the metal man. H-8-RED sat between them, rigid and still. It hadn't moved in many cycles, and the two guards had often expressed the sentiment that it would not, thus their presence here was unneeded.

"We should be at the arena now, to see the blood-match between the general and the trickster god," the first guard complained. "This thing is dead. We need not be here to watch over a lifeless suit of armor."

"I know," agreed his compatriot. "This is a once in a lifetime experience, and we are probably the only two Gnarfs in all the high royal province not to see it!"

"But we are stuck on guard duty," moaned the first. "We will never be allowed to leave here unless this thing were to suddenly melt away into a puddle of molten metal."

"Then why not dispose of it and leave? We can say it self-destructed, yes? These things are known to have that capability, are they not?"

"Do not be a fool! We cannot leave our post! The general would skin us and wear us upon his shoulders as a cloak!"

"It was only a suggestion..."

Their conversation dulled at that point, as they could both hear the roars from the coliseum ebb. But that was not the only noise ringing in the bay. A hum began to exude from the belly of the robot, and a tinging sound emanated from its ocular sensors, as they began to glow yellow. The distant cheers of the crowd had enraptured the two guards though, drowning out any audible elements of the robot's reactivation process. The next sound, however, they did hear, as a cold and clinical vocalization reverberated in the hold.

"Greetings."

Startled, the two guards jumped in fright, fumbling their polearms. But before either had a chance to recover, Red's precise programming kicked in, its powerful processors computing combat three steps ahead of its foes. With an inescapable grip, Red grabbed the polearm of the guard to its left with its own right hand, and the weapon of the guard to the right with its left hand. Arms crossed, the assassination automaton righted its stance, yanking both Gnarfs into each other with tremendous force! The hapless guards unconsciously thudded to the bay floor, as H-8-RED made a beeline for the bulkheads.

Chapter 18

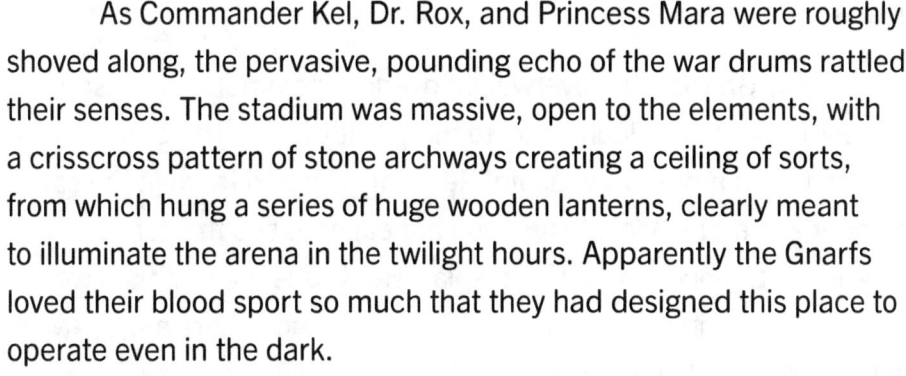

As Commander Kel, Dr. Rox, and Princess Mara were roughly shoved along, the pervasive, pounding echo of the war drums rattled their senses. The stadium was massive, open to the elements, with a crisscross pattern of stone archways creating a ceiling of sorts, from which hung a series of huge wooden lanterns, clearly meant to illuminate the arena in the twilight hours. Apparently the Gnarfs loved their blood sport so much that they had designed this place to operate even in the dark.

Their escort of guards took the crew to the front row of the bleacher style stone benches, a bulky wire netting separating them from the playing field below. One of the men leaned close and whispered, "King Bë-Konn's orders. So you can get a good view of the slaughter of your friend." He offered a spittle launching chuckle, pushing each one of them gruffly onto their seats.

From their observation point, Kel could see that the arena had been set up as a sort of maze, wooden blockades being placed around in a labyrinthine configuration. Random bladed weapons, mostly swords, were strewn about across the field, while hanging from the stone arches in the center of the area was a missile launcher that looked brand new and pristine, a network of ropes strung around it, reaching all the way to the ground. *They didn't loot that from a raid*, Kel mused. *Someone gave it to them. Payment from Lord Hex, maybe.* But her contemplations were stalled as the war drums built to a powerful crescendo.

On the opposite side of the ring, King Bë-Konn made his grand entrance, to the screaming delight of a thousand adoring subjects. He was trailed by Boxie and Flogg, both looking overly pleased to be watching the punishment of the general. Bë-Konn quieted the throng with a raised hand. The war drums ceased. *Thank goodness*, thought Kel.

"My Gnarfs," the overweight overlord commenced his speech, "I, your high king, welcome you to this great event!" The crowd cheered even more. Once again, Bë-Konn silenced them in the same manner as before. "Yes, I know you are eager to see this terrific, magnificent, blood splattering display. But this is the first time we have had such an event in many years, and I know there are a few in our gallery who do not know the rules for this matchup.

"The challenger will be released first, given a thirty second head start to hide and find supplies within the labyrinth. After the head start time is up, the champion will be unleashed to wreak his wrath upon his foe! Once both competitors are on the field, it's an all-out duel to the death, as one must kill the other to win. Lastly, if either combatant can find the middle of the maze, they can board the pulley operated elevator to lift themselves to the sunburst shooter dangling above. One final note to the audience, NO INTERFERENCE!! Ladies and gentlemen, this is Maze of Death!!"

An eruption of cheers and cries shook the coliseum as King Bë-Konn and his cohorts took their seats under a lavish pavilion strewn with cushions and pillows. Attendants stood on hand with giant jungle fronds used as fans, with several others holding platters loaded with fresh tropical fruits and juices. Indulging in these amenities, the distended despot gestured to the Gnarfs who controlled the arena entrances. "Proceed!" he shouted.

The lever was pulled, and the western portcullis started retracting, creaking and grinding as the counter weighted chains hauled it upward. Amidst boos and jeers, Prince Jym emerged from the shadows, shielding his eyes from the sun while they adjusted. He seemed shocked at the setup before him, as though he hadn't expected to see such a sight.

"They didn't explain the rules to him," Kel concluded.

"That's cheating, isn't it?" queried Rox.

"Probably," acknowledged the commander, "but how are we going to accuse the high king of Urkasak of cheating in his own kingdom, while playing his own game?"

"Not to mention the fact that we're surrounded by a myriad of bloodthirsty Gnarfs that would just as happily eat us as well," Mara unhappily mentioned.

Mustering all her lung strength, the commander yelled out, "Jym! Grab a sword and hide!!"

That garnered her a thump on the forehead from the closest guard's polearm handle. "The king said no interference! That is your only warning."

Rubbing her bruised cranium, Kel quipped to Rox and Mara, "Worth it."

She checked to see if her gamble had paid off. It appeared to have worked, as Jym bolted and darted through the labyrinth of barricades, winding his way around the edges of the arena. The young prince scooped up a dirty, grimy dirk with a quick spin and kept on moving. He was now directly in front of them, still maneuvering eastward along the wall.

"No, baby, go the other way," Kel muttered under her breath. "You're going to run right into – "

A horn blasted through the air, signifying that the thirty second head start time was up. The Gnarfs stationed at the eastern portcullis pushed down their lever, and the hefty iron gate screeched skyward, revealing the prince's opponent waiting therein. General Hämm emerged in full wartime regalia, his bronze breastplate gleaming in the sunlight. The belt of shrunken heads and giant skull helmet gave the general a truly terrifying visage. Upon his back rested a power pack, a short cord extending from it to the base of his chainsaw sword. Revving the spiked saw blade, Hämm issued a thunderous roar, and commenced the chase!

Having recovered from the nerve attack, Vin Trell was helped to his feet by Brownie and Whitey. He shook the strange sensation of helpless catalyzation from his mind and body. Turning to his mercenaries, nose twitching and teeth clenched, Vin growled, "Alert the Vardens. Put out an all-points bulletin. I am offering a three thousand bit reward for the capture of those two miscreants. I want them found and punished!!"

Sipping on slimy beverages in a crummy watering hole of a cantina on the main floor of Vortex, Schlaar and Shtrepp enjoyed their newfound financial freedom. Well, sort of, at least they didn't owe the Trells any more loan money. Now they just needed to find work and pay the nearest ferryman to get them off this space station.

Their surroundings certainly reflected their situation well, as the bar's mauve neon lighting flickered, and had burned out in many places. It cast a dull pink hue across the entire establishment, hiding the flaws and cracks in the stucco walls. Monitors hung in various locations, airing a live broadcast of some sport that was being played in another section of the station. The pounding music of Vortex wasn't as obnoxious in this locale, but the noise from the monitors was loud enough to rival it.

Suddenly, a robotic voice came through the strident screens, and the picture altered to show a still image of two individuals. "Alert! Alert! This is a station-wide APB. Captain Burnay Nado and his shapeshifting sidekick are wanted for immediate arrest and questioning. A three thousand bit reward has been offered for their capture. That is all." Static buzzed across the monitors for a second, then the picture resumed the live game.

"Did you see that?" Shtrepp asked, speaking in the Kriton tongue.

"Yeah, was that really..." started Schlaar, his words trailing off.

"Captain Nado and Schiff!" exclaimed Shtrepp. "Come on, if there's a bounty on them, this may be our chance!"

"Oh, don't be ridiculous," Schlaar moaned. "We got lucky last time, what are the odds that they'll run right past this cantina?"

Almost as if by natural reaction, both Kritons turned to look out the entrance. Nothing but the normal hustle and bustle of Vortex swarmed outside. Schlaar shot a mocking glance at Shtrepp as if to say, "I told you so," only to have Shtrepp's eyes light up as she pointed outside. Schlaar twirled back around just in time to see the captain barreling down the street, Schiff being carried on his shoulder.

"You have got to be kidding me," grumbled Schlaar. "How is that even possible?!"

"Let's go!" Shtrepp grabbed her partner's arm and yanked him from his stool, both readying their weapons as they rushed from the bar!

The blood-match raged on, as Jym rounded a bend, only to find himself face to face with his adversary! Kel watched in horror, seeing Hämm swing his chainsaw furiously, swiping an overhead arc straight down toward the prince's head. Dodging and rolling out of the way, Jym dashed at the giant general, sticking the dirk into Hämm's right leg.

"Argh!" grunted the muscly man. "I'll kill you for that, boy!"

"First blood!" bellowed Bë-konn from his cushioned perch.

Hollering their disapproval at this turn of events, the multitudinous mob continued to side with their champion. But that didn't deter Jym. Twisting and turning, the prince wound deeper into the maze. He jetted around corner after corner, until nearly tripping over a sawtooth saber that shone like silver in the sunshine. Looking at it as if it were the most priceless treasure he'd ever seen, Prince Jym paused to snatch the saber, proceeding to twirl and spin the blade to test its weight and balance.

Unfortunately, this short display gave his opponent time to close the gap, the now limping general slicing through one of the barriers with his motorized weapon. The burly brigadier sliced the blockade into splinters as he charged forward! Blood seeped from the stab wound on his leg, but Hämm appeared to take no notice of it, shrugging off the pain in desperation to conquer this courageous child.

A quick and heavy blow flew towards Jym's neck on the left and would have decapitated him had he not parried. This was followed by three more strikes in swift succession as Hämm attacked with a roundhouse swipe at the prince's right leg, an overhead swing at the boy's head, and one final thrust at the young monarch's gut. Jym responded by blocking each and every one, then returning with his own offensive. Gathering all his might, the prince struck at Hämm's head, attempting to turn the tables. Sparks flew as saber met chainsaw and the two combatants locked gazes with one another.

Screeches and squawks erupted from the onlookers as the battle intensified. Commander Kel was having a hard time observing any of the action now, as the fight was largely obscured by the northern maze walls. There was just enough visibility to piece together the events of the altercation. Heaving a gruff grunt, the general shoved Jym backward, nearly knocking the boy to the ground. Not wanting to hang around for more trouble, the prince again took flight through the labyrinth, seeking refuge behind the curvature of the walls and barriers of the quagmire.

Every speaker on Vortex received temporary relief from the thrumming, thumping tunes that played consistently throughout the space station. But that reprieve only occurred so that an alert could be announced. Captain Nado halted his flight to listen to the broadcast.

"Alert! Alert! This is a station-wide APB. Captain Burnay Nado and his shapeshifting sidekick are wanted for immediate arrest and questioning. A three thousand bit reward has been offered for their capture. That is all."

"Three thousand bits?" cried Nado.

"Sidekick?" cried Schiff.

"We've got to keep moving," the captain groaned, pushing onward.

The pair started peering around the packed avenues, hoping to spot a good place to duck inside and lay low for a few minutes. But as Nado resumed his grueling pace, a regiment of Vardens came at them, cutting off their forward escape! Using communicators on their wrists they instantly notified the entire force, and anyone else listening, of their prey's location. As the five crimson-clad mercenaries leveled firearms at the escapees, the captain pulled Schiff from his shoulder and turned around to block the incoming projectiles with his own body. Rifle reports rang out in the open street, but Nado felt nothing striking him. He looked up to see every Varden officer downed, then checked to see where the opposing shots had come from. Schlaar and Shtrepp stood a few feet from them, expressions of pride and pleasure on their faces.

"Schlaar? Shtrepp?" stammered the captain. "What are you doing here?"

"We came to pay off the loan with that ssskull," the female Kriton replied. "But no time for talk now, we need to get out of the open!"

Captain Nado and Schiff needed no additional incentive. They nodded and once again took off at an incredibly quickened rate. As they ran, Schiff bouncing along on the captain's shoulder, the willowy young woman inquired, "So, what are the odds that we'd bump into each other again like this?"

"Pleashe don't mention the oddsss," Schlaar hissed, rolling his eyes.

Their gang hadn't made it two blocks when another squadron of five more Vardens leapt into the chase, hounding their every step. Trying to continually outpace the massive militia was proving to be nigh impossible. But just as the captain was about to make a new suggestion, out from a side street stepped a humongous Gnarf, clearly one of Boxie's that she'd left behind. The frumpy fellow gave no warning, no heads up, no war cry, he simply charged straight at them! Caught between a rock and a hard place,

Nado prepared himself to bullrush the Gnarf Boxie and attempt to overrun him. However, as they drew closer, he could hear the big brute yelling at them.

"Duck!" shouted the Gnarf. "DUCK!!"

The zestful Zennian didn't give the decree a second thought. Holding tight to Schiff, he ducked under the Gnarf Boxie's gauntlet-covered right arm as it was swung in a haymaker right over the captain's crown To avoid an impact themselves, the Kritons shoulder rolled to either side of the pudgy pugilist, allowing him space to do whatever it was he planned to do. More quickly than Captain Nado would have anticipated, the Gnarf clobbered the first Varden trooper square in the jaw, sending him spiraling to the surface of the street with an electrifying hit!

Another electrically charged gauntlet rested on the Gnarf's left arm, which delivered a powered punch into the second merc's chest. He tumbled backward, tripping up one of his other comrades, while the brawling Gnarf bowled the last two over with a double clothesline. All the Vardens were incapacitated for the time being. The mysterious rescuer spun to face them, quite obviously winded from the fray.

"No...no more...running," he stuttered between breaths. "Come with me."

"Cap, you think this is a good idea?" Schiff asked.

"He certainly seems like he wants to help," replied Nado. "I think we should do as he says."

"That's what I was thinking too!" she chirped back. "I only wondered if you were thinking the same thing that I was thinking...again."

"Let's go."

Along with the Kriton duo, they dutifully shadowed their newfound protector to an elevator tucked away in the side of a trash filled alleyway. It only took a few taps on a keypad to unlock and open the lift, and they all piled inside. A tight squeeze for sure, but the captain reckoned it was best not to complain, considering the rather tight spot they were already in figuratively.

"Boxie had this one installed because she didn't want to have to walk all the way to the normal elevators," the Gnarf Boxie explained unprompted. "But the Yildi wouldn't approve any other location for the top end except that gross old alley."

"Don't you still technically work for Boxie?" Captain Nado questioned.

"Not anymore," answered the chubby chap. "You're Captain Burnay Nado, right?"

"I am."

"Then you're responsible for getting Boxie the 'Beautiful' to leave Vortex! Those of us who remain of Boxie's old embassy are forever in your debt. We hated living under her, lording over us as if she were royalty. But now that she is gone, we have rebuilt her embassy and freed all her slaves. Such petty grudges are not the way of the Gnarf people."

Schiff beamed, "I'm glad you feel that way."

"Yeah, she should have allowed us to eat them long ago."

"Never mind...," the little shapeshifter recanted.

"Good Gnarf, what is your name?" questioned the captain.

"I do not have one," their new companion answered. "Boxie stole our names from us. We cannot even remember them now. She made a god-race slave put a spell on us!"

"A spell?" Nado inquired.

"Yeah, she chanted 'you're getting sleepy' until we all got sleepy. The next thing we knew, we'd forgotten who we were. I am Gnarf Boxie Number Fourteen. That is my name."

"Huh," mused Captain Nado. "Well, at least it's good to have another buddy in the mix."

"Ooh," grunted the Gnarf, "I like the sound of that. That's my new name, Buddy. Thanks Captain Nado."

"You're quite welcome, Buddy."

"We alsho owe the captain a debt of gratitude," Shtrepp chimed in. "The ssskull he gave ush paid off a great loan we had with the Trellsss. With a three thousssand bit bounty out on them, we figured thish makesss ush even."

At that point, the elevator opened, and Buddy led them all inside the old embassy quarters. "We still have a small selection of weaponry," he informed them. "Contraband taken from would-be troublemakers. Take your pick of the stash."

"I don't suppose any of you have a ship?" Nado wanted to know, kneeling next to the locker to have a peek at the arsenal within.

"Boxie took everything with her when she left," replied Buddy. "She didn't even leave any short-range sky-beasts for quick fights."

"We paid a shuttle to ferry ush here," said Schlaar.

"And here ish where you shall ssstay," growled a voice from behind. They all whirled to see an unexpected sight.

"Gnash?!" Shtrepp and Schlaar simultaneously shouted.

"Nope," the intruder corrected, "I am hish brood-mate, Klensh. I ssstopped by Vortex to sssee if there wash any newsss concerning the Explorer 2000 and look what I ssstumbled into! Thish ish perfect. Now I can really tesht out my new hunter sssquad. Ha! What are the oddsss?"

"Pretty good, apparently," muttered Schlaar.

Now funneling into the room and flanking Klensh were a half dozen gnarled, marled, snarling individuals of various races, shapes, and sizes. Two Fangorians, another Kriton, a quirky looking Pyrian, and a couple of Ranjemans. The pointed ears, orange striped fur, and extended front fangs of the latter betrayed their hunger for the hunt. Every single one of them was armed to the teeth, carrying an assortment of artillery. Only one thing tied them all together, their matching prison brandings, burned into the left side of each one's face.

Guns were unholstered, fighting stances assumed, and opponents targeted as Klensh delivered his ultimatum. "I'm under ordersss not to harm you, captain. The shapeshifter, on the other hand, ish dishposssable. Ssstep out peaceably and we won't have to gun you down like you did to Gnash."

"Step out?" Nado stalled for time. "Rather forward. Shouldn't you have brought some flowers first?"

"Flowersss?" The albino Kriton seemed thoroughly flummoxed.

"It's only proper in the modern courting scene," Captain Nado carried on. "And besides, flowers are so well known for their… 'pistils'!" With that, the captain decisively drew two plasma firearms from the footlocker, providing cover fire for his allies. "Everyone get to cover, quickly!"

"Aah!" shrieked Klensh. "Immobilize that captain and kill the resht!!"

Barriers and blockades were being ripped, torn, splintered, and sundered all across the arena, General Hämm making a muddled mess out of the maze. It also gave Prince Jym fewer and fewer places to hide. He was barely able to stay ahead of the lumbering menace, but only just that, as Hämm's tremoring footfalls threatened to shake the lad into the open with every stomp.

He was closer to the southern wall now, where Kel could get a better view of their ward. Able to even see his facial expressions from this distance, the commander noticed that spark of bravery, coupled with a glint of mischievousness. "Don't do it," she murmured. As if sensing her thoughts, Jym met her stare and nodded. "He's going to do it," Kel said aloud.

"Do what?" queried the doctor.

"He's going to use his abilities on that sword," she replied.

"No, he can't!" Rox protested. "It could seriously harm him!"

"How else can he beat General Hämm?"

Having no response to that, Dr. Rox relented. They all watched Jym anxiously, hoping that the young boy wouldn't overdo it. Even from their obscured vantage, Commander Kel could see the warping and blurring around the edges of the prince's blade, and the blood trailing from his nostrils. Jym then lingered and listened for the general's approach. It wasn't too hard to perceive, as Hämm was still trashing the combat zone. Smash after smash, Jym's foe grew closer, until the last barricade between them was shattered. Exuding all his might, the prince pummeled the massive powerhouse of a Gnarf with an upward strike! Using the flat side of his blade, Prince Jym sent Hämm reeling, somersaulting end over end backward into the splinter-infested heap of rubble that the general had left in his wake.

Though weakened from this expenditure of energy, the young Vampyrial still had enough presence of mind to keep on the offensive. He raced to Hämm's crash site and batted the defeated villain's own blade from his loosened grip. Beaten and bruised, it was all too clear that General Hämm had lost this fight. The crowd immediately went completely silent, utterly shocked at this strange and sudden reversal.

"This fight is over!" announced the lad. "Now, king, hold up your end of the bargain!"

"This fight is NOT over!" Bë-konn roared. "Not until one of you is dead!"

"I'm not killing a helpless opponent!"

"Those are the rules, boy! You can either play along, or I kill every last one of you!" The high king raised his fat fist aloft. "Now cut that loser to pieces, or I give the order to my guards, and they start chopping."

They were at a standstill, until Kel heard an all too familiar sound ring in her ears like a heavenly choir, a clinical, cynical, metallic heavenly choir. "Greetings."

Yes! It was H-8-RED! Somehow that goofy, gear-brained robot showed up just in time. Two accurately aimed plasma cartridges burned through the armor of the sentries that menaced the crew in the bleachers, causing the guarding Gnarfs to abandon their posts. More plasma bolts that purposefully missed their marks scattered the swarm of spectators, and pandemonium began to break out in the arena. Other guardsmen struggled to reach the crew, the cowardly crowd gumming up the aisles and walkways. Red strode tenaciously to Kel's side from the upper entrance of the stadium.

"Red, I never thought I'd say this, but boy am I glad to see you!" the commander jested.

"That behavior was not predicted," was the only response Red had. "This unit's speech pattern protocols predicted that you would say, 'What took you so long?' To which this unit would reply, 'For optimal survival ratios, protocols dictate that friendlies must be armed in a combat scenario.' Thus, this unit made a pit stop to retrieve your confiscated weaponry from Boxie's vessel."

"Then stop gabbing and start passing it out!" Kel quipped. Complying, Red proceeded to arm the crew with their lost firearms. Kel had a sudden realization. "Wait, does this mean the Explorer is here?"

"Indeed."

"Good, as soon as we escape, take us to it."

While getting her .308 rifle equipped, the commander heard King Bë-konn cry out above the chaos, "Forget them for now! Get the boy!" That got her attention fast. She whirled and steadied her shot, the scoped sniper giving her the sensation and comfort of an old friend returning after a long absence. Kel lined up her shot, exhaling long and gently. BANG!

Before he could croak another command, Bë-konn's crown flipped from his horned head, a .308 caliber bullet pinging it with deadly accuracy. The commander made sure to lock eyes with him, slowly shaking her head. She then shouted her own orders. "Jym! Get out of there and meet us outside!"

Prince Jym took his own moment of victory as well, despite the blood trail seeping from his nostrils. "I'll be taking this," he stated, relieving General Hämm of his favored weapon. "And that." He indicated the missile launcher, pointing the sawtooth saber at it. Flinging the blade at the line that held the high intensity explosive in place, Jym cut the missile launcher down, catching the hefty weapon as he retreated through the western portcullis and out onto the open stone streets.

Guns aimed outward in a tight circle, the crew reconvened outside the coliseum, holding the entire Gnarf army, all wielding melee-based armaments, at bay. Not wanting to lose their current element of shock and surprise, the crew hightailed it after Red, boarding their very missed starship. The two unconscious Gnarfs that had been on guard duty were rapidly relocated to a safe spot, and the bulkheads were closed.

As soon as the thrusters had cleared the planet's surface, Commander Kel ordered, "Red, I'm plotting a course for Vortex station. Once we've achieved the necessary safe distance, activate the warp drive. Let's go rescue the captain and Schiff!"

Chapter 19

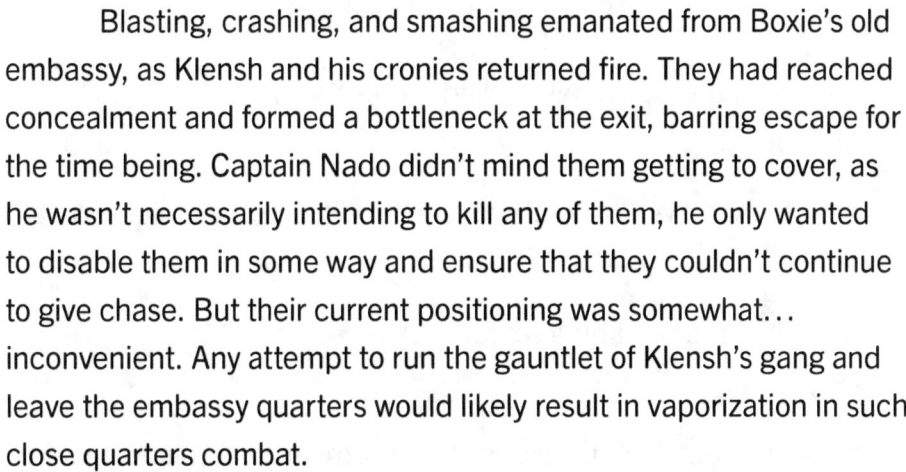

Blasting, crashing, and smashing emanated from Boxie's old embassy, as Klensh and his cronies returned fire. They had reached concealment and formed a bottleneck at the exit, barring escape for the time being. Captain Nado didn't mind them getting to cover, as he wasn't necessarily intending to kill any of them, he only wanted to disable them in some way and ensure that they couldn't continue to give chase. But their current positioning was somewhat... inconvenient. Any attempt to run the gauntlet of Klensh's gang and leave the embassy quarters would likely result in vaporization in such close quarters combat.

"Shoot out the lightsss!" Klensh yelled. "Ushe your infrared gogglesh!"

Lighting fixtures all around the chamber started shattering and popping, visibility dropping little by little. Momentarily, Klensh and his surly six would have the upper hand with those goggles. Unless...Nado knew that infrared technology was based on tracking heat, and that gave him an idea. With what light he had left, the captain commenced deftly disassembling one of his plasma pistols.

First, he ejected the magazine of plasma cartridges, giving him access into the inner workings of the firearm. The heating core that super-heated the cartridges was right along the inner wall of the magazine chamber. He could almost get it, but his fingers were too big to fit.

"Blast!" he exclaimed.

"Allow me," offered Schiff, her thin, spidery appendages able to effortlessly perform the task. "I don't know what you're doing, but it seems like you have a plan."

"Sure do," Nado said. He then called out, "Buddy! Is there a fire prevention system in here?"

"Yep!" the big Buddy replied. "Takes a minute to kick in though!"

"Perfect! Everyone get ready to shield your eyes and make a run for it."

"What are you about to do?" asked Schiff.

"I'm going to break the housing of this heating element," the captain answered. "That'll expose the electrical coil, which should be enough to start a fire hot enough to blind their infrareds."

"Huh. Good plan. Won't that burn your hands though?"

Nado shrugged. "It's better than a plasma bolt to the chest."

"Fair…"

Muscling through the pain of the heat on his hands, the last thing Captain Nado could see before the final light was extinguished was a crack beginning to form upon the housing. In the dark he heard two things. One was Klensh saying, "Alright, go get them." The other was the snapping of the sturdy casing in his tight grip. A soft orange glow exuded from the electric coil therein, so the captain wasted no time in finding some of Boxie's old cushions and, best of all, her nearly squashed mountain of pillows, a lumpy mattress at its base.

"There they go!" one of the thugs shouted. "They're headed for the back wall!"

"After them!" grunted Klensh.

Though he couldn't see them, Nado could hear Klensh and his horrid half-dozen edging closer to them. "They've gone behind the pillow pile!" another goon announced.

"Closhe in on them!" their leader growled.

Nado started lighting the mattress. It burned even faster than he expected, probably a result of Boxie the Beautiful's body oils still residing on the unwashed mound. The fire grew, burning ever hotter until it suddenly erupted, a veritable volcano of bedding!

"Now!" the captain hollered, shielding his eyes and running for the exit. The others followed suit, Schiff, Buddy, Shtrepp, and Schlaar right on his heels.

"Oh, crud!" they all heard Klensh shouting amidst similar cries from his compatriots. "I can't sssee a thing! Blasht!"

The bright fire lit the way for Captain Nado's group to flee to the exit. They'd gotten out of that mess, but more Vardens, bounty hunters, and fiends waited beyond, not to mention Vin and his mercenaries. So what to do now? They needed a rescue...

Vortex came into view once again as Commander Kel navigated the Explorer 2000 to the sizable station. As they maneuvered toward their berth, she addressed the robot. "Red, I've got to know how the Explorer made it to Urkasak. And what happened to you?"

"As you were boarding Boxie's vessel from the Puddle Jumper, this unit intercepted a message from Boxie's radio operator meant for Vin Trell," Red began explaining. "Unable to relay the message to you, this unit followed protocol and initiated a rescue operation. Upon assessing the situation you and the captain were in, this unit's self-preservation protocols activated. A temporary shutdown was initiated to prevent detection via energy scans. Rather predictably, additional Gnarfs within the dragnet hauled the Explorer to their home-world."

"Right," said Kel, a bit overwhelmed by the exhaustive explanation. "Well, good work, I guess. Let's dock and see if we can't track down Captain Nado." She spoke into the radio system. "Hailing the port-master of Vortex, this is the Explorer 2000, requesting a vector and a berth for landing."

They were given coordinates, and the Explorer 2000 set down in its original airlock bay from the last time they were on the station, the same port-master recognizing them on approach. "Oh, no!" they heard his voice crackle on the radio. "Not you guys again! If you're here to cause more trouble – "

"Don't fret," Kel assured him. "We're only here to pick up a couple of ferry charters and be on our way."

"That better be all it is!"

Commander Kel shut off the radio and started making her way to the bulkheads. "Come on Red. This time everyone goes, and that includes you. I'm not taking any chances."

"How are we going to locate Nado and Schiff?" Princess Mara inquired as they passed through the galley. "They could be anywhere!"

"Instead of searching for them, how about we get them to come to us?" suggested Dr. Rox.

"How would you propose we do that?" Kel questioned.

"Could we hack into the station's speaker system?" queried Jym.

"Not a bad idea…," mused the commander. "Red, let's see if our friendly port-master can help us out. He's got radio access, maybe it's connected to the station's PA system. Let's go!"

A quick jaunt to the port-master's office and they were facing the same slight Sorogan that had sold them out to the Gnarfs before. He still bore many of the battle scars of that last encounter, his bruises being slow to heal. The minute man balked at their approach, at first unwilling to allow them entry.

"It's an emergency!" begged Mara. "Please!"

"Oh, alright," the port-master conceded. "What do you want?" As the door swished open, Rox and Kel grabbed the man and pinned him to the wall. "Hey, wait a minute! You said you weren't going to cause any problems!"

"And we won't," Kel reiterated, "as long as you don't cause any either. Now, your radio, can it be patched into the station's speakers?"

"Yes, but only for...well, emergencies."

"This counts," stated the commander. "Red, log onto his terminal and see what you can do to patch us through to the speakers."

"This unit will comply," answered the austere automaton. A few seconds later, the robot had a report. "Commander, according to the station logs, there is an all-points bulletin out for the captain and Schiff. A broadcast accompanied this notification."

"Can you pull up that broadcast?" requested Kel.

"Indeed."

They listened to the robotic recording of the APB announcement, Kel's grin growing wider as it played. "I think I have an idea..."

Nado and company had finally found a place to hide and catch their breath for a minute, huddled behind an abandoned storefront. The locale reminded Nado of the many shops and markets on Zen I that had been shut down and closed, going out of business when the Galactic Community corporations had moved in. Reminiscent of those bygone days, the hideout brought up some bitter memories.

But he had to admit that the GC had done some good as well. Without it, there would be no Star Guard, probably the best thing to come of the Community. The advanced technology, increased level of protection, and access to the Community market did grant quite the advantage to many worlds.

No time to dwell on that now though. "Everyone rested?" the captain checked. They all nodded. "Then we have to keep moving."

As they were preparing to race back into the open, the station speakers blared another robotic alert, "Greetings. This is a station-wide notice. Captain Burnay Nado and his shapeshifting accomplice have been apprehended. I repeat, the fugitives have been apprehended. They are being remanded into the custody of airlock bay 193. That is all."

Schiff and Nado looked at each other, stunned. "Was that Red?" Schiff asked.

"Sure sounded an awful lot like it," confirmed Nado. "Airlock bay 193. We'd better get there before anyone else does."

"From here, you are about fifteen minutes away from that docking bay," Buddy informed.

"Start hoofing it!"

The party sprinted from hiding and dashed for the airlock!

"I sure hope that worked," muttered Rox. "What do we do if someone else shows up looking for them?"

"We give them a fight to remember," replied Kel. "And we keep that path clear as long as we can."

For about fifteen minutes, no one said anything. They waited, knots churning in their stomachs and thoughts blazing through their minds. What if Nado and Schiff didn't make it? How would they even know? What if all they'd accomplished was bringing down a frightful force on their own heads? Then they heard it. That telltale booming voice that they'd all recognize anywhere.

"Crew of the Explorer 2000? Are you in here?"

Commander Kel burst from the port-master's office and raced to embrace the Captain. "Nado, you made it! We thought we'd lost you!" She pulled Schiff into the hug. "Schiff, it's good to have you back!" Kel then composed herself. "Right, good to see you both alive and well. Shall we depart?"

"Hold it right there!" yelled another voice, light and airy. Vin Trell and his bodyguards were closing in from the northern corridor.

"That'sss my bounty!" came yet another. Klensh and his gang barreled toward them from the southern corridor.

"We'll hold them off," declared Buddy, Schlaar and Shtrepp standing resolute at his side. "You, Captain Nado, go and be safe."

A very confused Commander Kel stammered, "Wait, he's a Gnarf! He's helping you? What's going on here?"

"We'll explain once we're in the air," responded Nado. "Right now, let's load up and go. No more stops, no more sidetracks, we're taking the kids to those Hex II archives to finally get some answers!"

While Buddy and the Kritons stacked crates next to the entrance of the airlock bay as barricades, Nado and Kel ushered the crew on board the Explorer. A few well-placed shots and blows from their new allies sent Vin and Klensh packing! It bought just enough time for the airlock chamber doors to close and fully seal. The bay depressurized, the outer gates opened, and the Explorer 2000 was on its way to their ultimate destination in Taldish Sector, the mysterious and war-torn worlds of the Hexagon planetary system...

A somber and dismal atmosphere hung thick in the air of King Bë-Konn's throne room like an unwelcome stench. It was quite the different scene from the last time that Lord Hex was here. Rather than a proud, arrogant, stuck-up monarch, Hex now saw before him a deflated, demoralized dump of a Gnarf.

"High King of Urkasak," the marquis greeted, "why do you sit and mope when you should be cheering the success of your people? Unless, you don't actually have the crew of the Explorer 2000 as reported."

"They escaped," huffed the king. "You did not tell us that they had trickster gods with them. We were denied knowledge that would have prevented this loss."

"Bah!" spat Lord Hex. "The only thing you have been denied is the intelligence to pull off this task! It was simple, but still you failed miserably. And now I have no more use for you. I have other allies that will finish this quest for me."

"Assuming you can leave this planet alive," Bë-Konn intimidated. "One good thing did come from those trickster spawn. They told us how to safely devour your flesh and avoid cursing ourselves." The weighty monarch withdrew a sawtooth saber from behind his throne. "All I need to do is defeat you in single combat, and your essence is mine."

"Are you sure that's the wisest thing to do, king," taunted Hex. His lordship raised his right hand, fingers poised to snap. "I wouldn't try it if I were you."

"What can you do, Hex-man? Snap your finger and bring fire from the sky? Ha! You are lies and bluffs. You have no real power."

Not missing a beat, Lord Hex snapped his formidable fingers, an act that somehow sent a shockwave pulsing across the land. King Bë-Konn stumbled and nearly fell from the impact, righting himself at the last second. Scared and surprised, he peered around cautiously. Nothing seemed out of place, nothing damaged, no real harm done. The bloated beast began to belly laugh.

"As I said," snorted Bë-Konn, "no real power."

"No?" Hex retorted. "Look outside."

Unable to resist his own curiosity, King Bë-Konn peeked out the opening that led to one of his many terraces. A bright white light shone in the sky, intensifying and magnifying. Suddenly, without warning, an enormous laser burst through the clouds, striking the heart of the royal city! The beam burned everything in its path, remorseless and cruel.

"Wait, stop!" ordered the king. "Make it stop!" Lord Hex stood motionless, himself a fortress of malice and brutality. "Please!" Bë-Konn continued to plead. "Do not punish my subjects! Stop, please, I beg you, stop this!"

"No." Hex turned to go, speaking over his shoulder. "Let this be a lesson to you, Gnarf. This is what you get when try to double-cross a trickster god. The fire will only relent once I am safely back aboard my shuttle and bound for the heavens. Then, and only then, will it cease. Now every time you stare out of your little terrace you will see the desolation I have wrought, and you will remember the power and might of Lord Hex."

Swirling his cape with his usual dramatic flair, the malevolent marquis regressed back down the palace steps, the humbled king unceasingly imploring, "No! Please stop! Please! Not my people! Not my people!"

But his cries fell on uncaring ears, as the heavens continued their assault.

Aboard the Explorer 2000, Commander Kel and Dr. Rox were seeing to their captain's wounded hands. The burns from the plasma gun heating element were not severe but had certainly taken a toll. Rox applied aloe, disinfectant, and gauze, wrapping it securely with medical tape. At the moment, they drifted in open space, preparation time a necessity prior to their excursion into the Hexagon's solar system. Stories had already been swapped, tales traded, and laughs shared as they refreshed themselves, at least somewhat, with a dehydrated meal.

"How was Schiff?" Captain Nado inquired, all four of his mighty mitts outstretched.

"She'll be alright," responded the doctor. "Aside from some cuts and bruises, mild dehydration, and sleep deprivation, she's in fine health. I've got her resting in her quarters for now."

"Good," said Nado. "I hope Buddy and Shtrepp and Schlaar made it out alright."

"I'm sure they're fine," Rox assured. "As far as we could tell, there was no bounty out for them. I doubt Vin, Klensh, or their ilk would care much for that chase."

"Speaking of," interrupted Kel, "when are you going to stop leaping impetuously into every dangerous circumstance you can find, and start listening to reason?"

"We've done well so far," argued the captain.

"We've been lucky so far," corrected Kel. "We're about to head to one of the most potentially hazardous places in the known universe. We can't afford any more mishaps. We have a plan to approach, Red can pilot us via warp right to the edge of the planet's atmosphere, activating the warp deceleration device from Anise, while Mara assists with her dark energy manipulation to keep us from warping into the planet itself. But once we're groundside, then what? We need to make sure we have a plan. No flying blind!"

"Understood, Commander," Nado stated in mock obeisance. "Whatever you say, oh impassioned one."

"Captain, she's right," Dr. Rox chimed back in. "Let's make sure we know what we're doing before we do it, yeah?"

"Very well," the captain acquiesced. "We chart a course for the last known coordinates of the archives, and land as close as possible. We then stick together, one full group, heading inside. We'll need someone to stay on board and keep the ship on lockdown while the rest of us check out the archives."

"I'll stay behind," the doctor offered. "If someone gets hurt, you can always retreat to the Explorer to get patched up. Otherwise, I'd be useless on an expedition."

"Not useless," snipped Commander Kel, rolling her eyes.

"Alright, not useless," he conceded. "But less helpful than Red or Schiff for combat purposes, and we can't deny the kids finding whatever is within."

"Then the plan is set!" declared Nado. "Wow, that was easy!" He abruptly rose and exited the med-bay, leaving Commander Kel and Dr. Rox stammering.

"Wait, that's not a full plan! Oh, never mind..."

All additional obstacles had regressed from the area, the Gnarf and Kritons who had assisted the Explorer crew in their getaway running off and blending back into the crowds and throngs of Vortex. Demoralized and defeated, the other interested party had also retreated, leaving Klensh and his grimy goons alone at bay 193. They waited for pressurization before asking permission to enter.

The port-master's knees knocked and shook when he laid his eyestalks on them, as if he knew why they were there. "Please," he begged, "there's no need for any rough stuff, or manhandling. You want to know where they went, right?"

Klensh raised his one good scaly eyebrow. "Right."

"I'll gladly supply their heading, Hexagon II. That Explorer 2000 has caused me enough trouble. I hope you catch them!"

With a sour smile spreading across his ugly mug, Klensh uttered, "I'm shure we will."

Initiating their approach plan for Hex II, the Explorer crew had positioned themselves on the bridge for the difficult maneuver they needed to employ. With Red at the pilot controls, Captain Nado monitoring and conducting, Commander Kel working the navigational console, and Princess Mara centered therein for maximum control, all was in readiness.

"Commander Kel is our course set?" the captain checked.

"Aye Captain," she replied.

"Red, activate the warp drive," he continued. "All hands, prepare for rapid deceleration."

As usual, they could all see the darkened bubble envelope the vessel, blurring and bending the expanse around them. It was fast, took less than a few seconds in fact, and required incredibly precise timing. Deceleration took effect almost instantaneously, with Mara assisting. As the warp bubble receded, they could all see through the viewports a vast planet in the distance ahead of them and an enormous satellite moon to their immediate right. The planet itself was dark and swirling, little orange streaks thereupon giving the appearance of tiny lava rivers running throughout. This was Hex

I, the primary planet of the Hexagon system, a gas giant of epic proportions. Their destination, however, was the moon to their right.

Having bypassed any potential defenses Lord Hex might have had lying in wait for them, the crew strapped in for re-entry. They rode in silence, all anticipating the precarious nature of the surface below. A jolting and jerking told them they had landed cleanly, Kel's console indicating that they had reached the plateau outside the old archive ruins. Donning goggles and dust protection masks, the crew lined up at the bulkheads, activating the airlock functions and readying themselves for disembarkation. Prior to exiting, Dr. Rox gave Mara a once-over.

"You look okay," he reported. "Not even a nosebleed."

She shrugged. "The deceleration device did most of the work."

"Alright," the doctor smiled, "you're cleared to go. Go find your family, sweetheart."

As the doors lowered, they revealed an abysmal scene. Dust storms raged on the horizon, the high winds reaching all the way to the spacecraft itself. The only thing that gave them any kind of shelter were the sharp, rocky, black ridgelines that surrounded the small valley. Half buried in purplish grey sand was an ancient structure that looked more like an old temple than an archive. The main doors appeared to be locked tight, sealed and barred, while on either side sat two towers with rounded roofs, also nearly lost to the dust and sand. One of them, the one on the left, had a telescope extending through the roof, while the other sported a long conductive rod.

Trudging across the thick sand of the valley floor, the group trekked from the rear of the Explorer, making their way to the archive entrance. Dr. Rox closed the bulkheads behind them, so as to avoid getting sand in the inner workings of the ship. Unfortunately, upon reaching the entrance, it became very evident very quickly that they could not open the great gate that locked away the secrets they sought.

"Maybe we can find a way in through those towers," suggested Kel.

"Good thinking," Nado agreed. "You and Red take the kids and check the northern tower, and we'll take the southern tower."

"You want to split up?" Kel was incredulous. "What happened to sticking together as one?"

"If there is a way in, we'll find it faster this way! Let's just go."

Jym piped up. "Captain, can I come with you?"

"Of course!" the booming Zennian answered. "Alright everyone, keep in touch with the communicators. There's a lot of interference, but we can still get through."

The access point of the northern tower had long rotted away, nothing but a ruined, rusty rod left hanging on the hinges. Inside, everything was dark except a single buzzing screen that appeared to be broken. A series of symbols on the display first flashed in one color, then the monitor would crackle with static, and new symbols would pop up in a different color. So on it repeated in a cyclical manner. Commander Kel wracked her engineer's brain, but to no avail. She couldn't make heads or tails of it.

"I've no idea what this is," the frustrated commander carped.

"I can read it," said Mara softly. "It's old Vampyrial. Those refer to constellations or something. There are instructions as well. It says, 'embrace the wisdom of the hues'."

"What is that supposed to mean?"

At that moment, the communicator sparked. "Commander? Can you read me?" the captain's voice warbled. Though garbled a bit by static, it was clear enough.

"Loud and clear, Captain," Kel responded. "What's going on?"

"We've made it into the southern tower. Had to use a grappling hook and rope and climb inside through a hole in the roof. We can't see much, there's a panel here with a lot of different colored buttons on them. Not sure what they're for yet. What about you?"

"Wisdom of the hues," mumbled Kel, her mind now racing, her mechanical inclinations beginning to click into place. "That's it! Captain, press those buttons in the order we tell you."

"Copy that!"

With Mara interpreting, she and Commander Kel walked the other group through pressing their knobs in accordance with the color changing screen. When it had cycled back to the starting point, a grinding noise so loud Kel thought it could wake the dead reverberated throughout the entire valley, shaking dust from the consoles in the tower. She dashed outside in time to see the reinforced entrance to the archives opening to a black and empty maw. They were joined shortly by Captain Nado and his company, and together they all made their way forward.

"I don't think these doors have been opened in a hundred years," Nado mentioned excitedly. "That means we did it! We beat Lord Hex here! Whatever lies within, we can make sure it never falls into his clutches and can keep that information secure. Come on kids, let's see if there's anything in here to tell us about your parents. For now, the archives are all ours."

Chapter 20

Having already warped back to the Hex system, Klensh and his seedy gang waited aboard their gunship for the return of the Marquis du Hex. Shimmering and shuddering, the dreadnaught came into view, the colossal craft blocking out the sun as it coasted past. At the radio, Klensh tuned in to Lord Hex's frequency.

"You're back, milord," he greeted. "I'll washte no time. We've tracked the crew of the Explorer 2000 here, to Hex II."

For several minutes, there was no reply. Then the speakers buzzed to life. "Well done, Klensh." His lordship's voice was cold and calculating. "They must be here for the archives, there's nothing else on Hex II of any interest to them."

"You want ush to go in after them?" queried Klensh.

"No. If they're going through the archives, they might be doing me a favor. Land outside and set an ambush. Capture anyone you can. Even if you don't get the kids, I can arrange a prisoner exchange."

"And then I get my vengeance?" the murderous Kriton muttered.

"Yes, dear Klensh, then you get your vengeance."

Inching into the dusty, icy blackness before them, the crew activated their flashlights. Captain Nado's was mounted to his left lapel, opposite his communicator, while Commander Kel preferred a headlamp. Red's ocular sensors emitted bright beams that illuminated here and there as the robot peered all around. They were in a long hall, lined on either side with rows of metallic statues wielding shields and staffs. At the far end of the chamber, they could all make out strips of dim yellow light set into the wall that framed a secondary entryway.

"I wonder what's up with those weird statues?" Schiff questioned aloud. Her bright and chirpy voice echoed through the haunting hall.

"Not sure," replied Nado. "They could be images of Vampyrial warriors from a bygone era, but they are all positioned the same and look identical. Maybe they have plaques or something that denote their identity."

"We aren't here for that though," Kel reminded. "Let's just get to that door and see where it leads."

Arriving at the secondary portal, the commander recognized it as a primitive elevator. On approach, the yellow lights brightened, enlightening a pad on the wall in the shape of a handprint. As if in a trance, Princess Mara reached toward the imprint gently and slowly.

Grabbing her hand, Kel cautioned, "Hold on, it might be a trap."

"For you it would be," replied Mara, her gaze remaining utterly transfixed, "but not for me. It opens by Vampyrial touch only."

"How do you know that?" Kel questioned.

"I'm not sure…I just do."

Against her better judgment, Kel loosened her grip, allowing the princess' petite palm to press against the pad, causing a low hum to emanate from behind the machinery. Splitting in the center, the doors yawned, revealing the compact elevator inside.

"Let's go," Nado said softly.

They all boarded quietly, Mara and Jym reading the selection of buttons and choosing the corresponding switch that would take them to the archive chambers.

Minutes passed slowly and agonizingly as they rode to their destination, but eventually the elevator opened once more, this time to a somehow even duskier chamber than the first one. A pale teal light source glowed from several of the floor-to-ceiling shelving in here, everything piled with books, discs, and data-pads. Thick layers of dust blanketed the whole area, and dominating the center of the room they could all see a giant computer system that sparked and zapped periodically.

"If there are answers to be found, they're probably on that," noted Kel, indicating the computer. "Red, do you think you could help me get it back up and running?"

"This unit will comply," was the robot's unemotive response. The two set to work while Mara and Jym meandered the aisles between the shelves, checking the other sources of information. Captain Nado and Schiff joined the search, but most of the discs and data-pads were too damaged to activate anymore, while the books had largely been lost to the passage of time, worn and practically unreadable. They all gradually strode back to the computer system, hoping Kel and Red could get it working.

"Guys, I think we got it!" called the commander.

Powering up the machine, she stepped back to observe, waiting for the ancient apparatus to come to life. A dull teal light was emitted by the screen as an image appeared upon it. It seemed to be forming a pixelated face, but was distorted and warped beyond any recognition, coming across as something devilish or monstrous instead.

"I think maybe it's some kind of virtual intelligence," Commander Kel informed, as the enigmatic electronics chimed and whirred.

A deep-toned, mechanical, monotone vocalization issued from the speakers. "Archivist program online. It has been forty-four thousand, eight hundred and ninety-five standard Galactic Community cycles since this system was last accessed. Ready to process queries."

Receiving urging from Captain Nado and Schiff, the young monarchs stepped forward, Mara taking the lead. "Archivist, what do you know about Princess Mara and Prince Jym?"

"Searching," came the reply. "Searching...many files are corrupted. Unable to access all archival resources. Limited information available."

"Just give us whatever you have!" Jym demanded impatiently. "Tell us where our parents are! Tell us who where we came from! Tell us something!" His sister calmed him.

The Archivist responded, "Princess Mara and Prince Jym, siblings, children of the traitorous ones. Born on Hexagon III, fled to parts unknown post war. Recognized within the system as sole inheritors of the Prime Executor's Kathnarii ring." Along with that last statement, a drawer opened on the console, containing a small box.

"Kathnarii?" questioned Jym.

"An old order of warriors that have been long disbanded," answered the captain. "At one time, the Prime Executor was a member, but that was prior to the Great War."

"Wait, why are we the beneficiaries of the Prime Executor?" Mara inquired of the Archivist.

"Files and records identify the names of Princess Mara and Prince Jym as the direct descendants of the Prime Executor," said the computer coldly. "Those are the names of the grandchildren of Mantis."

"Now things are starting to make even more sense," mused Commander Kel.

"And somehow also less," added Schiff.

"We're the grandkids of the meanest, nastiest guy in the galaxy?" Mara pondered, becoming gloomy and depressed.

"But what about our parents?" Jym wanted to know. "And this ring?"

The Archivist droned on. "The only records of the parental figures of the prince and princess state that they were slated for relocation to Zen I prior to the collapse of the Vampyrial Empire. They are listed as traitors to the Executor. All other records were downloaded immediately prior to shutdown by the traitors, and the ring placed in holding."

"So, this was all for nothing?" Mara despaired. "We came all this way to get no answers."

"Not nothing," corrected Jym. "We have this ring, and we know that all the info about mom and dad was downloaded to another device by the traitors, that's them! They downloaded the info, so maybe the ring is a clue they left behind!"

"But the Kathnarii are long gone," moaned his despondent sister. "What are we supposed to do now?"

"The order is gone," offered Nado, "but not their space station headquarters. It's still out there somewhere, we'd just need to find it."

"So, we have a plan!" exclaimed Jym. "We need to find this Kathnarii base!"

"I think we've exhausted our resources here," declared the commander. "Let's get back to the ship before anything goes wrong."

"Not quite," Captain Nado reminded. He turned to the Archivist. "Archivist, is there a way to track living Vampyrials using your systems?"

"Negative," the computer returned. "Too much corruption has occurred for that functionality to be restored."

"Hm. Just to be on the safe side..." A couple of plasma bolts quickly torched the inner workings of the Archivist, its eerie face-like display freezing momentarily before dying. The captain holstered his gun with a flourish and motioned for them to board the elevator to leave. Following their sustained, sluggish ascent, they were all ready to get moving again, not desirous of pressing their luck when Lord Hex could descend upon them at any time.

A sandstorm had moved into the valley, obscuring the view though the main entry. Heat lightning was barely visible, highlighting the sharp ridgelines of the surrounding mountains. The crew stepped into the open, arms shielding their eyes from the churning debris. It was then they heard the raspy, wretched voice calling out to them.

"Put down your weaponsss and sssurrender!" Klensh yelled, his pack of miscreants hunkered in the dirt around their shuttle craft. "Lord Hex requessstsss your presssence at the highesht level!"

Captain Nado spoke in hushed tones to the rest. "Red, get the kids to the ship. Commander, you and Schiff make a run for it."

"What about you?" asked the commander pointedly.

"I'm going to hold them off."

"You can't hold all of them off! Let's come up with a new plan – "

"GO! GO! GO!" the captain called out, rolling through the dirt with guns blazing!

"You crazy, wacky…," fussed Kel, trailing off as they all bolted for the ship. Into her communicator she yelled, "Rox! Lower the bulkheads now! Hurry!"

Ahead of them, Kel could see that her message had been received as the Explorer's airlock doors lowered. The drawbridge-style outer ingress had just reached its halfway point when they all arrived. Red knelt low and leapt aboard, carrying both children with it. Kel and Schiff had to wait, which granted them time to see how Captain Nado was faring. It wasn't good. He was pinned down, the gruesome gang hemming him in. These guys were well armed, too well armed for the Explorer crew to handle. It was a miracle that no one had been hit in their flight.

"We just need to get aboard!" Kel shouted. "If Nado can get clear, we can blast them with the Explorer's lasers!"

She was about to board when she heard a scream. Commander Kel whirled to see Schiff covering her mouth and followed the girl's gaze to Nado. He'd been hit! The goons were bearing down on him, pelting his position with heavy fire. They saw him take another hit. He couldn't hold out at this rate.

"Hurry!" ordered the commander. "The lasers!"

But Schiff seemed to hear nothing, instead running straight into the fracas. She slid through the sand to the captain's side, throwing her lithe body across his wide-framed physique. With the arsenal that Klensh's colleagues had aimed their way, Commander Kel felt she had little other choice but to retreat into the safety of the ship. The last thing Kel saw of the skirmish, Klensh and his men swarmed the captain's position, knocking Schiff unconscious. She flipped the airlock switch, closing the bulkheads on her friends.

"What about the captain?" asked Rox. "And Schiff?"

"We rescued them once before, we'll rescue them again," she answered sadly. "We must get out of here before they get all of us. These guys are far more armed than anyone else we've faced. Even with Red, they'd outgun us. Come on."

Groggy and near delirious, Captain Nado awakened in a thick and heavy holding cell, Schiff curled up off to the side. His wounds had been treated and patched up, though they were still incredibly sore. He couldn't help but sense another presence in the room, the murky corners of this eerie chamber feeling as if every single one housed evil monsters waiting to leap out and pounce upon them.

Something moved! A shadow, a spirit, a dark essence, he couldn't be sure. It moved with a flowing grace, but also with power and purpose. Its tall and muscular frame domineered the area, striding forth with a long cape that billowed dramatically.

"Do you know who I am?" the being rumbled, its voice at once intimidating and seductive.

"If I were to hazard a guess," Nado replied, "you are Lord Hex, our greatest enemy, and a vicious worker of a great many evils."

"Evils?" chuckled the shadowed form. "Don't you understand Captain Burnay Nado? Everything I have done, I did for us." Huge hands reaching upward, Lord Hex took hold of his ever-hovering hood, pulling it back to reveal a Zennian face. He was nearly the spitting image of Captain Nado, with a square jaw, handsome features, and black, starry eyes. The only difference was that this person's hair was charcoal in coloration, and he also wore a suave, thin moustache.

It was unmistakable. "Graylon?" Burnay Nado stammered, his shock and surprise causing his very core to quake.

Graylon Nado, the Marquis du Hex afforded himself a long belly laugh. "Oh, yes. Did you never wonder why I didn't want you harmed?"

"But...all the things you've done," murmured Burnay. "How could you have placed my crew in such danger? And what about this dreadnaught? The assassin robots, the cloned 'shifters...you've been labeled as cruel and merciless. That's not the Graylon I remember."

"It takes that kind of person to do what needs to be done," Graylon coldly corrected.

"Why are you chasing the kids?" the captain wanted to know. "Why do you want them dead?"

"Dead? Oh, no, I need them alive. At least at first. I need their powers. Thanks to my unfettered access to the Hex worlds, I've taught myself a bit of Mantis' techniques, but to truly harness the full strength of the Vampyrial people, I need their DNA. Maybe a little, maybe a lot. Perhaps they'll survive the process, perhaps they won't. But if they do not, their sacrifice will be for the greater good."

Burnay was incredulous. "How can you make such a claim?"

"You know as well as I do that the Aronites and the Humans run the Galactic Community," spat his brother. "They lord and flaunt their supposed 'greatness' over everybody! Just because they were the most technologically advanced, they think it gives them the right to parade themselves as gods. But with the power of the Prime Executor, the threat of my dreadnaught's weaponry, an army of robotic killers, and a steady supply of shapeshifting spies, the GC would fall before me. Then, we could finally shape the galaxy into what we always wanted it to be! We'll reignite the Explorer Initiative program, open the council to more races, end the tyranny of their racist regime!"

"That is not what I always wanted," said the younger Zennian softly. "All I wanted was to see the stars with my brother."

"And in this way, we can!"

"I still don't understand," murmured the captain, his mind reeling from every new revelation. "How did you do all this?"

Graylon took a deep breath before explaining. "When we left to enroll in the GCCA, you took your trust fund and invested it in a standard Community education. I, on the other hand, took my coinage to Yawin and invested it there. I spent years amassing a fortune, which I used to bribe my way into the political scene. That is how. Any more questions?"

"No." Burnay seemed utterly defeated and deflated. He was lost in a sea of confusion and hopelessness, spiraling toward near madness it seemed. For the first time in his life, Captain Burnay Nado felt anxious and sick, out of control.

This did not deter his elder brother, however. "Help me, Burnay. You feel the same as I, we've known it since we were young. Help me get those kids and gain their powers, and you and I can reshape the whole universe! Our people can start exploring and charting, naming new sectors and planets after our kind, and so can many more. Join me." Graylon, the treacherous Lord Hex, stood with both of his right hands outstretched.

"I can't," replied the captain. "I can't go along with it. It's…monstrous."

Withdrawing his warm welcome, Graylon suddenly became closed and detached. "In that case, you leave me no choice. I cannot have you interfering with my plans, so you will remain here for now, unable to cause any further delays. I'll return for you when it is time to complete the prisoner exchange." And with that, the Marquis du Hex twirled his cape, replaced his cowl, and regressed.

Captain Nado slumped to the floor, sobbing.

Thankfully, it seemed that Hex's forces were uninterested in chasing the Explorer for the time being. Commander Kel took that reprieve as a chance to try and recuperate, reassess, and regroup. Wracking her brain for any semblance of a rescue plan proved fruitless, however, as she was confident that they couldn't take on Klensh's band of fiends, much less the dreadnaught. The starship floated on the opposite side of the moon for now, avoiding any conflict and staying out of sight.

It was then Red gave a report. "We are receiving a hail on the radio, Commander. Shall it be patched through?"

"Go ahead Red," answered Kel.

The voice on the speaker was intimidating and seductive, all at once deep and calm, yet with an undercurrent of sheer ferocity. "Crew of the Explorer 2000, this is Lord Hex. I am offering you a golden opportunity."

"Any twisted deal you have, we don't want!" the commander snapped back.

"Are you sure?" taunted Hex. "I have your captain and shapeshifter, and if you ever want them back, you'll agree to an exchange. I want those kids."

"What are you proposing?"

"Bring your vessel to the frozen lake at the northern plateau of Hex II. It is a place where it is difficult to hide, and I want to see you all coming a long way off. I've heard the tales of the crafty crew of the Explorer 2000. Once there, you Commander Ashe Leigh Kel, as well as Dr. Rox Garrison, will exit, unarmed, to escort Princess Mara and Prince Jym to the icy wastes. You will wait near your ship, while the children walk to me. Once I have them, you will continue to wait until we have boarded my shuttle for the return trip to my dreadnaught. I will then send Captain Nado and the shapeshifter down in another shuttle, and you can all be on your merry way. Understand?"

"Is that all?" Kel was impatient.

"Every last word," fumed Hex. "Refuse that, and I'll turn the dreadnaught's lasers against your home, the flotilla."

Thinking fast, the clever commander agreed. "You have a deal."

"And you have two hours. I'll see you at the plateau." The radio crackled and buzzed, silencing with those last words.

"You're going to hand us over?" snipped Mara, who had slipped to the bridge unnoticed. "I knew it was only a matter of time before you guys turned on us too!"

Kel shouted, whirling to face the girl, "Hold on just a minute! We're here to protect you, I promise!"

"Then what about that deal with Lord Hex?" Dr. Rox chimed in.

Smiling slyly, an act she'd witnessed Captain Nado perform many times prior, Commander Kel informed, "He specifically mentioned the full names of every occupant on the Explorer...except one." She looked at the automaton assassin sitting at the helm. "He doesn't know that we have his H-8-RED! Red, how are you with a .308 sniper rifle?"

Red began its recitation, "As stated multitudinous times before, this unit is an assassin robot of unrivaled sophistication. A sniper rifle is not out of scope. No pun intended."

Rubbing her hands together like a maniac, Kel said, "Guys, this is going to sound bonkers, but I may have cooked up a plan that's crazier than one of Nado's hare-brained schemes!"

As the metallic cage around them groaned and creaked, Schiff sidled over to the captain, who still sat slumped and sulking. "Hey Cap? You okay?"

"Not really," he replied ruefully. "My brother is...the villain. All these years I wondered where he had gone, and it turns out he's the bad guy. I don't know what to do now. I can't kill him, he's my family. But I can't let him get away with this either. I...I just don't know what to do."

"Cap, if I may?" the little shapeshifter offered. "That warlord is not your family. He may be related by flesh and blood, but that doesn't make you family. Trust me, I know. Family is the people who love you, care about you, and want to see you succeed and grow into a better person. They protect, cherish, and encourage! All I saw from Graylon was arrogance and demeaning speech. Now, you need to snap out of it. Your real family needs you. I chose you guys because the Explorer 2000 crew is the best family I've ever seen! You're the coolest and best big brother I've ever had! So, get up, stop moping, and let's find a way to bust this joint!!"

Her expression one of slight embarrassment, Schiff lowered her head and retreated. But Nado walked after her, placing a hand on her shoulder. "You're right. The Explorer crew is my family. Always have been. And if Graylon is planning a prisoner exchange, that means he's making one more play to catch the prince and princess in his clutches. We can't let that happen. Schiff, do you think you could blink us through the bars?"

"What?" She appeared shocked. "No, I told you I can't do that! We could end up outside in space!"

Captain Nado grasped her by both shoulders now. "You've put your trust in me as your big bro, now I'm putting my trust in the coolest little sister I never had. If anyone can help us escape this mess, it's you."

"Okay," Schiff breathed deeply, closing her eyes to concentrate. "Okay. I can do this. I can do this." Placing her own palms atop the captain's, she continued to chant, "I can do this. I can do this."

Though Schiff's words never ceased, Nado saw reality bend and reshape around him. He'd seen this sort of thing before, every time the Explorer entered warp travel, but never like this. In a flash of light, they found themselves on the opposite side of the cage bars! Schiff was still muttering, "I can do this. I can do this," over and over.

"Schiff!" exclaimed Captain Nado. "You did it!"

The small shapeshifter glanced about. "Whoa! I did it. I did it!! Thanks, Cap, it looks like I just needed someone to believe in me."

"As you've just pointed out to me, that's what family does," Nado said. He beamed broadly. "Now, if Graylon plans a prisoner exchange, that means he's going to meet with them. He didn't take us with him, so either he plans to give us later, or double cross the rest of the crew entirely. Either way, we can't leave this dreadnaught armed. Let's see if we can get the weapons system offline, then commandeer our own shuttle and get out of here."

"I could shift into one of his robot guard guys and make it look like I'm moving you to a new part of the ship," suggested Schiff cheerily. "That way we can get around mostly undetected."

"Good plan. I think I know what panels to look for to disable the laser systems. Let's go!"

Chilling winds whistled across the ice capped plateau, whipping the cold into a frenzy around the frozen lake thereupon. The Explorer had landed, as instructed. Commander Kel and Dr. Rox were now standing ankle-deep in the snow and ice. With them, Mara and Jym also waited, having donned their black hooded cloaks that they had received from "Uncle." A whooshing noise announced the incoming shuttle craft that eventually set down on the opposing side of the frosty lake. Using telescoping binoculars, Kel watched as Klensh and his grisly goons disembarked, followed by a large man in a hooded cape that could only be Lord Hex himself. The malicious marquis gave the command, waving his hand in the freezing air.

"That's the signal," Kel informed. "Mara, Jym, go ahead."

Their own black capes swishing and billowing from the winds, the young monarchs started their trek across the wastes. Hearts were beating painfully with each passing step, as they grew closer to the man who had been hunting them since Octagon V. With Mara to the right, and Jym to the left, they surged forward gradually. Rox looked fearfully to Kel, who only gave a slight nod in response.

The children had nearly reached Lord Hex's shuttle, where Klensh and the very heavily armed half dozen were ready to receive them. Breathing intensified in the lungs of every person on the field. This was the moment Hex had been longing for. He'd stop at nothing to see it come to fruition. The Marquis du Hex stuck out a massive hand, motioning for the kids to halt.

"Wait," he instructed. "Lift your faces. I want to make sure I'm getting the real deal."

Acting in accordance, both Jym and Mara raised their heads simultaneously. While the prince looked fine, the princess had a trail of blood gushing from her nose. Eyes widening in fear, Hex thundered, "What are you manipulating? What have you done?!"

That was it! It was do or die now, as Kel shouted into her communicator, "Now Red!" On the far side of the ice-covered water, one of Klensh's men went down, a .308 bullet striking him suddenly in the shoulder! A second later, the rifle report resounded across the plateau.

"It musht be their robot!" shouted Klensh.

"Why didn't you tell me they had a robot, idiot?" demanded Hex with sudden realization. "It could only be my H-8-RED. What is happening?!"

"Just this," replied Mara, pulling her left hand upward with vehement force! From under the frozen surface, something burst through, and Jym caught it cleanly on his shoulder. It was the missile launcher!

"Fire in the hole!" the boy yelled, blasting the explosive projectile from its mount, sending it screaming straight into Lord Hex's shuttle. The tiny spacecraft detonated in a ball of flame and smoke, creating confusion on the battlefield. Hex himself used his abilities to generate a shield of ice in front of him as another of his dastardly minions collapsed, the subsequent "bang!" following a second later.

"Come on!" Commander Kel called to the kids. "Get back here and let's go get the captain and Schiff!"

At that very moment, her communicator crackled to life. "No need Commander! We're on our way!"

Another telltale zooming sound echoed throughout the field as a second shuttle plummeted out of the sky, landing with a crash between Hex's befuddled brutes and the prince and princess. Captain Nado! How he managed these daring, last-minute, out of the frying pan, heroic measures she'd never be able to fathom. Upon landing, Kel observed Nado repositioning his shuttle to scoop the kids up and ferry them in a rapid return to the Explorer.

Without shutting the tiny craft down, the captain and Schiff leapt from within. "Get on the Explorer!" he barked. "By the way Kel, excellent plan. I saw most of it as we were flying in. Well done!"

"I thought it'd be something you'd like," she remarked coyly. "Alright everyone, get on board! Red, pull in and take the helm. But Captain, what about Hex?"

"You mean Graylon," corrected Nado.

"What?" Kel and Rox voiced at the same time.

"No time now, we'll talk later. Move!" Delivering his last booming command, Captain Nado activated the auto-pilot mechanism on the shuttle, rigging it to fly at top speed. It careened at an alarming rate, plowing through Graylon's and Klensh's locations, the two vile villains diving for cover! Nado's shuttle smashed into the wreckage of the first craft with a mighty impact, sending yet another fireball shooting into the sky.

Everyone assumed their usual stations aboard the Explorer 2000, and within seconds it was sailing over the frozen plateau. From the gunnery stations, the captain and Schiff laid down suppressive fire with the lasers on their foes' fortifications, ensuring that Graylon had no chance to recover prior to their departure. In moments, they were gone, leaving chaos and destruction below. The Explorer 2000 had made yet another dazzling escape!

Watching his dreams slip through his fingers yet again, Graylon could not repress a guttural cry that emanated from deep within. Falling to his knees and shaking all four fists at the sky, he screamed, "NOOOOOOOO!!!"

As the engines carried them from the surface of Hex II, the command crew on the bridge readied the vessel for warp travel. Working feverishly, Kel asked of Nado, "How did you guys get off the dreadnaught?"

"Thank Schiff for that," he replied. "She blinked us out of confinement, then used a guise to sneak us around the ship. And I wouldn't worry about them chasing us. We disabled the weapons systems...and probably accidentally a few other things."

"Nice work Captain," laughed the commander. "So, Lord Hex should have a tough time coming after us for a while."

"I just pulled wires," Schiff shrugged. "No clue what we were doing. But yeah, we made a mess."

"Do we have a heading?" queried Kel.

"Let's get out of Taldish Sector," Captain Nado directed. "I think we've exhausted all our options here."

The remainder of the crew joined them on the bridge. Jym chimed in. "Yeah, we need to research this Kathnarii headquarters and see what we can find about our parents."

"But in the meantime," Mara interjected with a weak smile, "I think we've found a pretty good family to call our own."

"Yes, we have," added Schiff.

"I even learned to love you, Red," the commander quipped at the robot.

"This unit is incapable of returning affection," was all it had to say.

"Way to ruin the moment..."

Everyone allowed themselves to chuckle and chortle, until Captain Nado cut back into the conversation. "Listen up crew, we still have a long way to go, and Graylon will be hounding our every step. We have to be smart, clever, and willing to listen to each other. Impetuosity will only get us hurt, captured, or killed, take it from me. For now, we head for Murrigan Sector, and my home planet Zen I. Hopefully, I know a place where we can lay low for a bit. Then we're going to hunt down Kathnarii base, and eventually we will reunite Mara and Jym with their parents!"

"Well said Captain," offered Kel. "I see your optimism hasn't waned despite everything."

"It is the second-best weapon in our arsenal," he commented.

"Second best? What's first?"

"Family." The captain then resumed his post. "Everyone, strap in for warp travel. Commander, set our course. Red, activate the warp drive."

The darkened bubble enwrapped the vessel, and the Explorer 2000 blinked into the distant stars, leaving Taldish Sector behind.

To be continued...

Epilogue

In the dark, dismal, dusty bowels of the archives, Lord Hex traveled with Klensh down the gradually descending elevator. That pesky Explorer crew may not have realized it, but they'd done Graylon quite the favor bypassing the trapped main hall, and exposing this place's secrets for him. They probably also didn't realize that he could read ancient Vampyrial, thus was well aware of what lay beneath the actual archive level.

Opening into utter blackness, the elevator completed its trip. Graylon reached for a panel, the controls thereupon casting old and dim light across the vast chamber. Lining the walls were dozens of what appeared at first glance to be stasis pods.

"Why do you need ssstasssisss podsh?" questioned Klensh. "I don't undersssstand."

"And you have just answered your own question, fool," Graylon growled. "I brought you here in case there are any additional booby traps or security measures that require protection. Don't make me regret that decision." He crossed to one of the large tubular cases containing a sage green, partially translucent, liquid. Many of them held what appeared to be people within, floating and wafting, seemingly dead. A small figure, barely the size of a child, had bubbles surrounding its fragile frame. "These are a cloning apparatus. This is where I believe Prime Executor Mantis held the keys to altering the Vampyrial race to grant them their powers."

"I thought he taught them thoshe abilitiesss?" Klensh wondered.

"No. My theory is that it was through DNA restructuring. I cannot perform the necessary procedure on myself without those kids, though. They are the only pureblooded Vampyrials in the known universe. However, this one here seems to be intact." Graylon motioned to the child floating in the nearby pod. He checked the controls and panels. "Blast! The sequencer is incomplete... nevertheless, if I cannot yet become the perfect specimen myself, perhaps I can create someone who can help me."

Utilizing a little knife, the manic marquis sliced his finger, dripping his own Zennian blood into the yawning portal used to accept samples. Turning on the machinery and watching it hum and quake to life, shaking dust and cobwebs from its surface, Graylon whispered to the little being, "You're going to help me catch that Explorer 2000. Hello, son."

Unbeknownst to Lord Hex, further down lay a secondary clandestine chamber, as all who knew the Prime Executor knew he loved his secrets upon secrets. In this dank hole, only one pod resided. It activated simultaneously with Graylon's experiment. Crimson lighting shone upon the lone pod, filled with a viscous, nearly opaque, goop. As it began to drain, a dark and shadowy figure was revealed. It smiled a wicked, fanged grin, as orange eyes opened…

———⦾———

What awaits the intrepid crew of the *Explorer 2000*?
Find out next time in:

EXPLORER 2000

Book Two
The Hunt for Kathnarii Base

About the Author

With several years of experience as an amateur novelist and playwright, and as a professional technical writer, JB Stephens is excited to bring this adventure into creation. He has a great love of science fiction entertainment, having studied in depth to create fictional worlds that are rooted in traditional and theoretical technology. JB lives with his wife and children in Lawrenceville, Georgia, and is happy to craft stories that are inspired by make believe games invented by his kids. His greatest joy as an author is being able to share a positive, godly message in all his writings.

www.ingramcontent.com/pod-product-compliance
Lightning Source LLC
Chambersburg PA
CBHW060356260626
47160CB00006B/2327